CW00687194

More Than a Cowboy

A Carmody Brothers Romance

Sarah Mayberry

TULE
PUBLISHING

More Than a Cowboy
Copyright© 2020 Sarah Mayberry
Tule Publishing First Printing, April 2020

The Tule Publishing, Inc.

ALL RIGHTS RESERVED

First Publication by Tule Publishing 2020

Cover design by Lee Hyat Designs

No part of this book may be used or reproduced in any manner whatsoever without written permission except in the case of brief quotations embodied in critical articles and reviews.

This is a work of fiction. Names, characters, places, and incidents are products of the author's imagination or are used fictitiously. Any resemblance to actual events, locales, organizations, or persons, living or dead, is entirely coincidental.

ISBN: 978-1-951786-95-3

More Than a Cowboy

Chapter One

SUCK ON THAT, gravity.

Sierra Carmody grinned as she watched a broad-winged hawk soar on a thermal twenty feet below the cockpit of the Bell 407. Maybe she was anthropomorphizing her ass off, but it seemed to her that the hawk loved being up here as much as she did.

All around her was the crisp, clear blue of a Montana summer sky, and below was a vast blanket of green and brown occasionally cut through with the snaking line of a road or railway or river. Even the mighty hulk of Copper Mountain was reduced to a plaything from up here, its rocky peak wreathed in fluffy white clouds.

Sierra flashed a smile at the man sitting beside her. Jack grinned back at her, his leathery skin creasing into deep lines.

"Perfect day for it," he said, his voice tinny over the headset.

"Couldn't be better," Sierra agreed.

He turned his attention back to the instruments, his gaze assessing everything with the practiced ease of a helicopter pilot with thousands of flight hours under his belt.

She glanced at her watch, conscious that their passenger,

Gideon Tate, was a stickler for being on time. She flicked the switch on the audio panel so he could hear her through his headset.

"Mr. Tate, we're fifteen minutes out from the ranch. Should be landing right on time."

"Good to know. Thanks, Sierra," Gideon said.

She could see Gideon in the small mirror that Jack had retrofitted to the windshield frame for just that purpose, his head buried in his paperwork. The man never seemed to stop working.

She switched the comm back so she and Jack could talk without disturbing their passenger.

"Gideon wants me to collect something for him from Billings next week, if you're up for another run?" Jack asked.

"Sure. Let me just make sure Jed and Casey don't need me for anything, but that sounds great." She bit back the urge to shower him with gratitude for thinking of her, knowing from experience that he would only become red-faced and brusque if she tried to acknowledge his generosity. Like always, she'd find some other way to show her appreciation for the extra flight hours—bringing him some fresh vegetables from the kitchen garden at home or taking on the task of putting the Bell into the hangar for the night.

Jack nodded, adjusting the cyclic to accommodate a crosswind that had just sprung up. She had no idea why she glanced in the mirror to check on their passenger. Maybe she'd heard something over the whir of the rotors or caught movement in her peripheral vision. Whatever it was, what she saw in the mirror had her reaching for her seat belt release.

"*Jack*. Gideon's collapsed," she said urgently.

"Shit."

Sierra pulled off her headset and twisted around, coming up onto her knees. Although the seats formed a solid bench across the front of the helicopter, there was enough space between the headrest and the ceiling for someone to squeeze through into the rear passenger area. She slithered over the seat in an awkward rush, her boot heels hitting the ceiling on the way over. Then she was on her knees beside Gideon's too-still form, her fingers on his neck, searching for a pulse.

"Thank God."

It was faint, but it was there—a delicate percussion beneath her fingertips. She snatched up Gideon's headset so she could communicate with Jack.

"He's alive."

"We'll be at Marietta hospital in ten," Jack said, his tone clipped. "What should I tell them?"

"His pulse is thready." She rubbed her knuckles on Gideon's sternum and his eyelids fluttered. "He's semiconscious, and his breathing is shallow."

The headset went dead and she guessed Jack had switched to external radio. She could feel the powerful growl of the motor as he banked left, then cranked up the speed. Her ears popped as the altitude rapidly decreased.

She concentrated on Gideon, checking his airway to make sure it was clear before releasing his seat belt and putting him into the recovery position across the rear seats. There was a blanket stowed under the forward seats and she yanked it out, spreading it over him to keep him warm. Then she sat on the floor so she could hold his hand, willing him to be okay.

He was only sixty-four. Far too young to die.

And he'd been kind to her—generous—despite the messy history between her family and his.

Or perhaps *because* of it.

She leaned close so he could hear her over the engine.

"Hang in there, Mr. Tate. We'll be at the hospital soon."

Maybe it was her imagination, but she could have sworn his fingers briefly tightened around hers.

The next ten minutes seemed to last an hour. Jack checked in on her continuously and she kept monitoring Gideon's pulse, terrified he was going to stop breathing. She'd completed a comprehensive first aid course last year and she tried to remember the protocol for CPR. Was it thirty chest compressions to two rescue breaths or twenty?

Please don't die. Please be okay.

"About to land," Jack said over the headset and Sierra sent up a prayer of thanks to the universe.

The hospital's helipad was on the roof and Sierra caught a glimpse of the luminescent "H" painted on the cement before the Bell touched down with a thud. A medical team stood at the ready beside the entrance, their uniforms flapping in the rotor wash. Sierra leaned across to release the passenger door and waved them over. Seconds later she was making herself as small as possible as the team crowded into the passenger cabin, utterly focused on their patient.

"Let's get him oxygen," a young blonde doctor ordered, her tone authoritative.

"Blood pressure is 180 over 120," a male nurse said.

"We need to get him to resus. Let's move, people," the

doctor ordered.

A trolley was wheeled over and Gideon was transferred with brisk efficiency. Then they raced toward the emergency entrance, the doctor leaning over Gideon's still form.

Sierra let out the breath she didn't even realize she'd been holding, more than a little overwhelmed.

"You okay?" Jack asked from the open doorway.

She nodded, and he held out his hand to help her exit. Her body felt stiff with tension as she slid to the edge of the seat and ducked her head to step down onto the rooftop.

"What do you think it was? A stroke?" she asked.

"Seems the most likely." He passed a hand over his chin. "I need to call Nancy."

Sierra's gut tightened as she thought about Gideon's family—his wife, Nancy, and his son, Garret. This was going to be a huge shock for them. "Can I help with anything?"

Jack shook his head, the gray in his faded red hair glinting in the afternoon sunlight. "I might be tied up for a bit, though. Reckon you can make your own way home from here?"

"I'll call home," Sierra said. "Don't worry about me."

She could see how heartsick Jack was and she gave him an impulsive hug. "You were awesome. No one could have got him here faster."

He managed a sad smile before pulling out his phone. He stared down at the keypad for a long beat, then summoned up a number.

"Nancy? It's Jack. I'm afraid I've got some bad news . . ."

Sierra moved away, giving him space to say what needed to be said. Pulling out her own phone, she dialed home.

It was stupid, but her eyes got hot with emotion when her oldest brother answered the phone.

"Jed, it's me. I need you to come pick me up."

THE RAIN STARTED when Garret Tate was just ten minutes out of Billings, slashing at the windscreen and overwhelming the wipers. He kept his foot on the gas anyway, conscious of the clock running down. He'd been in Rome on a work trip when his mother's panicked, tearful call lit up his phone yesterday, and he'd been wrangling with travel companies and officialdom ever since.

He wasn't about to slow down now, not when the doctors had indicated his father's chances of surviving the next forty-eight hours were no better than fifty-fifty. His relationship with his father hadn't been strong for a long time, but that didn't mean Garret didn't love him. That he didn't care. That he didn't want to say goodbye, if that was all there was left to do.

A truck blew past, throwing road dirt and more water at his rental sedan just as his phone came to life with a bright ring. His hands tightened on the steering wheel.

Was this The Call? Had he gotten this close to home only to be half an hour too late?

He hit a button on the steering wheel and his mother's voice filled the car.

"Garret, I know you're on the road. I just wanted to let you know Dr. Wilson said he's happy with your father's overnight results, so they're going to reduce his sedation. With a bit of luck, he should be waking soon."

Relief washed through him.

"Okay. Thanks for letting me know. I'm only about forty minutes away, give or take."

"Be careful in this weather."

"I will. See you soon."

He had a ton more questions, but they could wait until he was face-to-face with his mother. The important thing was that his father was still alive and well enough for the doctors to start bringing him out of the medically induced coma they'd put him in to help him recover from the major stroke he'd experienced yesterday afternoon.

That was a huge step forward. Hopefully the first of many.

Another truck passed, and he redoubled his concentration on the road because no one needed him to end up in a ditch or worse right now. When he finally pulled into a parking spot at Marietta General half an hour later, the rain had slowed to a light pitter-patter and his shoulders and back were aching from the tension of his long journey home.

He climbed out of the car and rolled his neck as he strode toward the building. Minutes later he was being led to the waiting room in the intensive care unit by a middle-aged nurse.

His mother sprang to her feet from where she'd been sitting on one of the two couches in the small space, her eyes red from tears and lack of sleep.

"Garret." She hugged him tightly, pulling away almost immediately as though she was afraid to let herself to take comfort for too long. "Thank you for coming so quickly."

"As if I wouldn't."

"Well, I know you and your father have had your differences." Her gaze was searching, and Garret wondered for the millionth time if she had any idea what had caused those "differences." Sometimes he was convinced she knew—that she had to know—but then she'd do something or say something and he'd wonder all over again.

"Any more news?" he asked.

She shook her head, her blond bob brushing her shoulders. "They've been in with him for a while. Wouldn't let me stay. They said they'll assess him when he's conscious, work out how much damaged he's suffered . . . Garret, what if he's not there anymore? What if the blood clot did so much damage he's gone?"

She lifted a hand to push back her hair and he saw that it was trembling. For the first time in her life she looked every one of her sixty-two years, and he made a bet with himself that she hadn't eaten or slept since she'd gotten news of her husband's stroke. It had always been that way—Gideon always came first, above everything, including herself.

"We won't know anything until they do the tests," he said, aware he was offering her zero comfort. But he was in no position to offer reassurances or promises. It would be naive to believe his father was simply going to wake from sedation with all his faculties intact.

"I've been so scared something like this was going to happen," his mother said. "He never stops working. Even when he plays golf he's working, hustling for a contract or networking. I tried to talk him into slowing down but he never listens."

Garret nodded, guilt biting at him. If he hadn't chosen

to walk away and forge his own path in Seattle, he would have been working at his father's side at Tate Transport the last eight years, sharing some of the load, and maybe this wouldn't have happened. Yes, he'd had good reasons for walking away, but right now, right this minute, they felt self-indulgent. Even self-righteous.

Movement drew his attention to the doorway as a tall silver-haired man in a well-cut navy suit appeared.

"You have to be Garret," he said, offering his hand. "The family resemblance is powerful. Dr. Wilson, we spoken on the phone."

"We did. Mom said you've been in with Dad?"

"I have. He's conscious and a bit distressed. I've explained the situation to him, but it's a lot to take in. I think he'd benefit from seeing his family for just a few minutes."

His mother was already moving forward, hope on her face. Garret followed her across the corridor and into a single room where a couple of nurses were adjusting various machines around the bed. His father's head was propped on a single pillow. There were oxygen prongs in his nose and a line snaking from the inside of his elbow to a drip stand. His face was pale despite his tan; his salt-and-pepper hair rumpled, and the right side of his face sagged noticeably.

"Gideon," Garret's mother said, rushing forward to take his father's hand.

Garret was aware of his pulse pounding in his ears as he waited for his father to respond.

Come on, Dad. Please still be there.

Slowly his father turned his head toward his mother, his eyes cloudy with confusion.

That could just be the drugs. He's probably high as a kite.

His father opened his mouth, but all that emerged was a slurred, garbled moan. His mother squeezed his hand, tears streaming down her cheeks.

"It's okay, Gideon. I'm here. You're okay," she soothed.

His father attempted to speak again, but the words were so slurred they were unintelligible. It didn't matter—Garret could hear the fear in his father's voice, the terror.

Jesus, this was awful. All his life, his father had been a vital, unstoppable presence. A force of nature. To see him cut down like this . . .

Garret turned away, sucking in a deep breath.

Keep it together, asshole.

It took him a moment to gain control, then he turned back and stepped closer to the bed, standing at his mother's shoulder.

"Hey, Dad," he said, and his father's gaze shifted to him.

There was no mistaking the recognition there, or the warmth.

"They're taking good care of you, Gideon. It's going to be all right. We're going to get on top of this," his mother said, stroking his arm lovingly.

Dr. Wilson moved forward. "Gideon, I'm going to need to run some tests now to see where we're at, so I'm going to ask Nancy and Garret to step outside for a bit. But they'll be back soon, I promise."

Gideon's gaze moved to his wife's face. She lifted his hand and pressed a kiss to it, then moved closer and dropped another one onto his forehead.

"I love you," she said softly, and there was so much tenderness in her voice Garret got a lump in his throat.

"I'll see you soon, Dad," he said.

He led his mother into the corridor, aware of the medical staff closing ranks around the bed as they left. His mother was pale, and when he put his arm around her he realized her whole body was trembling.

"Oh, Garret." She turned her face into his chest and burst into messy, noisy tears. "His face . . . He can barely open his eye. And his mouth . . ."

"It's early days yet, Mom. Let's wait and see what the doctor says," Garret said, because there wasn't much else he could say.

He was still trying to find his feet himself, trying to get past the confronting realization that while his father might have survived, his life would never be the same again.

It was half an hour before Dr. Wilson came to talk to them in waiting room.

"Okay," he said, letting out a long sigh as he sat down. "We've completed an initial neurological exam, and it's clear Gideon's suffered significant damage. There are still more tests to do, but at the moment I'd put him at a twenty-eight on the stroke scale. In the severe category."

His mother made a small, distressed noise.

"But that will change with rehab, right?" Garret asked.

Dr. Wilson paused a moment before answering. "At the moment, he has profound paralysis down his right side. He's lost his speech, and his swallowing reflex is weak. We'll put him straight into intensive rehabilitation and speech therapy, but there is no guarantee what gains he might make or how long it might take. Rehab is a process, and it's never a straight line. I'm sorry, I know that's not what you want to hear, but it's all I can tell you right now."

They talked about next steps—moving Gideon to a general ward, intensive rehabilitation—for a few minutes before Dr. Wilson excused himself.

His mother plucked a handful of tissues from the box on the table and blew her nose noisily after he'd gone.

"Hang in there, Mom," he said. "We'll make sure Dad gets the best care. And you know how stubborn he is."

She nodded. Then she took a deep breath, as though girding herself for a difficult conversation. "Garret, we need to talk about the business."

"Okay. I can call Ron—"

"No. You have to take charge, Garret. Not Ron. I don't want him swooping in and taking over everything."

His mother held his gaze, urging him to agree. He studied her face, trying to understand what was going on. Ron Gibson had been with Tate Transport for more than thirty years, working his way from truck driver all the way up to general manager. There was no one his father valued or trusted more, and Garret knew for a fact that the man was a frequent guest at the ranch. There was no one more qualified or better positioned to take over the day-to-day running of the business in the short term. Long term was another story, but that wasn't a discussion for today.

"I thought you loved Ron."

"Your father loves Ron. Tate Transport is your father's legacy, your inheritance. You need to be the one making decisions, not Ron. I want you to take over as CEO immediately."

Garret thought of his business partners back in Seattle and all the plans they'd made together. After years of back-breaking work, their fledgling coffee machine manufacturing business was on the verge of really taking off. The deal they'd signed in Rome was just the beginning.

But Tate Transport was responsible for the employment of more than a thousand people, some of whom had been with his father for decades.

There was no arguing with those kinds of numbers, or the look on his mother's face.

"Don't worry about the business," he said, aware that he was about to upend his whole life. "I'll take care of everything. I'll do whatever it takes."

Chapter Two

LATE THE NEXT day, Sierra sat back on her heels and contemplated the pile of weeds in front of her. She'd been out in the kitchen garden for hours now, weeding and tidying things up. She'd already put in a full day's labor doing ranch chores, but she'd needed to stay busy, to keep moving.

She couldn't stop thinking about those fraught, tense minutes in the Bell, even though they'd happened two days ago.

Gideon's hand in hers.

The minutes that had felt like hours.

The terrible sense of helplessness.

There was dirt beneath her nails and in the creases of her hands, highlighting the swooping curve of her lifeline. She contemplated it for a long moment, thinking about how quickly—how irrevocably—Gideon's life had been altered thanks to a microscopic blood clot in his brain.

He'd seemed so unassailable. Rich, powerful, dynamic.

But no one was immortal, and sometimes life turned on a dime. She knew that better than most people—thirteen years ago, her parents had died in a car accident when their car skidded into the path of Gideon's powerful SUV on a cold winter's night. Those few seconds had changed Sierra's family forever, just as a tiny blood clot had derailed Gideon's life two days earlier.

She dusted her hands off and was pushing herself to her feet when her phone rang with a call from Jack.

"Hi," she said, hoping against hope he wasn't calling with more bad news.

"Sierra. I need to ask a favor," Jack said. There was a thinness to his voice, an oddness that made her frown.

"Of course. Are you okay?" she asked.

"You doing anything now? Reckon you'd be able to come out to the Tate place to help me put the Bell to bed?"

"Sure. I can be there in ten," she said. She couldn't help noticing he hadn't answered her question. And since when had he needed help putting the Bell into the hangar?

"Okay. See you soon," Jack said, ending the call.

She could have sworn she heard the rasp of suppressed pain beneath his words and she tucked her phone into her back pocket as she strode toward the house.

Casey and his girlfriend, Eva, were dancing in the kitchen when she entered, doing some kind of silly take on a two-step that had them both in fits of laughter. She'd honestly never seen her youngest brother as happy as he'd been in the last few months since he'd met Eva and landed a recording contract for his country crossover band, The Whiskey Shots.

"Out of the way, losers," she said, shooing them away from the sink. "And maybe you could tone it down on the PDA. Constant exposure to other people's happiness is nauseating."

She pumped some hand soap into her palm and shoved her hands under the faucet. Casey tapped the back of her head, pushing her black straw cowboy hat down over her eyes.

"One day you'll understand," he said.

Sierra bumped her hat out of her eyes with her forearm and started scrubbing at her nails. "Jack needs some help over at the Tates'. Don't hold dinner for me, okay?"

She flicked off the tap and shook water off her hands, conscious of Casey's habitual bristle at the mention of the Tate name. Like her other two brothers, he was not a fan.

"Everything okay?" Eva asked.

"Don't know. Hope so," Sierra said, drying her hands on a hand towel before scooping up her truck keys and heading out the door.

The kitchen door slammed behind her and she took the porch steps two at a time. One advantage to being taller than most women was that when she wanted to get somewhere in a hurry, she could really cover some ground.

Her rusty old pickup started on the first go, and seconds later she was barreling down the driveway. She sat at the speed limit for the short drive to the Tates' place and parked beside Jack's SUV near the hangar. The Bell was out on the helipad, but there was no sign of him anywhere.

"Jack?"

"Here." His response came from inside the hangar, and there was no mistaking the edge of pain in his voice this time.

She strode through the open door and spotted him lying on his side near the old desk he kept in the corner for dealing with various administrative tasks.

"Jack! What happened?" Various nightmare scenarios flew through her mind as she rushed to his side, including that he'd succumbed to a stroke like his boss. He and Gideon were about the same age, give or take.

"Damn back," Jack said.

Her shoulders dropped a notch. A bad back wasn't great, but it wasn't life-threatening either.

"Dropped the keys, bent down to pick them up, and that was it. Couldn't move. Couldn't get up. Ridiculous," Jack said, clearly frustrated with his body's betrayal.

Sierra was aware he'd had a niggling lower back problem for a while now, but as far as she knew this sort of collapse was new to him.

"Has this happened before?" she asked. "Should we call an ambulance?"

"No ambulance," Jack said, lifting his head to glare at her as though she'd suggested he take up ballet dancing instead of offering a perfectly rational response to finding him incapacitated with pain on a hard concrete floor.

Men. Always with the stoicism.

"What about your doctor? Should I call him?" she suggested instead.

"Don't need any of that. I'll just lie here for a bit, and it'll settle. Just need you to put the Bell away for the night for me. They said there might be an electrical storm coming through."

It was all Sierra could do not to gape. Was Jack seriously suggesting she leave him lying on the ground while she went about the business of putting the Bell away for the night?

Unbelievable.

She bent so she could look him in the eye. "That's not going to happen, you stubborn idiot. Give me your doctor's name if you don't want a ride to the hospital in an ambulance."

Jack glared at her, his dark red eyebrows crowding together in a ferocious scowl.

"Looking at me like that isn't going to change anything," she said. "If you don't like my solutions, give me another one of your own to work with. Because leaving you lying here like this is not an option."

Jack's jaw worked a couple of times. "I've got some meds at home. Muscle relaxants. It's just a spasm. If I can get home, lie down for a while, I'll be good."

Sierra eyed him dubiously. "I'm happy to drive you home, but I'm assuming you've tried to get up and can't. Am I right?"

"Haven't tried for a few minutes. Might have eased a bit," Jack said.

"Well, okay. Let's try again. But slowly, because if it's not just a spasm, you don't want to do more damage." She was no doctor, but she figured back pain was not something a person wanted to mess with.

Grimacing, Jack rolled onto his stomach, then attempted to push himself up onto all fours. He barely got halfway before he gasped with pain and dropped onto his belly.

"Jack. God. Please let me ring an ambulance." She pulled out her phone, ready to dial.

"I'll be fine. I can do it. Just give me a moment," he insisted, his tone sharp.

"Everything okay in here?"

Sierra gave a start, her head whipping toward the hangar entrance where a tall, broad-shouldered figure stood silhouetted against the setting sun.

"All good," Jack called.

"Ignore him," she said. "He's done something to his back. We're trying to get him on his feet so I can drive him home."

The man entered the hangar, his stride long and easy, and even though it had been years since she'd last seen him, she recognized Garret Tate straight away. Dressed in designer jeans and a black sweater, his dark hair windswept, everything about him screamed *big money* and *big city*.

"What's the problem?" he asked, crouching on the other side of Jack's prone form. Even though he was a few feet away Sierra caught a whiff of his aftershave, something smoky and earthy and pineapple-y that made her blink, it smelled so good.

"Just a spasm," Jack said. "It'll pass. Just need my muscle relaxants."

"Which are at home," Sierra explained, meeting Garret's golden-brown gaze.

He nodded, then glanced behind the desk. "How about we use this chair? That way Jack'll have something to push himself up on."

He brought the chair around so it was next to Jack's prone form. "A friend of mine in college had a bad back. Used to wear a brace all the time for support," Garret said. "Is there anything we could use to create a brace? A towel, a bit of canvas? Something like that?"

Sierra watched in fascination as he unbuckled his belt, pulling the leather free from his jean loops with a deft flick of his wrist.

"Um. Let me think," she said, prodding her dazed brain back into action. "The tie-down sock is canvas. That could work."

She jogged out to the Bell and yanked open the cargo hold, pulling out the tie-down strap and detaching the rope that trailed from it. She jogged back, folding the stiff canvas into an approximation of a bandage as she ran.

"Perfect. Good work," Garret said, flashing her a small smile as she handed the canvas over.

Garret asked Jack to lift his hips enough so he could slip both the canvas and belt beneath him. Then he tightened the canvas around Jack's waist, cinching the belt to keep it in place.

"How's that?" he asked.

"Yeah. Feels better already, thanks," Jack said, and Sierra could hear the relief in his voice.

"Let's give standing a shot, then," Garret said.

It took them five minutes, but they managed to get Jack onto his feet. By that time he was white around the mouth and very pale. Sierra fetched his SUV and drove it into the hangar to minimize the distance he'd have to walk.

"I really, really want to take you to the clinic," she said as she and Garret assisted Jack to the car. "Just to be safe."

"I'll be fine. Just need to lie down," Jack insisted.

Garret gave her a look over the other man's hunched shoulders, indicating he shared her skepticism on that front.

"Then I'm calling Tally," Sierra said.

Jack's daughter lived locally. Maybe she'd be able to talk some sense into him.

"She's got Ruby's dance class this evening," Jack protested.

Sierra felt a rush of frustrated affection for her mentor. Trust Jack to memorize his granddaughter's schedule. He doted on Tally's two kids and was an active and enthusiastic presence in their lives. "If you were my father, I'd want to know you were in this kind of pain."

Garret cranked the passenger seat back as far as it would go and Sierra took Jack's arm and helped him ease down into the seat. By the time they were done, he was shaky and sweaty and Sierra simply held out her hand for his phone.

He handed it over with a resigned sigh, and she looked up his daughter's number and called her, aware all the while of Garret standing nearby, smelling like the best thing she'd ever smelled in her life.

She filled Tally in briefly before agreeing to meet her at Jack's place, then ended the call.

"You heard all that?" she asked Jack.

"Yes," was his grudging response.

She gave his shoulder a quick squeeze, because she could see this situation was putting a serious dent in his dignity.

Sierra turned to Garret and offered him a smile. "Thanks for the helping hand."

"You going to be okay at the other end?" he asked.

"We'll be fine," Jack responded before Sierra could.

"Apparently we'll be fine," Sierra said.

Garret smiled, and the part of her brain that wasn't worried about Jack offered the observation that on a scale of one to ten, Garret Tate was definitely an eleven.

Maybe even a twelve.

"Good luck," he said.

"Hopefully we won't need it," she said.

She walked around the car and slid into the driver's seat, suddenly very conscious of her dirt-streaked jeans and dusty flannel shirt. She wasn't wearing a scrap of makeup either. And lord knew how she smelled, given she'd been mucking out the stables earlier in the day.

Not as good as him, that was for sure.

Then she realized it was pretty dumb to worry about any of that, because even if she'd noticed Garret Tate was a hottie, there was no way a guy who lived in Seattle and who smelled like he did and looked like he did would have time in his busy schedule to notice her.

That was not the way the world worked.

"I'll try to be as gentle as I can," she promised Jack as she started the engine.

"I'm not made of glass," he snapped.

She put the car in gear and eased her foot onto the gas, passing out of the hangar and into the twilight. She couldn't resist a quick glance in the rearview mirror as she hit the driveway. Garret Tate stood where they'd left him, hands on his hips, a slight frown on his face as he watched them leave.

Then she turned into the driveway and he was gone.

THE LAST TIME Garret Tate had seen Sierra Carmody, he'd been nineteen and in his first year of college and she'd been a beanpole sixteen-year-old. Now she was . . . not a beanpole.

Far from it.

She had to be, what, twenty-seven now? All grown up.

Old memories washed over him as he returned the chair to its place behind Jack's desk. Once upon a time, he'd been close friends with Jesse Carmody. He'd been in and out of the Carmody house all the time back then, treating it almost like it was his own. He'd eaten at their kitchen table, played football in the paddock behind the house, ridden across their land with Jesse and Jed.

And then the accident had happened.

Garret straightened the chair unnecessarily, uncomfortable with the echo of old guilt. Maybe one day he'd be able to think about that night and not feel like dirt, but apparently it was not today.

He strode to the door of the hangar and was about to flick off the bright overhead lights when his phone rang. His mother was still at the hospital—she'd practically been living there since his father's stroke—and he half expected it to be her, letting him know she was going to spend the night in his father's room again.

Instead, he saw it was his father's general manager, Ron Gibson, returning his call. He'd been playing phone tag with Ron since yesterday, but it looked like they were finally going to connect. "Ron. How are you?" Garret asked as he took the call.

"Garret. How's your father? I've been getting text updates from your mom, but I'd appreciate anything more you can tell me," Ron said.

"He's doing okay. They're giving him a lot of intensive therapy to try to improve his swallowing reflex, and he's already working with a speech therapist, so hopefully you'll be able to talk to him yourself soon."

"Oh, man. That is so good to hear. I've been feeling sick at heart up here, waiting to know he's going to be okay." There was a quaver in his voice, not surprising considering he and Gideon had been working side by side for nearly thirty years.

"It's going to be a long road," Garret cautioned. "Which brings me to the reason for my call. Given he's going to be in rehab for a while, Mom's asked me to step into Dad's shoes for the foreseeable future."

There was a profound silence on the other end of the line.

"Well, I appreciate Nancy thinking about the business when she's got so much on her mind already, but neither of you need to worry about anything up here in Helena while you've got your hands full with Gideon. That's what I'm here for," Ron finally said.

"I appreciate that, but it's unlikely Dad's going to be returning to work for a while, and even if he does it would only be part-time. Given the circumstances, she wants to cause as little disruption to the business as possible. Obviously it's going to be a steep learning curve for me, coming in cold, so I'll be relying on you and the rest of the team to show me the ropes and get me up to speed," Garret said, keeping it as light as possible.

"Maybe I should have a word with Nancy, reassure her that I've got the situation covered up here. Gideon and I worked hand in glove. No one's better situated than me to keep things moving forward."

Or take over as CEO more permanently. Ron hadn't said it, but Garret didn't need to be a mind reader to guess where Ron's ambitions lay. A difficult ambition, given this was a privately owned, family-run business.

"I'd prefer for you not to bother her with this right now. As you said yourself, she's got a lot on her mind," Garret said. "She's spoken to the lawyers, and they're drawing up a contract. This is what she wants."

His father's general manager treated him to another long silence.

"I'll do whatever your father needs me to do," Ron finally said, his tone cool now.

"Like I said, I'll be relying on you to help me get up to speed. My plan is to fly in to the office first thing Monday," Garret said. "I'll commute back and forth so I can support Mom here in Marietta."

It was Friday now. That would give Ron the whole weekend to untwist his panties. "All right. I think it's unnecessary, but it's not my name on the company letter-head, so you suit yourself," Ron said.

"I'll see you next week, Ron. Have a good weekend," Garret said.

Ron ended the call without responding and Garret made a rude noise in the back of his throat.

So that went well.

After so many years with the business, Ron was entitled to a little umbrage, but it wasn't as though Garret planned to storm into the building and start restructuring—something he hoped Ron would work out pretty damned quickly because Garret had enough going on in his life right now without getting into a dick-measuring competition with his father's right-hand man.

He flicked off the light, then pulled the hangar door shut. It wasn't until he'd done so that he registered his father's helicopter still sat on the helipad. He knew it was Jack's habit to hangar it when it wasn't in use, but clearly that was not going to happen tonight. Well, there wasn't anything he could do about that either. He'd seen Jack hangar the helicopter dozens of times over the years, but he didn't have the first clue how to go about doing it himself.

He headed into the house, making his way directly to his father's study. Sitting at the desk, he opened his laptop and went straight to his inbox. Jay and Marco, his business partners in Seattle, had been more than generous when he'd filled them in on his situation. Between the three of them they'd decided to redistribute Garret's workload for a month, freeing him up to do what needed to be done in Montana. When those four weeks were up and Garret had a better idea of the lay of the land, they planned to get together to discuss ways and means of going forward. The most likely outcome at that point, Garret suspected, was that his two buddies would offer to buy him out. But no one knew better than Garret how tight their margins were as they moved into this crucial growth stage of their business, so Garret's counteroffer was going to be that he remain a silent partner in the business.

He still hadn't worked out if that was because he didn't want to expose his friends and partners to more risk, or if he wanted to maintain a link to his former life.

Maybe time would tell.

He was just finalizing an email summarizing outstanding tasks and projects for his buddies to take over when he heard the sound of a car arriving outside. The engine was too loud to be his mother's refined sedan, and curiosity brought him to his feet to look out the window.

It was Jack's SUV, returned to its usual spot beside the hangar. As he watched, Sierra Carmody climbed out, her slim, long-legged form outlined by the SUV's interior light. After beeping the car locked, she crossed to the hangar and slid the door open.

He frowned, wondering what she was doing. Then the lights flicked on inside and outside the hangar, flooding the helipad, and a few seconds later she appeared with the electronic tow cart Jack used to move the helicopter in and out of the hangar.

Clearly she intended to put the helicopter away for the night. Garret headed for the front door, making his way down the flagstone path to where she was positioning the cart to slide it beneath the helicopter.

"Hey. You need a hand with that?" he asked as he approached.

She flicked a quick smile over her shoulder. "Nope. All good, thanks."

"How's Jack doing?" he asked as she squatted to install clamp-on wheels to the rear of the helicopter skids.

"He's had his tablets, which he seems to think are a magical cure. I left him flat out in bed, his daughter fussing over him."

She switched on the cart and Garret watched with growing respect as she jacked up the nose of the helicopter, pushing the weight onto the wheels she'd just fitted before towing the helicopter into the hangar with the ease and confidence of long practice.

"So I'm guessing you've done this before," he said as she detached the electric cart from the helicopter and plugged it in to charge.

"Just a few times. I help Jack out whenever I can. Payback for him teaching me how to fly." She patted the helicopter's windshield fondly and Garret realized she meant she'd learned to fly in his father's Bell 407.

For a moment he was surprised his father had been so generous. Not that Gideon couldn't be when it was called for, but his generosity was almost always strategic and there was no strategy in helping a young woman gain her pilot's license. Then it hit him that Sierra wasn't just any young woman, she was a Carmody. Garret could easily imagine his father salving his conscience by being magnanimous toward Sierra—that seemed infinitely more in character than unmotivated beneficence.

He felt a little guilty for the cynical thought, given his father's current condition, but his father's stroke had not erased the past thirteen years of history between them. He still knew the things he knew about his father, and he couldn't unknow them.

"How long have you been qualified for?" he asked.

"About eighteen months," she said, walking around the helicopter as she gave it a quick but thorough visual inspection.

It was impossible not to notice her long legs as she moved, showcased by faded, work-worn denim. The last time he'd seen legs like that, they'd belonged to a supermodel.

"All right. I think she's good for the night," she said, dusting her hands together and turning to face him.

"Lucky I was here to offer my valuable assistance," he joked.

"Oh, definitely," she said, flashing him another one of her bright smiles.

The combination of her big green eyes and straight white teeth was more than a little dazzling.

Added to the appeal of her long legs, it was a pretty heady mix.

"I'm going to leave Jack's car keys in the desk drawer. Tally said she'd drive him over tomorrow morning to pick it up," Sierra said.

"Sounds like a plan," he said, watching as she slid the desk drawer closed and headed for the door.

He was so busy enjoying the way she moved he didn't realize she was preparing to leave until she stopped near the light switch and gave him a quizzical look.

Right. She probably wanted to get home. To her boyfriend or husband or whatever.

He took his cue and walked past her into the cool night, then blinked in the sudden darkness as she killed the lights. She exited seconds later and pulled the door shut.

"I'll text Jack when I get home and let him know his baby is all tucked in," she said.

"Thanks for taking care of that for us," Garret said, because it was clear she'd gone out of her way to come back here.

She waved a dismissive hand. "Least I can do, given the hours I've clocked up in the Bell." She pulled a set of keys from her front pocket. "I was really sorry about what happened to your father. I hope he's doing okay."

"He's getting there. But it's going to be a long road, I think. I know you were with him when it happened. Thanks for everything that you did."

"Jack did the hard bit," she said, shifting the keys in her hand. "Anyway. Good to see you, Garret."

"Yeah. You too."

Her gaze scanned his face briefly, as though she was trying to work something out. Then she turned and strode to her rusty old pickup. For the second time that day he stood and watched her walk away.

Weirdly, he was aware of a sense of disappointment. Which was nuts, because although he'd once spent a lot of time hanging out with her brothers, that had been a long time ago now and he and Sierra were essentially strangers. He didn't know her, and she didn't know him.

Unsettled, he restrained himself to a brief nod when she reversed her pickup and prepared to drive off. Then he turned toward the house, determined to put their encounter behind him.

Chapter Three

SIERRA SPENT THE whole weekend alternating between fretting over Jack and speculating about Garret Tate. It had been a long time since she'd last seen him and either he'd gotten a lot hotter while he was off in Seattle living his life, or she'd been too young to notice last time he'd been around. Either way, her curiosity was pointless, since it was highly unlikely their paths would cross again.

She was cutting vegetables for dinner on Sunday afternoon when Jack's daughter, Tally, called.

"Sorry to bother you," Tally said, sounding more than a little weary. "Do you have five minutes to talk?"

"Of course," Sierra said, setting down the tomatoes she'd just taken out of the crisper. "Is Jack all right?"

"No, he's not. Surprise, surprise. I have been at him and at him to go to the doctor all weekend, and he finally agreed after nearly passing out when he had to go to the bathroom. So we went to the clinic, and they took one look at him and sent him for X-rays. Long story short, he's got a bulging disk. The doctor said he'll be on bed rest for at least six weeks, possibly longer."

"Oh, wow. I'm so sorry to hear that. How is Jack taking

the news?"

"About as well as you'd expect. Dad being Dad, all he's worried about is letting the Tates down. Apparently Garret's stepping into Gideon's shoes, which means he'll be doing the Marietta-Helena commute on a regular basis, and Dad feels they really need him right now. I told him he should just let the Tates sort this out for themselves—he's sick, for Pete's sake, he shouldn't have to worry about replacing himself—but he doesn't want to serve up another problem to them when they're already under the pump."

"That sounds like Jack," Sierra said, all her spider senses tingling. She had a bad feeling she knew where this conversation was heading.

"He's hit up a few flying buddies already to cover for him, but they've all got their own businesses and they can't just abandon them for a couple of months. I told him he had the perfect person on his doorstep—you. He's always talking about what a great pilot you are, and you learned to fly in the Bell, right? But he doesn't want to make trouble for you with your family, since he knows how they feel about the Tates. He said he would never put you in that position. So that's why I'm calling, Sierra, because I have no shame, and I know it will be a load off Dad's mind if you could cover for him for those six weeks."

"Oh, boy," Sierra said. She pushed her hair off her forehead, her brain going a mile a minute. The last thing she wanted to do was to let Jack down, but what he'd said about making trouble for her with her family was accurate—her brothers hated the Tates. For years they'd ground their teeth over the lessons Jack had given her in the Tates' helicopter, barely tolerating the arrangement. She could only imagine how they'd take it if she announced she was stepping in to fill in for Jack, all so the Tates wouldn't be inconvenienced.

But this was Jack, and he'd been a good friend to her over the years. He was the reason she was a pilot, no bones about it. There was simply no way she would have been able to afford to pay commercial rates for all the flight hours required to gain her license without his generosity.

"Is that an 'oh, boy, yes,' or an 'oh, boy, maybe, let me think about it,' or . . . ?" Tally asked.

Sierra squeezed her eyes shut, warring loyalties and concerns ricocheting around in her mind. Six weeks was a long time for her brothers to cover for her on the ranch, especially when they were already juggling things to accommodate Casey's band commitments.

But none of that counted against the fact that Jack, her dear friend, needed her, and she was in a position to help him.

"I can do it," she said, because there was really no other answer.

She was rewarded with a relieved sigh from Tally.

"Thank you. I knew you'd come through for us. I'm going to hang up now and go tell Dad the good news. Once he's done tearing me a new one and telling me I overstepped by calling you, you'll no doubt hear from him with detailed instructions on just about everything under the sun."

Sierra couldn't help smiling at Tally's wry words. "That sounds like Jack. I'll stand by."

"You're a lifesaver. If I wasn't done with having kids, I'd name my next daughter after you," Tally joked.

Sierra's smile faded as she ended the call. It was great to be in a position to help Jack out and return the many kindnesses he'd shown her, but her chest was already getting tight with anxiety over breaking the news to her brothers.

It's only six weeks. Between us we can make this work.

But it wasn't losing her labor on the ranch that they'd object to—there were ways and means to get around that, including hiring a ranch hand for a couple of months—it was the fact that she was going out of her way to help the Tates.

"Damn it," she said, tossing her phone onto the counter.

Because she always thought better when she was working, she started chopping tomatoes for dinner. She'd already planned on making her mother's meatloaf, a perennial family favorite, but she mentally added an apple crisp to the menu because she was not above using food to set the stage for her announcement.

By the time the meatloaf was in the oven, she'd had a brainwave and she ducked out into the yard to make a quick phone call to her friend Cara, who happened to have a younger brother who might be in the market for some casual work. A quick conversation with first Cara and then Cara's brother, Davey, eased some of the tension banding her chest.

Davey was up for six weeks of work, if it was available. Sierra told him he'd be hearing from her brother shortly, then ended the call.

She had a solid solution to replacing her labor on the ranch. Now she just had to tell her brothers.

Even though she'd decided to just get it over and done with the moment her family appeared in the kitchen for dinner, she chickened out as Eva and Casey set the table and again when they all sat down to eat. Eva shared a funny story from her day, much to Jed's and Casey's amusement, and Sierra smiled when she was supposed to and pushed her food around her plate to make it look like she was eating when in reality she was rehearsing her announcement over and over in her head and bracing herself to speak up at the end of the meal.

Or maybe after they'd done the dishes.

You're totally turning this into something it isn't. You know that, right?

The problem was, while the Carmodys enjoyed a good squabble, they were generally always on the same page when it came to the big stuff. She was happy to give Jed and Casey a hard time when she thought they deserved it, but she didn't relish sowing discord in her family, especially when it touched on the memory of their parents and the dark days after the accident. She didn't want to be on the receiving end of her brothers' disapproval.

And she really didn't want to disappoint them.

She was so preoccupied with her thoughts she didn't realize Jed was talking to her until he gave her foot a nudge under the table.

"Hey. You still with us?" he asked, giving her a curious look.

"There's something I need to tell everybody," she blurted.

Not exactly the way she'd planned to introduce the subject, but what the hell.

"Let me guess—you're pregnant," Casey said, helping

himself to another serve of apple crisp.

"Don't joke about that," Jed said.

Eva nudged Casey with her elbow. "Sierra doesn't even have a boyfriend."

Sierra could see the conversation was about to get hijacked.

"Jack went to the doctor today and apparently he's got a bulging disk. They've told him he's looking at a minimum of six weeks of bed rest, possibly more, and his daughter, Tally, asked if I'd be prepared to take over his job with the Tates until he's recovered. And I said yes."

For a moment there was nothing but silence. Then Casey let the serving spoon drop into the crisp dish with a loud clang. "What the hell, Sierra? Why on earth would you go out of your way to do the Tates a favor?"

"The favor is for Jack," she said.

"They've got more money than god. Let them find themselves another pilot," Casey said, his lip curling. "Why should we bend over backward and make do without you to accommodate them?"

Eva scowled at him. "Come on. I know you have your reasons for not liking the guy, but Gideon Tate is not Stalin. Don't make Sierra feel bad for helping out a friend."

Casey shifted in his chair and looked like he was ready to argue the point. Sierra glanced at Jed, who hadn't said a word.

"You wouldn't have to make do. I spoke to Cara, and her younger brother, Davey, is looking for ranch work. He's twenty, keen for the experience, and he said he'd be happy to take whatever hours we've got to offer," she said.

"Get me his number and I'll have a word with him," Jed said, his expression giving nothing away.

Sierra waited for him to say more but he didn't. She scanned his face, nonplussed, trying to decide if he was holding anything back. This was not the way she'd imagined this conversation going. Casey's reaction, yes. But Jed was not sticking to the script she'd written in her mind.

"You're not pissed with me?"

"*I'm* pissed with you," Casey piped up. "The Tates are entitled assholes. It's not our job to make their lives easy."

"I heard you the first time, Casey," Sierra snapped. "For the record, they have been nothing but nice to me. And yeah, I know it's probably out of guilt because of Mom and Dad, but would you prefer they'd treated us like dirt for thirteen years instead?"

Casey glared at her, and she knew he was working hard to hold on to his temper. She figured she could thank Eva's presence for the fact they weren't already yelling at each other at a million decibels.

Eva deliberately changed the subject then, asking Casey when he was expecting the cover art for The Whiskey Shots' debut album, and slowly the tension drained out of the room.

Sierra could tell Casey was still stewing, but it was Jed she was worried about and when he slipped out to check on the horses after dinner, she waited a few minutes and then followed him.

She found him feeding Pedro half an apple, his palm flat as the horse lipped up the treat.

"You are such a softie," Sierra said, leaning against the

stall door.

"He's a good horse," he said simply.

"You didn't say much back there."

"Not much to say. Like you said, you're helping out a friend."

She forced herself to give voice to her real fear, the fear that was always attached to her accepting anything from the Tates. "You don't think I'm being disloyal to Mom and Dad?"

Jed's brow furrowed. "It was an accident."

"Sure, but you and Casey and Jesse still hate the Tates."

"I don't hate anyone." He wiped his hand on the side of his jeans. "I don't like feeling beholden to the Tates. I didn't like it when Gideon offered to buy this place out of charity, and it never sat comfortably with me that he gave you free use of his helicopter so you could get your hours up. We don't need handouts."

"But you're okay with me filling in for Jack?"

Jed shrugged. "He's your friend and he's been good to you. And like Eva said, Gideon Tate is not Stalin. He's just lucky his car could take a hit better than Dad's old pickup." He ran a hand down Pedro's neck, his expression unreadable. "Can't keep letting the past dictate the present. That night has caused more than enough misery."

She guessed he was thinking about Jesse's estrangement, how he'd kept his distance from the family for years because he blamed himself for their parents being on the road that night. Then Jed shifted and the light hit his face and she saw something else in his eyes, something sadder and more private. She understood suddenly that he was thinking about

Mae, the girlfriend he'd cut loose in order to take on the responsibility of being the head of the family.

It had been thirteen years and he'd never so much as looked at another woman. Not seriously, anyway.

"Why don't you call her?" she asked impulsively.

Jed's brow furrowed as he shot her a look. "She's getting married."

Pretty revealing that he didn't bother to ask who she was referring to.

"I'm not telling you to elope with her. Just have a coffee. Let it go. Look into her eyes and say goodbye, finally."

Jed was already shaking his head.

"Then let me set you up with one of my friends."

"Pass."

"Why?"

"I'm too busy with this place."

"Bullshit. Casey's got time for Eva and his music. I've got time for my flying. Jesse's got time for the rodeo, CJ, *and* this place. You've got to have more in your life than work, Jed."

He rolled his eyes. "Okay. I'll make a note to take up a hobby."

He moved to go but she refused to stand back from the stall door so he could exit.

"What are you going to do when we've all got our own places, our own families? What are you going to be left with when we've all flown the nest that you kept safe for us?"

Jed stared at her, and for a moment she could see the regret and resignation in his eyes.

"You want to move so I can get out of here?" he asked,

gesturing for her to step back.

"You can run but you can't hide from this stuff, Jed," she warned him as she stepped out of the way.

"How about you concentrate on the favor you've agreed to, and I'll concentrate on this place," Jed said, his tone a warning that further forays into his personal life would not be welcome.

Sierra weighed the wisdom of persisting for a heartbeat, then decided to let it go—for now.

"I'm not giving up on you," she told her brother as he headed for the house.

True to form, Jed didn't say a word in response.

SIERRA ROLLED OUT of bed a whole twenty minutes before she needed to the following morning, she was so amped for the day. It was impossible to pretend she wasn't excited about the next six weeks now she'd gotten the messy business of talking to her brothers over and done with.

She was going to fly every single day, give or take, for six weeks. It didn't get better than that.

She'd never talked about it openly with anyone, but her long-term dream was to be a full-time pilot. She wasn't quite sure what that might look like yet—working for one of the tour guide operators based out of the Big Sky ski resort perhaps, or doing charter flights out of Billings or Bozeman. Maybe even air rescue, if that was an option.

Of course, a job like Jack's would be amazing, too, but private pilot gigs were as rare as unicorns. Maybe even rarer. Which was one reason why Jack was moving heaven and earth to ensure the Tates weren't inconvenienced by his illness.

Anyway, whatever flying full-time might look like for her, it was still a long way off. Until the ranch was well and truly out of the red and Casey was more established with his music career, her family couldn't afford for her to go chasing her dream. In the meantime, this gig covering for Jack would look great on her CV as well as getting her flight hours up. As a newly qualified pilot, every hour she clocked up helped increase her bona fides and employability, not to mention improving her knowledge and experience.

She'd laid out clothes for herself the previous night, a uniform of sorts that roughly approximated what Jack typically wore—chinos, navy polo shirt, tan belt, lace-up boots, and a navy ball cap—and she checked the weather on her phone as she dressed. They were forecasting perfect flying conditions—clear skies, low wind—so there was no need to adjust Jack's usual flight path to Helena.

Jed was in the kitchen when she entered and he poured a cup of coffee and slid it across the counter toward her.

"I made oatmeal," he said, and she blinked at him.

"I beg your pardon?" she said, pretending she hadn't heard properly.

Jed was notorious for not having the patience to make oatmeal, which happened to be her favorite breakfast food.

"Wanted to say I was sorry for not being more support-ive last night. I should have hosed Casey down at dinner. You're doing the right thing, helping Jack out."

It was so typical of her thoroughly decent older brother that he'd felt the need to address a perceived wrong.

Sierra smiled at him. "Thanks, bro-daddy, but I can handle Casey."

"Thought we agreed we never needed to hear those words again," Jed said, filling a bowl with steaming oatmeal.

She'd coined bro-daddy in junior high as a joke and he'd always hated it.

"It felt like a special occasion."

He gave her a dry look and she laughed, buoyed by his support. Casey would come around, too, she knew. He'd never been able to hang on to a bad mood for long.

She added honey and milk to her bowl and made short work of her oatmeal before finishing her coffee and hitting the bathroom to brush her teeth. Ten minutes later, she was heading for the front door.

The Tates' spread was just ten minutes' drive from the Carmody ranch and it wasn't long before she was pulling alongside the hangar set off to one side of the Tates' sprawling house. Originally a humble ranch-style home similar to the one her parents had built, it had been extended over the years and embellished with feature timber porch supports and impressive landscaping. She'd heard the Tates owned a place in Helena as well, but this was Gideon and Nancy's original home, the house they'd started their hugely successful transport business from all those years ago, and Gideon obviously considered it his true home base even though his company headquarters was in Helena.

It took her ten minutes to move the Bell out onto the landing pad using the battery-operated tow cart. By the time she'd untied the rotor the sky was a soft apricot color as the sun made its first appearance over the horizon.

She did a visual check, walking around the aircraft, looking for the usual—oil, water, or fuel leaks, and any cracking or signs of fatigue in the rotors and skids. As Jack had taken pains to explain to her last night when he called, the helicopter had a full tank, so she didn't have to worry about refueling. Instead, she inspected the passenger cabin to ensure it was ready, leaving the flask of coffee she'd made at home there for Garret, as per Jack's instructions. She checked the weather report one last time—still clear—and was just pocketing her phone when she heard the distant sound of a door closing.

Her stomach gave an odd, unsettling little jump at the prospect of seeing Garret Tate again. She hadn't allowed herself to think about him too much once she'd agreed to take over Jack's job, but there was no denying the buzz of anticipation in her belly as she climbed out of the cockpit.

He was walking toward her from the house, and she adjusted her ball cap nervously as she drank in the sight of him. He'd been wearing casual clothes Friday night, but this morning he was all clean lines and crisp edges in a navy suit with a white shirt and navy-and-red-striped tie. His dark hair was neatly styled, his jaw clean-shaven. The cut of his suit jacket highlighted the width of his shoulders and the slimness of his hips, while his pants hinted at muscular thighs.

The whole effect was more than a little overwhelming and Sierra felt blind-sided.

This man was not just easy on the eyes—he was inordinately, disturbingly hot.

Definitely a thirteen. Maybe even a fourteen.

"Morning," Garret said as he stepped onto the helipad.

"Morning," she said, offering him what she hoped was a cool, professional smile and nod.

As though that would make up for all the highly unprofessional mental ogling she'd just indulged in.

He paused in front of her and she was treated to a waft of his insanely delicious aftershave.

"Thanks for covering for Jack at such short notice. I appreciate it," he said.

"Not a problem. Happy to help out. And I promise I'll get you to Helena in one piece as an added bonus."

He laughed. "Very reassuring, thanks."

She opened the passenger door for him. "There's coffee in the thermos flask. We should be in Helena by seven thirty."

"Thanks, Sierra."

He climbed into the cabin and set down his briefcase, a sleek, modern take on the traditional businessman's accessory. She waited until he'd clipped his belt on before shutting the door and climbing into the cockpit. She put her headset on and checked he'd done the same using the mirror. He hadn't, and when he glanced up and met her eyes she mimed him doing so. He gave her a small acknowledging smile before sliding his headset on. She rewarded him with a thumbs-up, then turned her attention to the Bell.

Okay, here we go. Don't fuck it up, Carmody.

Taking a deep breath, she started running through her preflight checklist.

GARRET FELT THE mechanical vibration of the motor

starting up, followed by the rising whir of the rotors engaging. Even though he had plenty of work to get through, he waited until the Bell lifted gently from the helipad before opening his briefcase, watching Sierra's face via the mirror.

There was an intensity to her expression that told him she was taking this temporary job very seriously. Jack had assured him she was one of the best pilots he knew when he called Garret to apprise him of the situation last night. She certainly looked like she knew what she was doing as she deftly operated the pedals and cyclic with quiet confidence.

He frowned as it occurred to him that he was paying her a lot more attention than if she was Jack. Not the smartest way to kick off their professional relationship.

He switched his focus to his computer and didn't look up again until Sierra announced they were approaching Helena airport. She landed the Bell with the gentlest of bumps and when he glanced at the mirror he saw she was smiling, clearly pleased with herself. A minute later she climbed out of the cockpit and came to open the passenger cabin door, letting a wash of cool air into the cabin.

"Right on time," he said as he stepped down onto the tarmac.

"Helps when the wind is in our favor," she said with a modest shrug.

"What's the latest we can leave for Marietta this evening?" he asked.

Sierra pushed the door shut and secured the latch. "We start losing light at seven thirty, so six thirty would be our latest possible departure time at this end."

"Then I'll be here by six thirty," he assured her before

giving her a nod goodbye.

He crossed to where his father's car was parked next to the hangar, shrugging out of his suit jacket for the short drive into Tate headquarters. He slid it onto the coat hook behind the driver's seat, glancing idly toward the helipad as he pushed the door closed.

Sierra was inspecting the main engine compartment, and he paused to admire her easy, agile athleticism as she stepped down off the skid.

And, yes, her ass, because it looked nothing short of sensational in her slim-fit chinos.

A gust of wind caught the end of his tie, making it dance in front of his face, and Garret realized he was staring inappropriately. Again.

He turned away abruptly. No matter how attractive he found Sierra Carmody—and, clearly, it was pointless to deny he found her *very* attractive—the moment she'd stepped into Jack's shoes she'd become off-limits. She was a Tate employee now, and that was a hard line he would never cross.

He had no place noticing how she moved or how nice her ass was. In fact, it kind of made him a creep. She was here to fly him from A to B, and how she looked while doing so had nothing to do with anything.

He was frowning again as he started the car and steered it away from the hangar. Apparently his subconscious—or, more accurately, his libido—had decided his life wasn't messy enough at the moment.

Perfect. Just what he needed, another complication.

Chapter Four

I T WAS A short drive into the office and when Garret cruised into the underground garage he noticed with interest that while a half dozen spots were occupied, the one reserved for his father's general manager was notably empty.

It was still relatively early, but Garret had hoped he and Ron could get straight into it this morning. Garret had a lot of questions and a lot of background to catch up on, and he was keen to hit the ground running. But apparently his general manager was not an early bird.

Not today, anyway.

He made his way to the fifth level and headed for his father's office, where he found a neatly dressed woman with salt-and-pepper hair and clear gray eyes stationed at a desk outside the door. She was a new face to him, which meant she must have joined Tate Transport within the last seven years.

"Mr. Tate. Good Morning. I'm Mandy. We spoke last week," the woman said, standing and offering him her hand.

"Hi, Mandy. Good to put a face to the name," he said.

"For me too," she said with a tight smile. "I didn't get a chance to say so last week, but I'm very sorry for your father's illness. It was a huge shock to all of us."

"Thanks, Mandy. We got lucky—he's still with us. I'm concentrating on that part at the moment."

Her smile was more relaxed this time. "That's a good way to look at it."

He glanced into his father's office. "I might as well dive right in."

"Of course."

Conscious of his father's assistant watching him, Garret stepped over the threshold and into his father's most prized domain. This was the place where Gideon Tate had always been at his happiest, his sharpest, his best.

A huge polished walnut desk stood in pride of place, wide and deep and imposing. A well-used leather chair sat behind it, positioned to take advantage of the view across the rooftops of downtown Helena. The opposite wall was covered with photo frames of various sizes, the pictures depicting his father laughing and shaking hands with various local and national luminaries. Golfing heroes, politicians, even the occasional B-list celebrity smiled out at the world alongside his father, assuring visitors that Gideon Tate was a man who knew all the right people.

The last time Garret had been in this room, he'd told his father he was moving to Seattle to start a business with his college roommates. It had been . . . unpleasant, to say the least.

"Can I get you a coffee before you get started? Or maybe a juice, or something else, Mr. Tate?"

Garret snapped out of his reverie and offered Mandy a smile. "Thanks, but I'm good for now. And it's Garret. I have a feeling we're going to be spending a lot of time with each other."

That won him another small smile and a nod. "All right. If there's nothing else you need, I'll leave you to it," Mandy said, already on her way out the door.

Garret moved behind the desk. Setting down his brief case, he sank into his father's chair. Discomfort washed over him. It didn't feel right, sitting on this side of the desk, in his father's place.

Get used to it, buttercup. This is the way it is now.

When Garret was in his teens, he'd dreamed of working side by side with his father one day. It was something he and his father had talked about a lot. At sixteen, Garret had started to think about what courses he should take at college, and which departments he should intern with during summer break—all with an eye to joining Tate Transport as his father's heir apparent once he'd graduated.

Then the accident happened, and everything had changed between them.

And now it had changed again.

Flipping open the screen on his father's laptop, he clicked through to the email inbox. An email had come in since he landed and he narrowed his eyes as he read that Ron was unfortunately going to be absent from the office for the entire day with unavoidable off-site meetings. He apologized to Garret for the inconvenience, but looked forward to talking to him tomorrow.

Garret sat back in his chair.

It was impossible to pretend Ron's absence on Garret's first day in the office was anything other than a power play.

It solidified the feeling Garret had had ever since their first phone call. Apparently Ron was determined to be a douche about him taking over his father's role.

Fuck him. Like he said, it's not his name on the letterhead.

Ron might be his father's right-hand man, but Tate Transport was bigger than any one person. And maybe Ron making himself absent could be turned to Garret's advantage. After all, there was something to be said for finding your own way into a new role, rather than being led into it.

Pulling up a new email message, he typed up a request to his department heads asking for a brief overview of their current projects, full financials, and any outstanding matters they felt required attention, due by close of business the next day.

He fired it off with a grim smile on his lips. Ron might not be keen to share his sand pit, but that wasn't going to stop Garret from digging in.

SIERRA HAD A number of maintenance inspections to run to keep her busy during the day, but it didn't stop her thoughts from drifting to Garret.

The first time she told herself it was because she was curious about him. The second time she told herself it was because she empathized with him, today being his first day at his father's company, which had to be a daunting prospect. Stepping into his father's shoes with no notice or hand over would not be easy or pretty, she imagined.

The third time she caught herself thinking about him, it was hard to come up with an excuse for her own preoccupation—apart from the obvious one, which was that she was attracted to him. It was an unwelcome moment of clarity, given she'd just agreed to work for him for six weeks in Jack's stead, so she batted it away and promised herself she'd think about it later.

At four thirty she started her preflight checks so she could be ready for Garret in case he arrived earlier than anticipated. She was glad she had when he pulled into his parking spot just after five. He looked less crisp and a lot more rumpled at this end of the day, his hair standing up in unruly spikes, his jaw shadowed with whiskers.

It didn't make him any less hot, she couldn't help noticing as he walked toward her. In fact, if anything, it made him more approachably sexy, as though he'd just climbed out of someone's bed after a hard night of doing amazing things to that lucky someone.

Good lord. Can you hear yourself?

She could, and it was both embarrassing and confusing. She'd never responded this powerfully to a man in her life. But it seemed that everything about Garret made her aware of the fact that she was a woman and he was a man.

Not great when the only thing she should be thinking about was the fact that she was a pilot and he her passenger. And her boss.

"Mr. Tate. Good timing. We're all ready to go," she said.

"Thanks, Sierra."

He seemed more distracted than this morning, burying himself in his computer the moment he'd fastened his seat belt. Every time she checked the mirror during the flight home he was either frowning at the screen, typing, or checking something on his phone.

As she'd recognized earlier, he'd taken on a huge task by jumping into a business the size of Tate Transport on such short notice. And it wasn't just what he was taking on; it was what he was giving up too. He'd been living in Seattle for years. He must have a whole life there. A house or apartment. A career. A girlfriend. Maybe even a wife?

She pondered the notion that he might be married for a moment and then discarded it. It seemed unlikely he could have gotten hitched without her hearing some echo of the news, given how small Marietta was and how much people liked to talk. Of course, if she wanted confirmation of his marital status, she could probably tap into the local whisper network to verify what his situation was. Ashley's mother was good friends with Nancy Tate. She'd probably know all about Garret's—

WTF. This man is your BOSS, even if it's only temporary. Jack is relying on you to cover for him. What the hell is wrong with you?

It was a good question. A tide of heat rushed into her face and she spent the next few minutes fiddling with the instrument panel unnecessarily, willing the warmth to leave her face. This was a big opportunity for her—six weeks of flying, great experience, a step in the right direction in terms of her career ambitions. And Jack was relying on her to do him proud. There was no place in any of that for her to develop a crush on her employer, which she was well on her way to doing.

She needed to get a grip. She needed to stop thinking about Garret Tate as anything other than a passenger whose safety she was responsible for. This was not singles' night at Grey's Saloon. He was not a hot prospect. And she had a job to do. Period.

The stern talking-to seemed to help. For the rest of the flight, she successfully kept her eyes front and center, away from the temptation of the mirror. Thanks to a strong crosswind, it took them five minutes longer than usual to touch down at the Tates' property. Once she'd switched off the engine, she whizzed through her postflight shutdown routine and climbed out to open the door to the passenger cabin.

"Thanks for today, Sierra." Garret offered her a distracted smile as he exited, his thoughts obviously elsewhere.

"See you tomorrow," she said.

His phone beeped with a text and he pulled it out as he headed for the house, once again absorbed in work. She refused to allow herself to watch him go—finally, a bit of self-discipline—and concentrated on hangaring the helicopter for the night.

That was the way it was going to be between them from now on as far as she was concerned—all business all the time, no exceptions. Even if it killed her.

SIERRA CARMODY WAS wiping condensation off the Bell's windshield when Garret left the house the next morning, her dark, wavy ponytail swinging across her shoulders. The moment she heard his approach she glanced over her shoulder, a friendly smile on her lips.

Her green gaze was bright and clear, her cheeks a little

flushed. "Morning."

"Morning."

"There's coffee in the cabin, skies are clear, and we're ready to take off when you are."

"Sounds good to me," he said. "Let's do it."

She moved ahead of him to open the helicopter door and they were in the air less than five minutes later, the engine noise muffled by his headset.

If he was a different sort of man he would put this time alone with Sierra to good use. He'd talk to her, find out more about her life. About her. He'd make her laugh and lay the groundwork for a dinner invitation down the road. If he played his cards right, it wouldn't be long before there was more than dinner on the menu.

At least, that was the way he imagined it must work. He was no expert. He'd simply watched his father operate over the years. Gideon had had affairs with two of his employees that Garret knew of. There was a decent chance there were more, but once Garret had gone away to college, he hadn't been in a position to notice anymore. But it stood to reason that his father hadn't changed the habits of a lifetime—he'd always believed the rules didn't apply to him.

Garret had different values, which he'd spent the last thirteen years demonstrating to his father via his absence from Marietta, the business, and his parents' lives.

Sierra might be gorgeous and sexy. She might intrigue him—but she was utterly, incontrovertibly off-limits now she was an employee of Tate Transport.

So instead of flirting with Sierra, he spent the trip going over the list of queries he'd compiled for Ron and making more notes for himself on matters to follow up with Mandy.

When Sierra set them down in Helena with a barely perceptible thud, he thanked her and was on his way with minimal interaction, everything strictly aboveboard and businesslike. As it should be.

Twenty minutes later he was in town, riding the elevator to the fifth floor.

Mandy was behind her desk when he arrived, and she passed over his messages and mail when he paused to wish her good morning.

"Thanks for these. Could you please let Ron know I'd like to see him when he gets in?" he asked.

"I'll make sure he knows," Mandy said, the picture of professionalism in a neat black suit and pale blue shirt.

It was just after nine when Ron appeared in Garret's doorway, a welcoming smile on his craggy face, acting for all the world as though he hadn't pulled a total dick move the previous day.

"Garret. How are you settling in? Mandy looking after you?" he asked, striding forward to shake Garret's hand. He'd played college football and had an inch on Garret, along with twenty or so pounds. His grip was firm, his pale blue gaze holding Garret's intently the whole time they shook hands. A classic alpha-dog move Garret had seen his father pull many times.

"Mandy's been great. How were your meetings yesterday?" Garret asked, keeping his tone light and casual.

"Great, great," Ron said, his smile broadening. "Mantis want us to take over all their motor vehicle transport. Contract should be signed by the end of the week."

"That's a big score. Congratulations," Garret said. Mantis was a large car dealer network with locations across the state. The contract would be a good addition to the bottom line.

"Your dad set the deal up, I just knocked it down," Ron said modestly. "Listen, I was really sorry I couldn't be here on your first day, but I really wanted to nail Mantis down."

"Have you got time to sit with me now? I've been reviewing some files, talking to a few people, and I've got a lot of questions," Garret asked.

"Sure thing. Just let me grab a coffee."

Garret waited until Ron was settled opposite before launching into a series of queries about the company's current contracts, fleet makeup, and key clients. To his credit, Ron took pains to explain everything thoroughly yet succinctly, and by the end of the session Garret felt as though he'd filled in a lot of blanks.

And maybe it was his imagination, but he felt as though Ron had relaxed his guard a little, too, when he saw that Garret was willing to take the time to listen and learn from those more experienced than himself.

With a bit of luck, maybe Ron wasn't going to be a problem after all. Maybe it was just going to be a case of Ron needing a little time to adjust and digest the fact that his status and authority in the business were not going to change just because Garret was sitting in his father's chair.

It was a nice dream, but his sense of optimism didn't survive the morning. At eleven Mandy entered his office, a frown on her face.

"I know you've got a call in five, but Theo just emailed

me," she said, referencing the head of the sales department. "He wanted to warn me that the report you asked for is going to be incomplete for his department because Ron is sitting on the financials."

Garret put down the contract he'd been reading. "Did Ron give any reason for holding them back?"

"Not that Theo passed on," Mandy said, her expression diplomatically neutral.

Garret paused to digest the full import of her news for a second. He'd spent an hour trying to smooth the waters with Ron this morning, and the whole time the other man had known that he'd already countermanded Garret's first direct order in the business.

Which made it official: Ron was fucking with him.

The realization made Garret feel more than a little stupid for his moment of optimism that morning, which in turn made him less inclined to be understanding toward the other man. He understood that his father's sudden illness and the unexpected management change was a big gearshift for everyone, but Garret was not up for games. He couldn't afford them, not when he was already running to catch up and get a grip on a multimillion-dollar enterprise with thousands of employees.

If Ron wasn't interested in being number two to Garret's number one, then it was time for him to leave the business.

The thought made Garret's gut tighten. He knew without asking that his father would urge him to do everything in his power to keep Ron happy and on deck, but Garret couldn't afford to have a general manager who didn't respect him or his authority. An attitude like that would soon seep into every level of the business.

"Postpone my call and ask Ron to come see me, please," he said.

Mandy acknowledged the request with a single nod before exiting the office.

"You wanted to see me, boss?" Ron asked five minutes later as he breezed in.

"Grab a seat," Garret said, indicating the guest chair in front of his desk.

"Feel like I've been called into the school principal's office," Ron said, his tone light. "Hope I'm not about to get detention."

He smirked and waggled his eyebrows, supremely confident. Garret sat back in his chair and considered the other man, letting the silence stretch, refusing to allow Ron to frame their meeting as a childish role play.

"What's up?" Ron finally said, his smirk fading.

"I'm trying to work out why you'd hold back the financials for the sales department," Garret said. "Maybe you could fill me in on what your strategy is?"

What remained of Ron's casual demeanor slipped away as his eyes grew cold. "What exactly are you insinuating?"

"I'm not insinuating anything. I'm asking you a direct question. I asked for a comprehensive report from each department head yesterday, and today I learned that even though you managed to be absent from the office on my first day in, you've held back the sales department financials I requested. I'd like to know why."

"I'm still pulling the numbers together," Ron said. "Theo's a good people person but he's not great on admin. I thought I'd do him the favor of making sure he didn't look like a moron."

"I'm happy to take whatever you currently have, on the understanding that it's not completely up-to-date," Garret said immediately, calling the other man's bluff.

"I'm not handing over half-assed data. Anyway, I don't see why you need all this bullshit paperwork, anyway. I can tell you everything you need to know to sit in that chair—namely, trust me. I've been making sure this business runs smoothly for years. Your father trusted me to get the job done, and if the way I ran things was good enough for him, it should be good enough for you."

The impatient contempt in the older man's expression was very revealing. Garret had been hoping it wouldn't come to this, but Ron had left him with no choice but to play hardball.

"Here's what's going to happen, Ron. You're going to get me those sales financials. And then we're going to talk about how things are going to work around here, if you'd like to continue in your role."

A tide of red rushed up Ron's neck and into his face as he leapt to his feet. "You slick little asswipe. You think you can come in here and kick over everything your father and I built over the last thirty years? Who the fuck do you think you are? I was prepared to give you the benefit of the doubt, but you just proved everything your father ever said about you. When he hears what's been going on, you're going to get the wake-up call of your life."

"Not gonna happen, Ron. You're not talking to my father. He doesn't need the stress, and it would be pointless, because I've got full legal authority to do whatever I want to do with this business."

Ron's face got even redder as he glared at Garret, his chest lifting and falling rapidly, his hands flexing at his sides. A part of Garret's brain measured the distance between the other man and himself, just in case Ron really lost his shit.

"This is *bullshit*. You'll be hearing from my lawyer." Ron stormed to the door, opening it with enough force to send it smashing against the wall. Then he was gone, leaving a vapor trail of anger and resentment behind him.

Seconds later, Mandy appeared, her face pale with shock. "Is everything all right?"

"Did he head back to his office or leave?" Garret asked.

"He took the elevator," Mandy reported.

Which meant he was leaving the building. Good. Garret didn't want him around while he made his next moves.

"Could you ask his assistant to come see me, please? Then I need you to get me David Hannam on the line for a meeting in half an hour with myself and Sabrina." Hannam was the company lawyer, while Sabrina headed human resources. Garret needed their twin expertise in order to exit Ron from the business as quickly and cleanly as possible.

It would be expensive to pay Ron out, but his continued employment with Tate Transport had just become untenable.

"We also need to take immediate steps to revoke Ron's access to the internal network and this building."

Mandy blinked. "Oh. Um. Of course. I'll talk to Vinnie in IT. We might need to get someone in to reconfigure the security system."

"I'll leave it in your capable hands," Garret said.

She blinked again. Then she nodded. "I'll make it happen."

"And I'd like to see every head of department in my office at two o'clock. I don't care whatever else they have on, they need to cancel it."

Mandy nodded, her color coming back a little now. "I'll go see them personally, make sure they understand."

"Thank you."

Garret stood and removed his jacket after she left his office. He felt wired and jumpy with adrenaline, and he stood at the window and forced himself to breath steadily, conscious of his racing heartbeat and clammy palms. Classic fight-or-flight reactions.

It was a huge pain that Ron had decided to be a douche over the business succession but there wasn't a whole lot Garret could do about it except cut the man out of the chain of command as quickly and cleanly as possible.

A thought occurred and he reached for his phone and called his mother, hoping he'd beaten Ron to it.

"Garret. Your father and I were just talking about you. How is everything going?" his mother asked brightly.

Garret figured that meant he'd gotten in before Ron, which was a very good thing.

"Mom, I don't have time to talk now, but you need to know that Ron has just burned his bridges with Tate Transport. He's pretty fired up, and there's a high chance he's going to try to go over my head to you or Dad. So I'm going to ask you to not take any calls from him until I've had legal advice, okay?"

There was a moment of stunned silence. Then he heard his mother moving.

"I'm just going to step outside for a moment, Gideon," he heard her tell his father.

"Mom, I really don't have time to get into the details right now."

"I don't understand. Did you and Ron have words?" his mother asked, her voice hushed, presumably so his father wouldn't overhear. "What was it about?"

"He made it very clear that he is unwilling to work under me," Garret said dryly. "In the most insulting way possible."

"I see."

A knock sounded tentatively on the door and Garret turned to find Brianna, Ron's assistant, standing in the doorway. Blonde and blue-eyed with a plump, smiley face, Brianna had been Ron's assistant for more than a decade. She wasn't smiling now. Her face stiff with wariness. He held up a finger to indicate he needed a moment.

"Mom, I need to go. But we're clear on the call situation? The last thing Dad needs right is Ron in his ear."

"I've got your father's phone, so there's not a problem there. And I won't take any calls from Ron until you tell me to."

"Great, thanks. I've got to go now, sorry."

He ended the call and waved a hand to indicate Ron's secretary should enter.

"Brianna, sorry about that. Grab a seat."

Chapter Five

SIERRA SPENT THE morning checking and testing software updates for the Bell's avionics before heading into the terminal in search of coffee and something to eat. She ran into some old friends of Jack's as she paid for her chicken salad sandwich and wound up eating lunch with a table full of pilots. There was a lot of laughter and good-natured shit-slinging and she was still smiling when she left the terminal building to head back to the Bell. She was halfway there when her phone buzzed with a call from Garret.

"Garret, hi," she said.

"Sierra. Sorry for the late notice, but I'm going to need to stay overnight here in Helena."

"Okay, not a problem," she said. Jack had advised her that every now and then he'd had to overnight in Helena when Gideon's plans had changed, and she'd packed a bag carrying fresh underwear, some toiletries, and a clean polo shirt into the cargo hold, just in case.

"That was easy," Garret said, his tone wry.

"All part of the service."

"Nice to know one part of my life is working smoothly. Maybe you could walk me through how this usually operates. Do I need to get my assistant to organize a hotel room for you tonight?"

"My understanding is that there's a guest room at your lake house that Jack used to stay in when he had overnighters, and I'm more than happy to do the same."

"Right. That makes sense. Good plan. You're going to need a key to get in, and the security code."

"I've got a key on the set Jack gave me, but the code would be handy, thanks. And the address."

"I'll text it to you, along with the code. Keep your taxi receipts. I'll make sure you're reimbursed," he said.

"Thanks. I guess I'll see you later, then. And if things change . . ."

"I'll call," Garret assured her.

Sierra pocketed her phone after he ended the call, wondering what had gone wrong at his end to necessitate an overnight stay in the city. He'd sounded tense, distracted. But Tate Transport was a big company. It stood to reason he'd have his work cut out for him, getting on top of all the moving parts.

Her phone vibrated to signal it had received a text and she checked to make sure Garret had sent her both the address and the code. He had, and she saved them into a private folder.

The Tates had an arrangement where they could rent hangar space if the Bell was overnighting in Helena, but it took an hour or so for Sierra to track down the right person and get her hands on a tow cart to move the helicopter under shelter. It was late afternoon by the time she called a taxi to take her to the address Garret had sent her.

The taxi took her out of town and she chatted to her driver while taking in the scenery out the car window—tall trees, blue sky, stretches of open land, then the deep, true blue of Lake Helena. The views disappeared when they turned off the lake road and into a private graveled driveway. They rumbled down a gravel road and around a bend, tall trees flanking the road, and then suddenly, just like that, they'd arrived. The trees fell away as the taxi drove into a landscaped clearing and Sierra gasped as she got her first look at the house perched on the shore of the lake.

A luxurious, overblown take on a traditional log cabin, it was built from local stone and timber and seemed to sprawl in every direction with dramatic pitched roofs, numerous balconies, and expanses of shiny glass.

The taxi driver leaned forward and peered through the windshield, eyebrows raised as he took the house in.

"This your place?" he asked, shooting her an assessing look.

Sierra huffed out a laugh. "God, no. I'm just a pilot."

And co-owner of a struggling ranch. She estimated the modest house she shared with her brothers would safely fit into one wing of this imposing residence—with room to spare.

She'd always known the Tates were wealthy, but this was next level. Seriously next level.

She settled the fare, pocketed her receipt, and stepped out onto the sweeping driveway. The taxi driver gave her a friendly wave before using the generous turnaround to head back the way they'd come.

Sierra stood and stared at the imposing entrance after

he'd gone, trying to get her head around it. Projecting forward from the house proper, it featured a steeply pitched portico that rose three stories high and was supported by what looked like two enormous tree trunks. An oversized front door with elaborate lead-light sidelights was sheltered beneath it, and the entryway itself was paved with richly colored terracotta tiles. On either side of the portico was a collection of pots and wine barrels filled with carefully curated greenery that complemented the rugged natural surroundings.

"This is insane," she whispered to herself.

She stopped to inspect one of the portico supports on her way to the front doors and confirmed that, yes, it had been formed by stripping the branches and bark from a whole tree trunk. The security keypad was located discreetly on the wall near the front door and she tentatively punched in the number Garret had provided her, half expecting it not to work.

The lights on the panel went from red to green, so she tried the key. It worked, too, the oversized door swinging open with the barest of nudges, despite its size and heaviness. Feeling like Alice in Wonderland, she stepped over the threshold.

"Sweet baby cheeses," she breathed.

Rustic beams soared overhead in the entry hall, the space beneath them filled with an enormous rustic chandelier bristling with light globes. The floor was covered with massive slate flagstones and a round antique table sat in the middle of the space, an empty vase in the center. No doubt it was usually filled with an elaborate floral arrangement when the Tates were in residence, creating a breathtaking display for visitors when they entered the house.

Talk about shock and awe.

Eyes wide, she ventured farther into the house, her jaw dropping more with each new discovery—the vast living room with a fireplace as large as her whole freaking bedroom and a custom leather modular lounge suite that could easily accommodate ten people; the kitchen with its antique wood cabinets and acres of marble counters; the study with its squishy leather chairs, floor-to-ceiling bookcases, and yet another beautiful fireplace.

And the view—the view was *insane.*

Every room featured enormous windows designed to make the most of the sweeping vistas of the lake. There wasn't so much as a glimpse of another house, power lines, or other signs of civilization to mar the sense of privacy. Sierra stood in the living room and stared out at the crystalline blue water for several minutes, astonished that someone could actually own a view like this.

Setting down her bag in the kitchen, she took herself on a more extensive tour, discovering what was obviously the master suite and other family bedrooms before finding a more modern, simpler space in the west wing of the house. She found a room that roughly matched Jack's description of where he usually stayed on the second floor of the modern wing, tucked away in a corner. Smaller than the family suites, it was still lavishly appointed with its own private balcony, marble bathroom, and a king-sized bed covered in crisp white linen.

"Better than any hotel I ever stayed in," she muttered to

herself before taking a picture and texting it to Jack, asking him to confirm she'd identified the correct bedroom before she made herself at home.

She went back downstairs and let herself out onto a large deck while she was waiting for him to respond. The land fell away toward the lake and she had to descend a flight of stairs to reach the lap pool and pool house. She stooped to test the water. Yep, it was warm.

Of course it was warm. Rich people didn't swim in cold pools.

A trail meandered artfully across the slope and down to the water's edge and she followed it past a firepit with a circle of Adirondack chairs, all the way down to the private dock that stretched into the lake. Her footsteps thudded on the weathered timber as she walked out over the water. The sun was blindingly bright out here, magnified by the mirror of the lake, and she shaded her eyes with her hand and breathed in air scented with the smell of green living things and wet earth.

Imagine living like this. Imagine owning all of this.

But she couldn't. It was so far beyond everything she'd ever known, she might as well be visiting another planet.

To think she'd been lusting after Garret Tate yesterday and wondering if he was single—as if she had a chance at catching his eye. She laughed out loud at her own audacity, the sound echoing off the water. What could she possibly have in common with a man who lived like this?

Nothing. He might as well be another species.

Her phone chirped with a message. Jack, confirming she'd found the right room.

This house is astonishing, she wrote back.

How the other half live, Jack texted.

You can say that again.

They exchanged a few more texts—Jack assuring her he was following doctor's orders, Sierra assuring him all was going smoothly with the job—then she made her way back up the trail to the house and let herself into the kitchen. Faced with several hours of free time, a rarity in her life, she was momentarily stumped. Then she remembered the vast bathtub in her en suite bathroom.

"Why the hell not," she said.

Then she headed off to see how the other half bathed.

DINNER TIME FOUND her scrolling through the Uber Eats options for Helena and surrounds. A brief scan of the menu at a local Chinese restaurant got her stomach rumbling and she ordered Kung Pao chicken, fried rice, and a serving of egg rolls. Then she sat at one of the stools in the kitchen and read a book on her phone while she waited.

THE BOOK WAS so good it felt like barely five minutes had passed when the Uber app buzzed to let her know her meal was nearly there. Standing, she swept her still-damp hair over one shoulder and made her way to the front door.

Headlights swept across the decorative glass side lights on either side of the front door just as she arrived.

"You just made my night," she told the teenage driver as he handed over her food.

He flicked a look over her shoulder at the entrance hall and raised his eyebrows, obviously thinking she had better things to be excited about.

Little did he know she was just an interloper.

His reaction made her thoughtful as she closed the door, though. Having this kind of money brought a whole world of expectations with it. A whole world of privilege, too, but still. She couldn't imagine what it must have been like for Garret, growing up surrounded by all of this opulence. Despite all the evident luxury, this did not feel like a home.

She was just turning to take her food to the kitchen when she heard the distinct sound of another car engine approaching. She hesitated, then decided it probably wouldn't be a good look to be hovering in the front foyer when Garret arrived home. In fact, the best thing to do would probably be to disappear altogether and eat in her room.

Her brilliant plan was thwarted by the fact that there were one million and one cupboards and drawers in the kitchen and she'd only just found the one holding plates and bowls when she heard Garret's step in the hallway. He appeared in the kitchen doorway moments later, shirtsleeves rolled up, tie missing, looking just as rumpled and weary as he had at the end of the day yesterday.

"Hey. What smells so amazing?" he asked, sniffing the air.

"Kung Pao chicken. There's more than enough for two if you want some?" she offered.

"I can't take your dinner," Garret said quickly. "The housekeeper keeps the freezer stocked with a bunch of stuff.

I'll just defrost something."

He dumped his suit jacket and briefcase on one of the leather upholstered stools and went to the fridge.

"I need a beer. You want a beer?" he asked.

"Um. Sure. Thanks." Maybe it would make her feel less nervous. Or self-conscious. Or whatever it was she was feeling right now.

Not comfortable, that was for sure.

He pulled two imported beers from the imposing fridge and twisted the tops off, sliding one across the marble counter toward her.

"Cheers," he said, tilting his bottle toward her briefly before lifting it to his mouth.

Sierra watched as he swallowed deeply, the muscles of his throat working, his eyes closing as he savored the small pleasure.

She didn't need to ask to know he'd had a shitty, stressful day—it was written all over him—and even though they were not friends and hardly knew each other, she made a decision.

Reaching into the drawer for a second bowl, she started dishing up the food, dividing it evenly. Garret set his bottle down on the counter with a contented sigh, then frowned as he registered what she was doing.

"Seriously, Sierra, I can't take your dinner."

"You're not. You're saving me from indigestion," she said.

She rested one of the two egg rolls on top of the heaped food in his bowl and offered it to him. "Help a girl out."

Garret hesitated, then he smiled, making the corners of

his eyes crinkle attractively. "Hard to resist a call to offer humanitarian assistance," he said, taking the bowl from her outstretched hand.

"Only a monster would refuse," she agreed.

He nudged one of the stools toward her, indicating she should sit before taking the next one for himself. "Seriously, though—you just saved my life," he said.

"You can return the favor by telling me where I can find a fork," she said. "It just took me ten minutes to find the bowls."

"Yeah, this kitchen is a bit crazy."

He crossed to a set of built-in drawers near the sink, extracting two forks and holding them up in the air as though he'd just uncovered buried treasure.

"*Voila, madame*," he said, handing her one before returning to his stool.

"French. Very impressive. What a pity we're eating Chinese," she said.

He smiled as he dug into his food. "What happened to me being a hero for finding the forks?"

"In your own home."

Garret surprised her by grimacing. "This is not my home."

"And yet, here we sit," she said before biting into her egg roll.

It was lukewarm, but she was so hungry it tasted amazing and she made a happy sound as she swallowed her first mouthful.

"This is no one's home. I don't even know why my parents bought it." He took a bite of his own egg roll. "Mom has always preferred the Marietta house, hence the fact that my father commuted every day via helicopter except in the worst of winter. This place is a big white elephant."

"I thought white elephants were supposed to be useless and unwanted? Hate to break it to you, but a lot of people would kill to have a house like this."

Garret looked around the kitchen, patently unimpressed. "Well, I am not a fan."

"Not big enough for you?" she asked, poker-faced.

"Yes, that's exactly my problem with this place. It's not big enough." He shot her an amused look as he forked up a mouthful of fried rice.

They were both silent for a moment as they concentrated on their food, and Sierra tried to think of something suitably small-talky to say.

"How's Jesse doing?" Garret asked, beating her to it. "I keep seeing his name in the sports section. Seems like he's going pretty well on the rodeo circuit?"

"He's doing great, thanks. Managed to avoid breaking anything this season. And it looks like he's heading to Vegas for the finals."

"I guess he must be riding against that woman who's joined the circuit? I forget her name, but I was reading about her in a magazine a few months ago. Looks like she's shaking things up a bit."

"Funny you should mention CJ," Sierra said, smiling as she pictured her brother's badass girlfriend. "She and Jesse are seeing each other."

"Yeah? Even though they're competitors?" Garret looked intrigued by the notion.

"It works for them. A little too well. They should come with an adult content warning."

He laughed, then focused on his food again. It was now her turn to offer a conversational gambit, but her brain remained stubbornly blank.

"How's everything going with Tate Transport?" she finally asked. Lame, but safe, she figured.

He took a long pull from his beer before answering. "Well, the polite version is that things are going great. The truth is that it kinda sucks, and today was a nightmare."

She wasn't expecting such brutal honesty, and she blinked. "Oh."

He shook his head. "Sorry. You don't want to hear all my bullshit. Help yourself to another beer if you'd like one."

His cheekbones were pink, and she guessed he was regretting his moment of candor.

"Is this a being-thrown-in-the-deep-end thing, or a leaving-your-whole-life-behind thing, or is something else going on?" she asked.

"None of those things, although I guess they all factor into it a little." He flicked her an assessing look. "Fair warning—you're going to regret opening Pandora's box here. Brace yourself for a gut-spill."

"Spill away. Happy to be of service. Sometimes just getting fresh air on something gives you a new take on situations."

Garret pushed his empty bowl away and swiveled to face her more fully.

"Okay, a little backstory for context. When my father started Tate Transport, one of his first drivers was a guy called Ron Gibson, and over the years he's worked his way up to general manager. Dad's right-hand man, essentially."

Sierra nodded. "I know Ron. I've copiloted with Jack when he's been on board."

"So you know he's like family. He's always been on the scene. He and Dad are thick as thieves. I was hoping I'd be able to lean on the guy while I got up to speed, but right from the get-go Ron's been encouraging me to step back and let him run things and just concentrate on Dad."

Sierra frowned. "You think he resents you parachuting into your father's role when you haven't been involved in the business?"

"Hell, yeah. I was hoping I could win him around, prove I had no plans to mess with his role, but today we had a run-in and he pretty much blew everything up. Told me exactly what he thinks of me, stormed out of the building."

She stared at him, imagining Ron raging his way through an office building. "Wow. That must have freaked everybody out."

"Just a little." He rubbed the back of his neck as though remembering his day was giving him a headache.

"So what happens now?"

"He's out," Garret said, and she could see it gave him no pleasure to make the pronouncement. "I can't afford to have someone working against me in such a senior role. Even if he used to be Dad's number-one guy."

"No wonder your day sucked," Sierra said.

He gave a rueful laugh. "Yeah. That was just my morning, by the way."

Without saying another word, Sierra stood and went to

the fridge. When she returned she put a fresh beer in front of him. "You've earned that."

"Thanks."

She watched as he took the cap off with an economical twist of his hand, the muscles in his forearms flexing briefly. He was in pretty good shape for a guy who worked in an office, she couldn't help noticing.

"There's this thing I do sometimes when my life isn't going to plan," she said as she resumed her seat. She gave him a dry look. "Prepare yourself for some homespun wisdom. We've reached the inspirational part of the evening."

"Thank god. I need a little inspiration in my life right now."

"What I do is make a pragmatic assessment of how long things are going to suck for. A week, two weeks, a month. Then I remind myself that I have survived a lot worse. Hey, presto, perspective," she said.

He nodded, mulling over her strategy. "What if my best assessment of how long things are going to suck is longer than a month?"

He was joking, but she could see the worry behind his eyes.

"Well, then you're going to need a shit snorkel," she said.

His chest lifted as he huffed out as surprised laugh. "A shit snorkel. Interesting. Please elaborate."

"Everyone has their own version of the shit snorkel. For some people it's reading their favorite books. For others it's running for miles on end. For others it's this stuff." She indicated his beer. "You gotta have something to help you wade through the crappola. Bonus points if it's not self-destructive. So on second thought, maybe you shouldn't have this."

She took his beer away from him.

"Hey. Give that back," he said.

She pretended to think about it before sliding it his way again.

"Thank you," he said dryly.

"You're welcome."

He smiled at her, his golden-brown eyes warmly appreciative, and she couldn't help but smile back. Then she realized it was far too quiet in the kitchen, probably because they were too busy smiling at each other.

She was pretty sure that sharing meaningful eye contact with her new boss while they were also sharing his enormous luxury home for the night was probably not the smartest move she could make right now.

Clearing her throat, she slid off her stool. "Do you have any idea when you want to fly out tomorrow?"

"Probably the usual time."

"Okay. I'll make sure we're ready to roll," she said as she stacked the bowls, keen to find some busy work to dispel the tension.

"Leave those. You cooked, the least I can do is tackle the dishes."

"I have no idea where the dishwasher is, anyway," she admitted, glancing around the space.

He stood, moving closer to take the bowls from her. He was taller than her, a rarity, and she felt a frisson of awareness as his broad shoulders filled her vision. Then he was turning away from her and pulling down a cupboard door that was actually a cover for the dishwasher.

"Like magic, it appears," he said. "Because god forbid there be kitchen appliances on show in the kitchen."

"So gross," she said. "Don't even talk about it. I can't even."

He didn't laugh this time, but she could still tell he was amused. He bent to put the bowls on the lower rack of the dishwasher and Sierra gave in to the impulse to sneak a quick peek at his butt.

She knew it was wrong, especially after the smiling-at-each-other-too-long moment, but she felt a strong compulsion to find out if his ass was as good as the rest of him.

And the answer to that burning question was yes, it very definitely was. Taut and muscular and showcased beautifully by his tailored pants.

She would bet he looked nothing short of amazing in a pair of jeans.

And even better naked.

Okay, missy. That's enough of that foolishness.

Sierra averted her eyes before she could get busted and took a couple of good, long steps backward. "Okay. See you tomorrow."

She didn't wait for him to reply, pivoting on her boot heel and hustling out of the kitchen as though the seat of her pants was on fire.

She made her way to the west wing, thrown off balance for the second time today. When she'd arrived here this afternoon, the conspicuous wealth on display had led her to recalibrate her take on Garret and conclude they couldn't possibly have anything in common. It had been a welcome realization, because it had given her yet another bulwark against the unwanted and inappropriate attraction she felt toward him.

But he'd just spent the last half hour proving how relatable and approachable he was. He'd given her a glimpse into his world and what he was dealing with and had shown himself to be both humble and down to earth.

In short, he'd just destroyed most of her defenses and good intentions without even trying, and she'd responded by getting lost staring into his eyes while smiling like a goofball.

So much for all her good intentions and them being different species who had nothing in common.

Chapter Six

GARRET MOVED AROUND the kitchen, tidying away the containers from their takeout meal. Then he grabbed his beer and briefcase and made his way to the study. He set down his beer on a side table, then toed off his shoes and dropped into one of the armchairs in front of the fireplace.

For a moment he let his head fall back against the soft leather and closed his eyes. Fuck, he was tired. And wound up. He wasn't sure how the two states could coexist at the same time, but he was living proof it was possible.

You're going to need a shit snorkel.

He smiled as he remembered Sierra's pragmatic words. She was funny as well as smart and gorgeous.

She looked different with her hair down too. Less sporty and ready-for-anything and more approachable. And those eyes . . . Those eyes were something else. All the Carmodys had green eyes, but on Sierra they were particularly striking. When she smiled they seemed to glow, and when she laughed—

Please do not fucking do this, you tool.

He opened his eyes, letting go of the memory of Sierra laughing with him in the kitchen. The asshole in his head was right—he needed to rein it in and maintain the line.

No more looking into Sierra Carmody's eyes and trying to make her laugh. That shit was stopping right now.

This very second.

He reached for the beer and swallowed a long, cold mouthful. Then he dug into his briefcase and pulled out his laptop. There were multiple emails from his lawyer, David, outlining the procedure for exiting Ron from the business. There were also emails from the various department heads, confirming their availability for the one-on-one meetings he'd asked for tomorrow morning.

One benefit of Ron ejecting himself from the general manager's chair was that Garret no longer needed to tiptoe around the other man's sensibilities, hence the invitation for the executive team to brief him directly about their areas of responsibility.

A silver lining, at last.

By the time he was done reviewing his lawyer's advice, it was nearly ten. Aware he had another long day ahead tomorrow, he shut down the computer, then padded through the silent house. He'd had the choice of six guest bedrooms on the main floor, and he'd chosen the most modest one. Which really wasn't saying much.

A king-sized four-poster bed sat against the wall, positioned to take advantage of the view out over the lake. A walk-in closet opened to the left of the bed, and there was a lavish marble bathroom to the right. Garret stripped to his boxer-briefs and went into the marble echo chamber to brush his teeth.

For some reason he thought of Sierra as he stared at himself in the mirror, toothbrush in hand. It was strange to think that last week they'd barely been acquaintances, yet today they'd shared a meal and were now about to spend the night sleeping under the same roof.

For a split second he allowed himself to picture her upstairs, getting ready for bed. An image of long, bare legs and smooth skin filled his head, and he shut it down hard.

Nope, he just wasn't going there.

Bending, he spat out toothpaste and rinsed his mouth, then flicked off the light and went to bed.

HE HAD A crappy night, but all his nights were crappy lately. He was simply too wired to relax enough. The alarm on his phone went off at six and by six thirty he was driving away from the lake house, back toward the city center.

Mandy had beaten him in yet again, and he gave her an appreciative smile as she set a cup of coffee on his desk.

"Mandy, when the dust has settled, remind me to make sure we're paying you what you're worth," he said.

"I'm very happy with my salary package, Mr. Tate," she said firmly.

One happy employee. He decided to count it as a win.

By midday he'd had one-on-one meetings with all but a couple of his senior managers and was feeling easier about what Ron's removal would mean for the business. He'd been impressed with the team, and they'd left him feeling confident he wouldn't need to hold their hands until a new general manager could be appointed.

The upward trend of his day stalled when he met with

Theo, the sales manager, after lunch and received the missing financial report. It only took a moment for Garret to spot the gaping hole in the data.

"That's why I wanted to give this to you myself," Theo said, reading his reaction. "The missing piece of the pie is the executive account that Ron controlled. I don't have any detail on it."

Garret did some rapid math in his head. "That's a five-hundred-thousand-dollar piece of pie we're talking about."

"Yep. My understanding is that it was supposed to cover business dinners, junkets for account managers, incentives, that sort of thing. But I don't really know the details," Theo said.

"And my father was fully aware of this?" Garret asked.

"He and Ron set it up together," Theo said.

Then he broke eye contact to look down at his shoes, his throat bobbing nervously, and Garret's heart sank.

Shit.

No wonder Ron had been so reluctant to hand over all the financial reports.

"Thanks, Theo. You're around today if I've got any more questions, right?"

"Absolutely," Theo said, then he practically raced out of the office, clearly relieved to have completed an onerous task.

Garret stared at the printout in front of him. Five hundred thousand was a lot of money to spend on dinners and incentives. Although maybe that depended on what a person called an incentive.

His mouth was dry as he picked up his phone and hit the button to connect with Mandy.

"Could you send Brianna in, please?" he asked.

Brianna arrived minutes later, pale but composed.

"We need to talk about the executive account," Garret said.

"I don't know anything about it. Ron handled all of that." She said it quickly, as though she'd had her answer prepared already.

"All right. I'll need you to forward any documentation relating to it to Mandy, please. Immediately," Garret said.

"I don't have access to any of that. Ron kept it all on his laptop. He did that with all the sensitive information."

"Then I'd like to see Ron's laptop, please."

All the color leached from Brianna's face. "I—I don't have it. Yesterday, before Mandy asked me to come see you, Ron called and asked me to bring me some things from his office down to the garage. He said he'd forgotten them."

Garret closed his eyes briefly. "You took him his laptop."

"And some folders from the bottom drawer of his desk." Brianna's voice trembled with anxiety.

"Any idea what was in those files?" Garret asked.

She shook her head, her eyes glassy with tears.

A maximum of five minutes had passed between Ron storming from the building and Brianna arriving in his office to talk yesterday. Nowhere near long enough for Brianna to have collected Ron's things and taken them down to the parking garage and still be back in time to talk to Garret. Which meant she'd done so *after* he'd told her Ron was no longer an employee of Tate Transport and that she was to report any communication with Ron to himself or Mandy.

He should have sent her home on the spot, given she'd

worked for Ron for so long. In his defense, he hadn't known about the so-called executive account at that time, and he'd taken steps to ensure Ron didn't have access to the office physically or virtually.

Still, he felt stupid. An increasingly familiar sensation.

He really needed to stop giving people the benefit of the doubt.

"I don't suppose there's any point in asking if Ron backed his laptop up?" Garret asked.

"Not that I know of."

He considered her for a beat, long enough for her to shift uncomfortably in her seat.

"Anything more you'd like to say?" he asked.

She shook her head.

"Okay. So here's what's going to happen. I'm going to ask the security people to review the surveillance footage for the parking garage from yesterday and check the time stamps. If it shows what I think it's going to show, I'll be asking you to clear out your desk. Under supervision."

Brianna swallowed audibly, then her chin came up. "You don't need to check the security footage. And I'm more than happy to clear out my desk. I don't want to stay here without Ron."

"Nice to know you're loyal to someone," he said.

She stood, her blue eyes condemning. "Ron was right—you're going to ruin everything your father worked so hard for."

He picked up the phone and buzzed Sabrina in human resources. "I'm going to need you to supervise Brianna's departure from the building."

There was a small pause. "I'm on my way."

Garret shut the office door after the two women had left. Then he ran his fingers through his hair and yanked his tie loose.

"*Fuck.*"

This was bad. Missing files, an opaque account worth half a million dollars that only Ron and his father knew the details on. No one went to so much trouble to conceal business activities unless there was something sketchy going on. His mind raced as he tried to think through the implications.

It was possible Ron had been embezzling money from his father, but his gut told him that wasn't the case. Theo had said very clearly that Ron and Gideon had set up the executive account together.

So whatever was going on with that account, whatever was in those files, there was a very good chance his father was well aware of it. That he'd participated in it.

Garret sank into his chair. His father's business had contracts with the state government, national businesses, big corporations. He'd already seen the tenders that had been prepared for future business pitches. He knew the kind of money that was at stake every time Tate Transport threw its hat in the ring.

It didn't require too big a leap of imagination to suspect that his father and Ron had looked for ways to ensure the outcome of important tenders. Ways that were more impactful and persuasive than a nice dinner and a friendly golf game. Offering kickbacks to decision makers was a tried and true gambit of corrupt businesses the world over for a reason—it worked.

He just hadn't expected to find it happening at his father's company.

He stared at the tooled leather of the desktop. The first step was to confirm what he suspected. Ron might have taken the files, but he couldn't destroy the money trail. Garret needed someone who could backtrack from the money so he could start defining the scope of Ron and his father's malfeasance. Someone good and discreet.

He didn't know anyone like that, but he knew someone who might.

He reached for his phone and made a call.

SIERRA HAD THE Bell prepped and ready to launch when Garret arrived at the airport just before six. He gave her a cool nod of acknowledgment before climbing into the passenger cabin, a far cry from the warm, engaging man she'd eaten with last night.

She took her cue from him, keeping conversation to a minimum before firing up the engine. Still, her gaze kept straying to the mirror once she'd reached altitude. There was something different about him today. She'd seen him tired and overworked, but tonight he was giving off a different vibe. Angry, almost. Intense.

And for the first time he didn't bury himself in work the moment he sat down. Instead, he stared out the window, a deep furrow between his eyebrows.

She wondered what had happened. Another run-in with Ron? Or had some other issue cropped up?

So none of your business.

True. But she couldn't help but feel for Garret. She'd only been fourteen when her parents died and Jed had quit college to come home and look after them all, but she could still remember him sitting up until late in the evening, poring over the accounts, trying to make sense of their father's record keeping. Garret was doing that on a grand scale and then some.

They were halfway to Marietta, flying over the Missouri River, when she checked the mirror and got busted as he looked away from the window. She shot her gaze to the front immediately but could feel telltale heat climbing into her cheeks.

She told herself it was perfectly normal for a pilot to check on her passenger but that didn't make her feel any less busted. Probably because she knew she was lying to herself. She was checking on Garret because she couldn't seem to help herself where he was concerned.

After a minute or so, her headphones came to life.

"I keep meaning to ask you, how did you get into flying?" Garret asked.

Her gaze flew back to the mirror and he offered her a crooked smile.

"Humor me." He said it lightly, but she sensed an undercurrent of seriousness beneath his words.

"It's a long story. Get comfortable."

"I'm holding an imaginary martini. Begin," he said, waving a hand grandly.

"Your father offered free fun flights at the Marietta Fair one year. I got to sit up front with Jack while he flew."

There was a short pause while he waited for her to say more. When she didn't, she heard him laugh briefly.

"Glad I got comfortable for that."

"Drink your martini," she said.

"Really wish I could," he said with a sigh.

She checked the mirror again and he was once more staring out the window, his expression bleak.

"What did you do in Seattle?" she asked. "I mean, for work."

Anything to get the tight look off his face.

"Some college friends and I have a business start-up."

"What sort of business?"

"Coffee. We started out as a boutique bean roaster, but a couple of years ago we branched out into importing espresso machines from Italy."

"Gotta say, I love the smell of fresh coffee," she said.

"It's even better when it's roasting."

"So I guess that makes you a coffee expert? Did I offend you with my flask the other morning?"

"I appreciated the gesture," he said with careful neutrality and Sierra burst into laughter.

"Very diplomatic."

"I freely admit I'm a coffee snob," Garret said.

"Oh, well, as long as you admit it."

He laughed, and she felt absurdly pleased that she'd managed to shift his mood.

"Here's a deal—I'll get you some good coffee. Then you can tell me if you think it's any better than your usual," he said. "What sort of setup do you have at home?"

"I don't know what brand the coffee maker is, if that's

what you're asking. Mr. Coffee, maybe?"

She caught his wince in the mirror.

"That hurt you somewhere deep inside, didn't it?" she asked.

"I'm guessing you drink the coffee no matter how long it's been in the pot, too, huh?"

"Coffee is coffee," she said, knowing it would get a rise out of him.

"Someone needs to take you in hand," he said, shaking his head.

"Many men have tried and failed." The words slipped out of her mouth before she could catch them.

His gaze found hers in the mirror, and she saw the flare of interest in his eyes. It took her longer than it should have to shift her gaze back to the horizon.

He didn't say anything else and she didn't dare check the mirror again. Instead, she waited a few minutes before announcing their descent.

Neither of them spoke again until after they'd landed and he was climbing out of the cabin.

"Usual time tomorrow?" she asked, her tone professionally polite.

"Thanks." He hesitated, his gaze shifting over her shoulder toward the house. "Things are going to be a bit unpredictable for the next little while. So maybe come prepared for overnighters, just in case."

"Not a problem."

His focus came back to her. "Thanks for being so flexible."

"Thanks for being kind about the coffee."

His mouth quirked up into an almost smile. "See you tomorrow, Sierra."

He headed for the house, suit jacket under his arm, briefcase swinging.

Sierra kicked herself for the entire half hour it took to put the Bell to bed for the night. Why had she felt the need to slip that little joke in at the end? Why hadn't she just left things as they were, especially after that moment of mutual awareness last night at the house?

Thoroughly annoyed with herself, she slid behind the wheel of her old pickup and headed home.

Casey was finishing prep on macaroni and cheese when she arrived, his hair damp from the shower. Before Eva came into his life, he'd rarely showered before dinner. Now it was the first thing he did when he finished work for the day.

The civilizing effect of love.

"Starting to wonder if we were going to see you tonight," he said as she walked to the fridge to grab the water jug.

"I would have called if I had to stay overnight again," she said.

Her brother started grating cheese, then flicked an assessing look her way. "Eva tells me I should apologize for giving you a hard time about working for the Tates."

Sierra poured herself a glass of water before cocking an eyebrow at him. "Is that it? That's your apology?"

Casey laughed. "You're not buying it?"

"Dude, you're not selling it. I'll buy when you sell," she said, crossing her arms over her chest and giving him her best "I'm waiting" look.

"All right. It's a good opportunity for you. I know you

want to fly full-time if you can. And Jack's a good guy. Helping him out is the right thing to do. Sorry for being an asshole. I just . . . I hate that Gideon Tate got to walk away from the accident and nothing changed for him. I know it's not exactly rational. I know it wasn't Gideon's fault. But we lost everything, and he lost nothing. And then he tried to throw more money at us like that was all we needed to make everything okay."

"Sold," she said, and Casey smiled.

Out of all her brothers, they were the closest, probably because there was only a year between them, and it was good to clear the air.

"You enjoying the job so far?" he asked.

"I love it," she said.

He nodded. "Good. I'm glad."

The kitchen door opened, and Eva and Jed walked in.

"She's back," Eva said, smiling with delight.

"It was only one night," Sierra pointed out.

"We missed you," Eva said, giving her a quick hug.

Jed grabbed a glass and poured himself water from the jug Sierra had left on the counter. "Speak for yourself. I got to watch football without anyone bitching about me hogging the remote. It was glorious."

"It's incredibly sad that that's all it takes to make you happy," Sierra pointed out.

"I'm a simple man," Jed said.

"So many places to go with that one," Casey said. "I'm going to need a minute."

Sierra smiled into her glass of water. It was nice to be home, nice to slip back into the rhythm of her family.

She wondered what Garret was doing right now. Nothing like this, she guessed. He'd probably come home to an empty house, and dinner was most likely going to be something frozen before he drove himself to the hospital to support his parents.

She stilled when she realized her thoughts had gravitated to him yet again.

No, it was worse than that—she wasn't just thinking about him. She was *concerned* for him. He'd confided in her in a moment of weakness last night, and that was all it had taken for her to overinvest. That and a couple of moments of lingering eye contact.

"Give me a yell when dinner is ready," she said, pushing to her feet.

She headed for her room, dumping her bag on the bed. She had laundry to do before she repacked. And maybe she needed a bigger overnight bag, since Garret had indicated the likelihood of there being more stays at the lake house in the near future.

"Knock, knock."

Sierra glanced over her shoulder to see Eva in the doorway, hands tucked into the front pockets of her paint-splattered skinny jeans. The colorful tattoo on her forearm stood out vividly against the white of her T-shirt, and her short blond hair stuck up in places as though she'd been running her hands through it.

"Hey. What's up?" Sierra asked.

"I was about to ask you that," Eva said. "Everything cool with the job?"

"Of course. It's amazing. Someone's paying me to fly for

a living. What's not to love?" Sierra said lightly.

Eva pursed her lips, eyes slightly narrowed. "Hmm. That was pretty convincing, but just a little off. Want to try again?"

Sierra stared at her friend. Then she sat on the end of her bed and let out a sigh.

"The job is great. Really. I'm just feeling a little . . . distracted. Which is super unprofessional. And really self-sabotaging."

Eva sat beside her. "If you're worried about Casey being a dick the other night, he's already admitted as much."

"I'm not worried about Casey. He apologized to me before dinner. This is a *me* problem. Me and my hormones. Or maybe I should say my libido."

Eva frowned, trying to work out what she was saying. Then realization dawned and her eyes widened. "Oh. *Garret Tate* is the distraction."

Sierra pictured Garret the way he'd been last night, laughing and warm and—might as well admit it—sexy as hell in his parents' over-the-top kitchen.

"Yes. Yes he is."

"You want to jump him," Eva said.

"I wouldn't go that far," Sierra said, frowning.

"So you don't want to have sex with him?" Eva asked. "I'm confused."

"I am definitely . . . interested," Sierra admitted grudgingly. "But I don't *want* to jump him. What I want is to be able to look at him and feel nothing except a sense of responsibility for getting him from A to B in one piece."

"Ah. You're conflicted. I do love me some good conflicted yearning," Eva said. "Tell me more."

Sierra gave her a look. "This isn't a joke. Garret is my boss. I'm filling in for Jack, who is the consummate professional. I mean, he *never* puts a foot wrong, and he's relying on me. And all I can think about is making Garret laugh and how good he smells and how hot he is."

"Okay. Let's start with that. How hot is he?" Eva asked.

"Too hot."

"Hotter than Casey?"

Sierra gave her the side-eye. "I'm not using my brother as a benchmark for another man's hotness."

"Sorry, you're right. That was creepy. We need another metric." She narrowed her eyes in thought for a beat. "What about movie stars? Is he Chris Evans hot?"

"Definitely."

Eva raised her eyebrows. "Okay. Is he Chris Hemsworth hot?"

"Easily."

"He's easily hotter than Chris Hemsworth?" Eva asked incredulously. "Are you sure you're not wearing your horny goggles?"

Sierra gave a reluctant laugh. "I don't know. Maybe. But that's part of the problem, right? I can't stop thinking about him. He's got some stuff going down at his father's business right now, and I keep thinking about how he's had to give up his life in Seattle to step in and save the day . . ."

"So he's hot, and you're worried about his happiness?"

"That makes it sound even worse," Sierra said.

"It makes it sound like you like him," Eva corrected. "Not exactly a crime."

"It is when he's my boss." Sierra scrubbed her face with her hands and made a frustrated sound in the back of her throat. "I wish I could just erase the part of my brain that notices things like how nice his eyes are. It's driving me crazy and it's only been three days."

"Here's what I think," Eva said. "You need to stop beating yourself up for noticing this Garret guy is a hottie. You have eyes, and you like men. It's just a fact of life that sometimes you're gonna run across people you find really attractive. That doesn't mean you have to go shopping for a hair shirt. This is not George Orwell's *1984*. You don't have to punish yourself for thought crimes. You simply acknowledge that he floats your boat, and you move on because the job is more important than a roll between the sheets."

Sierra nodded. This was good advice. Eva was right. She was overreacting, giving herself a hard time just because she and Garret had noticed each other.

"Orrrrrr . . . You jump this guy and have a great time while you can, because it's not very often that you meet someone who really does it for you," Eva said, her smile wide and mischievous.

Sierra reached behind her for a pillow and bopped her friend on the back of the head with it.

"Not helping."

"I'm sorry." Eva laughed and scooted off the bed and out of range. "I've never been very good at coloring inside the lines. You think I planned on falling for your brother when I came to town to try to win the grain elevator contract? You think CJ thought it would be a great idea to fall for Jesse at her very first professional rodeo?"

Sierra stared at her, challenged. "This isn't like that."

"Okay. If you say so." Eva patted her on the shoulder. "I'll just point out that when you talked about how hot Garret is, you also talked about how you felt bad for his current situation. You're already invested, sweetheart. Maybe that's just because you've got a huge heart. Or maybe it's because you've met someone you really connect with."

Eva gave her shoulder a final pat before exiting, leaving Sierra to mull over her words for the rest of the night.

Chapter Seven

GARRET ARRIVED AT the hospital fully intending to brief his mother on what was happening at Tate Transport, but when he entered his father's room he found her reading the newspaper to his father and it hit him how tired and old she suddenly looked. Her hair was showing gray at the roots, and she hadn't bothered with makeup. She was wearing a pair of track pants and a T-shirt *outside of the house*, something he would have thought was a sure sign of the apocalypse in pre-stroke times.

Every ounce of energy she had, every atom in her body, was focused on his father's recovery, and it hit Garret that telling her what was going on wouldn't change anything or improve the situation. It would only give his mother one more thing to worry about.

And what did he have to tell her at the moment, anyway? That there were some accounting anomalies that needed looking into, and that Ron had taken some documents and files when he left. Until he knew more, it was pointless to add another burden to his mother's already heavy load.

His mother broke off from her reading, her mouth curving into a tired smile. "Hello. You didn't have to come in again. We know you're pulling long hours at work."

"I wanted to see you guys," Garret said.

His father was watching him with bright eyes, and he held out his hand for Garret to come closer to the bed. Grief and anger twisted together in Garret's belly as he moved forward to take his father's hand.

"You're . . . a good . . . sssson," Gideon said, squeezing Garret's hand.

But are you a good father?

The thought generated a stab of guilt and Garret forced a lightness he didn't feel as he returned the gentle pressure and asked his father about his day.

He stayed for an hour and was just pulling into the garage back at the ranch when his phone pinged with an email. He was relieved to see it was from Frank Nestor, an old family friend and someone he trusted implicitly. He'd asked Frank earlier if he could recommend a good forensic accountant, someone discreet and effective. Tate Transport had both internal and external accountants already, but given the anomalies within the organization, Garret figured it was smart to engage an outside firm, someone without a horse in the race. Someone with expertise at tracking down hidden payments. And it looked like Frank had come through for Garret.

I made a few discreet inquiries, and the same name came up a few times: Mae Barringer. She's based in Helena but works all over the country and has a great rep. I'm sorry you're in a place where you need this kind of help. Let me know if there's any other assistance I can provide.

Garret stared at the email. Why did everything in his

goddamned life have to be so complicated right now?

Because he knew Mae Barringer. He'd gone to school with her at Marietta High. She'd been a few years ahead of him, but he'd spent a bit of time with her because she'd been going out with Jed Carmody, and Garret had been close friends with Jesse Carmody at the time.

Pre-accident, of course. Sometimes it seemed that all the good things in his life had been pre-accident.

He wasn't thrilled with the idea of using a Marietta local for such a potentially sensitive project. He was pretty sure Mae's mom still lived in town, and even if she was based in Helena now, Mae probably had other connections locally. Even though he was sure that any forensic accountant worth their salt would take discretion and privacy very seriously, it felt unnecessary to use someone he knew personally.

And yet Frank had said her name kept coming up when he asked around. What was the point of asking for a recommendation if he didn't use it?

"Screw it."

Garret opened up a blank email before he could talk himself out of it. In his normal business life back in Seattle, he hadn't spent half his time second-guessing himself. He, Jay, and Marco had built their knowledge base as the business grew, and there had always been someone else to bounce ideas off and dig deep when research was required. It was freaking exhausting feeling so paralyzed and out of his depth all the time.

He tapped out a quick message to Mae, then fired it off. For better or worse, it was done, and he could move on to the next thing on his list.

You're going to need a shit snorkel.

The memory of Sierra's words made him snort out a reluctant laugh. Goddamn it, she was right—he was definitely going to need something to get him through the next few months.

Or someone.

He batted the thought away. He'd spent half his life determined to be better than his father. Now was not the time to start compromising on that commitment.

Weary to the bone, he went to find something to eat.

"MORNING," SIERRA SAID.

"Morning."

Garret's eyes were hidden behind sunglasses today, despite the fact the sky was overcast and the sun barely up.

Good. The less opportunity for eye contact, the better. That was how she'd gotten into trouble with him yesterday.

She moved ahead of him to open the passenger door, holding it as he stepped into the passenger cabin. She closed it after him, then climbed into the cockpit.

The Bell fired up beautifully, and she checked the mirror to make sure Garret had secured his seat belt. He had, and she switched the headset on.

"Weather is clear to Helena, apart from a little low-lying cloud. Should be landing on schedule," she told him.

"Thanks." He was busy opening his laptop, ready to disappear into his work again, and she told herself that was also a good thing.

Lots of good things happening this morning. Good, professional things.

She engaged the clutch, lifted the collective a little, and the Bell rose smoothly into a hover. She did a quick instrument check, making sure everything was in the green or sitting within operational range. Then she opened up the throttle a little more and the Bell glided up and forward.

It was a fifty-minute flight to Helena, but she limited herself to just three mirror checks in that time, a triumph of self-discipline. Before they landed, she allowed herself one quick glance before she disturbed him with an announcement.

"We're five minutes out," she said. "And I wanted to let you know the Bell is due for a full maintenance inspection soon. We can wait till Jack is back on board, or I can get it out of the way now."

Garret started packing away his laptop. "Go ahead and schedule it. Is there anything you need from me to make that happen?"

"I'm pretty sure the aviation mechanic will have your billing details on file, but if they don't, I'll hassle Mandy for them."

"Great. I appreciate that." There was a warm note to his voice, as though he wasn't just being polite but genuinely valued her effort to make his life easier.

She concentrated on landing then, communicating with the control tower to make sure she was clear to approach. Minutes later the skids touched down gently in a landing that would have earned her a smile and a thumbs-up from Jack. She flicked switches to their off positions on the overhead console, then pulled off her headset and slid from the cockpit. The handle to the passenger cabin was warm from the morning sun as she disengaged it and opened the door.

Garret was ready to go and stepped out onto the tarmac. She noticed he was becoming more comfortable with the overhead rotor now, not ducking or crouching like a lot of people instinctively did as he paused to pocket his phone.

"Have a good day," she said, turning to secure the door behind him.

"You too."

He strode off, and she refused to allow herself to watch him go.

Maybe talking to Eva hadn't been as dangerous as she'd thought last night. Maybe having her choices laid out so starkly had given her the clarity and self-discipline she'd needed.

She was just completing a postflight visual inspection when her phone buzzed with a call. When she pulled it out, she saw it was Jed.

"Hey, what's up?" she asked.

"You got any idea where the replacement seals are for the water pump? Casey and I have practically torn the barn apart looking for them," Jed said, frustration rich in his voice.

"You tried the tool kit under the sink in the laundry room?"

"Shit. No."

"Well, that'd be why you can't find them."

"Goddamn. Why didn't I just call you straight away? You always know where everything is."

"That's because I'm the organized one." She leaned

against the side of the Bell. "I didn't get a chance to ask last night—how's Davey working out?"

"He's a good kid. A little green, but a hard worker. Once he gets the hang of everything, he'll be great."

"Awesome. Glad he's working out," she said, even though there was an odd feeling in her chest.

She'd worked alongside her brothers all her life. They'd sweated together, cursed together, laughed together. She knew she could rely on any of them, utterly and completely, with the certainty of long experience.

"What's wrong?" Jed asked.

"Why does anything have to be wrong?" she countered.

"Because you went quiet for more than five seconds."

Her brother knew her too well.

"It just hit me that I'm going to miss you guys," she said, her throat suddenly tight with emotion. "I mean, this is my dream job, don't get me wrong, but it's a big change."

"Jesus, Sierra, it's only six weeks, and we're not going anywhere. And if you think you're getting out of helping on the ranch in your downtime, you're smoking something you shouldn't be smoking."

"You're supposed to say you'll miss me too," Sierra said.

"You know I will," Jed said, his voice low and serious. "But you said it yourself—you guys have all got your own lives to live. Casey's going to be a rock star. Jesse's going to be a rodeo star, if he doesn't get beaten to the punch by CJ. And you're living your dream right now."

"What about you?" she asked.

"I've got the ranch. That'll keep me plenty busy." He paused briefly. "And maybe we can talk about you setting me up with one of your friends someday."

Sierra blinked, sure she must have just misheard. "Ex-squeeze me? What did you just say?"

"You heard."

She let out a whoop of surprise and triumph. "Are you fucking with me right now or are you serious?"

"Keep your pants on. I said we'd talk, that's all. Don't go setting anything up yet."

She was tempted to tease Jed some more but she could hear the discomfort in his voice.

"Okay. I won't put out the alert just yet. But I'm not letting you off the hook on this," she warned him. "I'm going to recruit CJ and Eva, and the three of us are going to find you the perfect woman."

"Awesome. Something to look forward to," Jed said dry-ly. "All the women in my life trying to fix me up on a date. What could possibly go wrong?"

Sierra ended the call with a smile on her face. Jed was finally going to let her interfere in his private life. Like he said, what could possibly go wrong?

GARRET CHECKED HIS watch for the third time in as many minutes. Then he shot his cuffs and moved his water glass a whole inch to the right.

He was nervous. Big surprise. Talking to Mae Barringer about delving into Tate Transport's financials was the first step in a journey to places he really didn't want to go. But what choice did he have? He'd studied business law as part of his Bachelor of Business Management at UPenn. He had a fiduciary duty as acting CEO of the business to ensure the company was compliant with state and federal laws. And the only way to do that was to find out what the scope of the problem was so he could find a way to fix it, ideally without destroying the business in the process.

He'd chosen an out-of-the-way restaurant for the meeting, wanting to avoid scaring the horses by having Mae come to the office, and he kept his eye on the door, hoping he'd recognize her when she arrived.

Left to its own devices, his mind drifted back to his favorite distraction of late—Sierra Carmody.

She'd looked good this morning, her cheeks slightly flushed, the ends of her ponytail still damp from the shower. She'd been briskly professional the whole flight, as had he, both of them on their best behavior.

Hadn't stopped him from thinking about her, though. Remembering how her hair had looked the other night, the dark wavy mass loose down her back, and the way her eyes lit up when she laughed.

Stop being a sleazy douche.

What the hell was wrong with him that he couldn't stop thinking about her? Very deliberately, he pictured the two women his father had had affairs with over the years, one Gideon's secretary, the other his office manager.

As a passion-killer, it was pretty effective.

Movement drew his focus to the entrance as a short, curvy woman with sleek dark auburn hair arrived. Her gaze scanned the restaurant before finding him and she smiled in recognition. He stood, trying to hide his surprise as she made her way to his table.

Because the face and body of the woman walking toward him belonged to the Mae Barringer he remembered, but the hair and clothes belonged to someone else entirely. Back in Marietta, Mae had lived in jeans and her long, curly hair was almost always confined in a thick plait that hung between her shoulder blades. Today's Mae wore killer heels and a severe, precisely tailored suit, her hair brushing her jawline in a sleek, sophisticated bob.

It was quite the transformation and not what he'd been expecting at all.

"Garret, good to see you," she said as she reached his table, her blue eyes smiling into his as she offered him her hand.

"Mae. Hey," he said, registering the firmness of her grip. Her freckles were gone, he noticed, hidden beneath a layer of expertly applied makeup.

Her gaze swept over him briefly, assessing him in the same way he was assessing her.

"You haven't changed a bit," she said.

"You have," he said, and she laughed.

"Apparently you *can* take Marietta out of the girl," she said. "Shall we?"

She pulled out the chair opposite him and sat as he resumed his seat.

"How long have you been back in Montana?" she asked.

He'd forgotten how clear and direct her gaze was. A good characteristic for a forensic accountant, he imagined.

"Only a couple of weeks. Ever since Dad's stroke, essentially," he said.

"I was so sorry to hear about that. How is your mom

coping?"

"She's taken it on like it's a personal challenge. Dad's going to be doing rehab at home once the hospital is done with him, and she's determined to claw back every scrap of quality of life she can for him."

"People can do amazing things when they're motivated by love," Mae said.

A phone beeped with a notification and Mae rolled her eyes.

"Sorry. Let me switch that off." She pulled her phone from the side pocket of her expensive-looking handbag and toggled her phone to silent. Then she sat back in her chair and raised her eyebrows. "You said on the phone that you've come across a few anomalies at your father's business that you'd like me to take a look at?"

Apparently the chit-chat part of their meeting was over.

"That's right." Garret took a deep breath. This was it, the moment of no return. The moment his father's possibly illegal business dealings shifted from the realm of the theoretical to the real.

"My father and his general manager have set up an 'executive account' that's ostensibly part of the sales budget. Nearly half a million carved out of the budget, but no transactional details on record."

Mae's eyes narrowed briefly, as though she was committing the information to memory. "Okay. I assume you've quizzed the general manager and asked for the missing details?"

"He tried to stall me initially. When I pushed for more information he threw a temper tantrum and stormed out.

Which was when I dug deep enough to uncover the five-hundred-thousand-dollar hole. Unfortunately, he took his laptop and any data pertaining to the account with him when he left the business."

"Is he usually the temper-tantrum type?" she asked, head cocked.

Garret thought about it for a moment. "If you'd asked me a week ago, I'd say no. He always struck me as being pretty easygoing. Then again, as far as I know, he and my father always saw eye to eye, so there was no need for fireworks."

"I'm just wondering if the dramatic storm out was an excuse for leaving the company without having to hang around to answer difficult questions. If what you suspect is correct, that laptop hard drive has been destroyed by now."

"Yeah, I figured that was probably the case."

"That's not going to stop us from getting your lawyer to draft a letter demanding its return, however," Mae said with a quick smile. "We're going to want to start creating a paper trail so that you can prove you made all the right moves if any of this blows up."

Garret's instinctive flinch must have shown on his face because Mae quickly shook her head.

"Sorry, I didn't mean to scare you. There's no reason for this to blow up or go public. Even if something unethical or illegal has been going on, your general manager is going to want to sort things out quietly," Mae said. "And I can give you guidance on how to rectify any unpaid taxes if something like that comes up. There's always a deal to be made."

There was an unassailable, confident calm beneath her

words and Garret felt some of the tension leave his shoulders and neck. This was not going to be fun, and the results were probably going to give him a headache, but he was confident he had found the right person to start unpicking the mystery for him.

"When can you get started?" he asked.

She gave a small laugh. "That was fast. You don't want to know my fees first?"

"I'm sure you're worth whatever you charge. I need to know what I'm dealing with, and I'd like it to be sooner rather than later."

She reached for her phone again. He watched as she tapped through to her calendar, her lips pursing as she reviewed her obligations.

"Technically I'm not free to look at anything new until the end of the month. But this feels like the sort of situation where we're going to want to at least define the scope of what we're dealing with as quickly as possible. If you can get me whatever you have ASAP, I'll get someone from my team to start looking through things tomorrow. We're going to need a lot of access. Bank records, reports, people on your staff."

"Whatever you need, just let me know and it's yours."

Chapter Eight

THEY TALKED FOR an hour, and by the time Garret handed over his credit card to pay for lunch he felt as though he had shed a minor burden. Only temporarily, of course, and it was likely to become a major one, but for now he could sit back and allow Mae to do her thing and get on with getting a grip on the day-to-day running of the business.

Organizing the access and data Mae required for her team chewed up a chunk of his afternoon and by four he had so many things left on his to-do list he realized he'd once again be missing the departure window to fly back to Marietta before nightfall. He texted Sierra, letting her know she should make herself comfortable at the lake house, then dove back into work.

He didn't think about her again until he was driving along the lake road, the setting sun a glare in his eyes. He needed to be smarter about the way he interacted with her tonight. No sharing takeout meals and exchanging banter in the kitchen. No more flirting and sharing.

Just business. Cool, controlled business.

He parked the Lincoln in the cavernous four-car garage

and walked the short distance to the front door. The house was profoundly quiet when he entered, and even though it was hard to be absolutely certain in a house this large, his gut told him no one else was home.

He headed for the kitchen, trying to pretend he wasn't disappointed and failing miserably.

There was no rule that said Sierra had to be here. She was free to do whatever she wanted in her own time. If she wanted to go to a bar, or out on a date, or—

He caught himself. What she was doing or who she was doing it with was none of his business.

He dumped his briefcase on the counter. Then he stood with his hands on his hips. He had more work to do—there was always more work to do—but he needed a break for an hour or two. If he'd thought to grab some groceries, he could have made a start on dinner, but he hadn't. He really needed to get on top of the domestic part of his life. Cooking a meal would be a good return to routine, something he needed to cultivate. This was his life now, he needed to stop living as though filling in for his father was a temporary state.

Tate Transport was his responsibility now. Warts and all.

He walked to the window and looked out over the yard. The glint of water on the pool caught his eye and suddenly he knew what he wanted to do. A swim would help blow all the cobwebs away. Back in Seattle he'd been a regular swimmer and runner. Like cooking, he needed to add exercise back into his life and there was nothing stopping him from hitting the water right now.

He strode to his room and stripped to his boxer-briefs in record time. Grabbing a towel, he made his way onto the deck and then downstairs to the pool.

The sun was turning the horizon a deep crimson orange as he dropped his towel onto one of the sun loungers and walked to the end of the pool.

He curled his toes over the edge of the coping. Then he launched himself into space, his body taut with potential. The water closed over him, warm and welcoming. Sucking in air, he started to swim, using the economical freestyle stroke he'd mastered in high school.

He could feel the stress of the day washing away with each successive stroke. The meeting with Mae, the issue with the payroll software, a roster problem out at the depot . . . It all fell away as he concentrated on getting the most from his body as he cut through the water.

He swam until he could feel it in his shoulders and arms, a pleasant burn that meant he'd know about it tomorrow, in a good way. He swam to the shallow end of the pool and hauled himself up the stainless-steel ladder, water sluicing down his body as he stepped onto the pool deck. He shook his head like a wet dog and felt the tightness of goosebumps as the cool night air met the water on his skin. Then he padded barefoot to the lounger. He was reaching for his towel when some instinct made him glance over his shoulder.

Sierra stood frozen on the trail to the lake, her face pale in the twilight, her startled gaze glued to his body. Then her eyes found his and for a long beat they simply stared at each other, their gazes clashing across twenty feet of pool deck and landscaping. She didn't say a word, didn't so much as blink, yet he was suddenly conscious of his own near-nakedness, the heat in his recently exercised muscles, the trickle of water down his back, the way he was standing. The thump-thump of his own heartbeat sounded heavily in his ears as he took in her long legs in a pair of hiking shorts and the tumble of wavy hair over her shoulders.

The growing darkness almost seemed to shimmer with the intensity of their mutual awareness, and the only thought in Garret's mind was how good she would feel when he closed the distance between them and pulled her body against his own.

Then a dog barked nearby, triggering a call and response from another dog in the neighborhood, and the moment was gone, shattered, over.

He bent to pick up the towel at the same moment that Sierra sprang back into action, ducking her head as she strode toward the house. She had to walk past him to get to the stairs but she didn't so much as glance sideways as she passed by. Then she was taking the stairs two at a time, her long legs making short work of the climb.

Garret was pretty sure she couldn't have moved faster if someone was chasing her with a chainsaw. Which told him pretty much everything he needed to know about how she felt about the undeniable awareness between them.

Namely, that she knew it was bad news, in the same way he knew it was bad news.

And that is a good thing. Don't ever doubt it.

He blotted his face with the towel before roughly drying his body. Then he climbed the stairs and let himself into the house. He wasn't surprised in the least to find no sign of Sierra when he entered the kitchen. He walked quickly through the empty rooms to his bedroom. His skin smelled faintly of chlorine so he rinsed off briefly under the shower before pulling on a pair of jeans and a long-sleeved black T-shirt.

He was barefoot as he returned to the kitchen, his feet silent on the polished wooden floors, which was probably why he caught Sierra closing the fridge, a bottle of beer in her hand.

Her eyes widened when she saw him, giving credence to his guess that he'd snuck up on her. Then she gave him a quick smile.

"Hi."

"Hi."

"Um, you want one of these? They're not as fancy as yours but it's still beer," she said, offering him the bottle in her hand.

"Thanks," he said, more because it felt wrong to deny her than because he wanted a beer.

"I was just about to order a pizza," she said, her gaze bouncing around as though she wasn't quite sure where to look. His chest, his shoulder, his eyes, his chest again. She pulled her phone from her pocket and offered it to him. "I'm getting a supreme with extra olives, and I'm really bad at sharing so you need to order your own."

He hesitated briefly before taking her phone. He'd decided on the drive home that he was going to be careful around her, and the moment they'd just shared by the pool only underscored the need for distance and caution. A smart man—a man committed to staying the course he'd set for himself—would say thanks but no thanks to pizza and beer.

A smart man would retreat to the study and disappear into work.

Garret scanned the menu on her phone screen. "I'll take a large spicy chicken, thanks."

He handed the phone back and Sierra tapped the screen a few times, one hip braced against the counter. Like him, she'd changed into jeans, pairing them with a soft-looking blue shirt.

"Done."

"Thanks," he said.

"Not a problem."

An awkward silence fell, and for the life of him he couldn't stop himself from thinking about those heated, taut seconds by the pool.

Danger, danger. Retreat, retreat.

"I've got some files to review, but I'll keep an ear out for the door," he said.

"Sounds good." The smile she gave him was perfunctory.

But that was *fine*. He could live with perfunctory. Sierra Carmody was not his friend; she was an employee.

He took his beer to the study and opened his computer. Thirty minutes later the doorbell rang, and he pushed to his feet. Extracting his wallet from his back pocket, he walked to the foyer and pulled open the oversized front door.

His hand tightened on the handle when he saw Ron Gibson standing there instead of a delivery person.

"What the fuck is this bullshit?" Ron said, flicking a piece of paper at Garret.

It hit his chest but Garret caught it before it fell to the floor. One glance told him it was the letter his lawyer had drafted this afternoon on Mae's instructions, demanding the return of the laptop and any other Tate Transport documents Ron had in his possession.

"Would have thought that was fairly self-evident," Garret said mildly.

"You little pissant. Do you have any idea how hard I've worked to build Tate Transport with your father?" Ron took a step closer, his face flushed, and Garret caught the sharp smell of whiskey on his breath.

"You want to have a conversation about the business, make an appointment to come see me. And bring your lawyer," Garret said.

"No. We're working this out now, man to man," Ron said, gesturing imperiously for Garret to get out of his way so he could enter the house.

All too aware that Sierra was inside somewhere, probably overhearing this ugliness, Garret took a step forward and pulled the door shut behind him. No way was he letting this drunken prick into the house while she was there.

"You're drunk, Ron," he said. "Go home, sleep it off, and maybe we can talk then."

Ron literally spluttered with frustration and rage. "You think you're so smart with your Ivy League degree and your rich-kids toy start-up. You know why you have all of that shit, Garret? Because Gideon and I made the hard calls. We drove across the country on no sleep. We nursed broken trucks till we could afford to make repairs. We sweated blood and tears for Tate Transport, and you're not taking it away from me."

Spittle foamed at the corners of the other man's mouth

as he loomed over Garret, using his extra inches to attempt to intimidate him. Garret hadn't been in a fight since senior year, but he recognized all the signs of a man about to tip over into violence.

Normally, he'd do what he could to take the heat out of the situation, but he'd just spent the past few days wading through the sewage this man had trailed through his father's business, and Garret had plenty of his own anger to vent.

Adrenaline spiking in his blood, heart pumping, he lifted his chin. "Spare me the loyal lieutenant bullshit, Ron. We both know you're nothing but a lying, cheating piece of shit who's been gaming the system for years."

Ron surged forward, fists raised, but Garret was ready, his arms coming up to block the blow—and then suddenly Ron was reeling backward, coughing and spluttering, as a hard jet of water hit him square in the face. For a split second Garret blinked stupidly with incomprehension. Then he saw Sierra standing off to his left, holding the pistol-grip nozzle of the garden hose with both hands as she aimed it with devastating precision at a stunned, backpedaling Ron.

A string of expletives filled the night air as the other man tried to block the jet spray with his hands, to no avail. Only when he retreated and turned his back did Sierra let up.

"What the fuck?" Ron spluttered.

"Do we need to order him a taxi?" Sierra asked, shifting her focus to Garret briefly.

She was so calm, so utterly in control of the situation, Garret felt a bubble of surprised laughter fill his chest.

"I'll call his wife," he said, reaching for his phone.

"Don't you fucking dare," Ron bellowed, turning back

toward Garret.

Sierra gave him another blast in the face. "Back off."

"You little bitch," Ron gasped, hands flailing in a futile attempt to protect himself.

Sierra dropped her aim then, blasting him full in the crotch, sending Ron scuttling backward with a startled yelp.

The man was a slow learner.

Garret couldn't hold back a grin as he called up Ron's home number. He was about to dial when Ron threw a final expletive over his shoulder and strode to his car. Dripping wet and mad as hell, he got behind the wheel and left rubber on the driveway as he took off with a noisy rev of the engine.

"That seems like a safe choice," Sierra said, frowning as she stared after the car.

She was so matter-of-fact, so capable, so utterly unfazed by the situation, the laughter he'd been suppressing finally found a release.

Her eyebrows lifted in surprise as she took in his mirth. Then her mouth curled into a wide smile. It took him a moment to compose himself enough to talk.

"I would give my left testicle to have that on film," he finally managed.

She laughed. "Sorry. Next time I'll bring my selfie stick. Should we be worried about him driving?"

"Yes. But there's not much we can do about it now he's gone. He lives locally, so he'll be home soon."

Headlights appeared around the bend in the driveway as he spoke and Sierra lifted the garden hose, ready to leap into the fray once more. They both relaxed when they saw the pizza logo on the side of the car.

"Perfect timing. I'm starving," Sierra said.

He huffed out another laugh as she turned away to deal with the garden hose, leaving him to settle with the driver and collect their pizzas. He waited for her on the threshold as she wiped her damp hands down the front of her jeans and came to join him.

"Didn't realize I was getting a bodyguard as well as a pilot," he said as he held the door open for her.

"I know, right? You're a lucky guy," she said. "I figured it was better than dealing with the police and paramedics."

She shot him a questioning look then, and he realized that despite her apparent confidence, she was nervous about how he might react to her intervention.

"At least one of us was thinking," he said as they walked to the kitchen. "Thanks for saving me from myself."

"My pleasure. And I mean that. The look on his face was priceless."

Her words prompted an image of Ron's baffled outrage as he reeled backward, and Garret laughed again. "Hell, yeah."

He slid the pizza boxes onto the counter.

"You want to go change before we eat?" Sierra asked.

Which was when he realized the front of his T-shirt was damp with overspray. He'd been so caught up the cold hadn't registered.

"Won't be a sec."

He walked to his room and grabbed a sweater. It wasn't until he was tugging his wet top off that he registered his still-accelerated heart rate and the fine trembling in his hands.

He stopped for a moment, taking a few calming breaths, breathing into his belly. Trying to dispel some of the adrenaline still racing through his system. Then he pulled on his sweater and made his way back to the kitchen and the heroine of the hour.

Sierra had set out their twin pizza boxes side by side on the counter, next to a couple of fresh beers.

"Nope. Don't think beer's gonna cut it tonight," he said, then he pulled open the panel that hid his father's wine fridge.

He found what he was looking for on the top shelf, a dark green bottle with a nondescript label. "Glasses are in the cabinet to your left," he instructed, pulling open a drawer to hunt for a bottle opener.

She set a couple of Bordeaux glasses in front of him and he poured two large glasses. Then he handed her one and raised his own in a toast.

"To the best hose wrangler in Montana," he said.

She laughed. "To growing up with three brothers."

She took a mouthful of wine, her eyes widening. "Wow. That's really nice."

"It'd want to be, for five hundred bucks a bottle."

Sierra nearly choked. "What? Is that a joke?" She peered at the wine in her glass.

Garret considered the wine in his own glass, taking a mouthful and swirling it around his mouth before swallowing. "Cherry. Praline. Oak."

Sierra was still staring at him. "Garret, seriously—is this really a five-hundred-dollar bottle of wine?"

"Probably not."

"Thank god."

"A 1987 Penfolds Grange Hermitage is probably worth closer to seven hundred these days."

She blinked. "But—won't your dad be upset we're drinking this?"

"Fuck him," Garret said, flipping the lid open on his pizza box.

He could feel Sierra watching him as he helped himself to a slice of the pizza.

"Well, okay, then." She set her wineglass down as carefully as if it held radioactive fluid, then opened her own box.

The pizza was good, hot and fresh, and Garret inhaled his first slice, washing it down with wine. Sierra made short work of her own first slice before taking up her wineglass again. She took a big mouthful, then copied his ostentatious mouth-swishing before swallowing.

"Mmm. Bananas. Sardines. Moldy bread," she said. "Might be a trace of Bengay in there too."

He leaned against the backrest on the stool, amused. "You should send those tasting notes to the winemaker. I'm sure they'll be flattered."

"For sure. Every winemaker aspires to Bengay top notes." She helped herself to another olive-laden slice of pizza. Then she gave him a quick, assessing glance. "So, in case you were wondering, I heard pretty much everything. I gather the plot has thickened at Tate Transport?"

"Just a little." Garret drained the last of his wine and reached for the bottle to top off his glass. He glanced at Sierra and raised his eyebrows, silently asking if she wanted a refill, and she slid her glass his way.

"Wouldn't want it to go to waste," she said.

"Trust me, it won't. Not tonight." He took a long pull of wine, then sighed. "I think my father and Ron have been paying bribes to win contracts."

Sierra's eyes bulged as she swallowed pizza and inhaled at the same time. She coughed, her eyes watering, and he reached out to give her a helpful couple of pats on the back.

"Holy shit," she said when she was capable of talking again.

"Actually, I think this is just very grubby, run-of-the-mill shit," he said.

"Is this confirmed? I mean, is there a chance you're wrong?"

"Sure. A slim one. I've got a forensic accountant looking into things for me, following the money. Since Ron took all the records with him when he had his tantrum the other day."

"Jesus. And he had the audacity to turn up here tonight and try to tear *you* a new one?" She shook her head in amazement.

"I'm starting to think there's no underestimating Ron's sense of entitlement where Tate Transport is involved. Given he's probably known where the bodies are buried for a number of years now, I guess that's only natural. No wonder he and Dad were always so buddy-buddy."

Sierra was silent for a beat, her expression troubled. "Have you spoken to Gideon about any of this?"

"Not yet. He's in no fit state to handle the stress." He sounded angry, which made sense, because he was fucking furious.

"I'm really sorry, Garret. You must be feeling pretty gutted."

That was one way of putting it.

"I just hope I can find a way through, that's all. A lot of people depend on Tate Transport for their paycheck."

They were both silent for a moment.

"So apart from unearthing graft and corruption at the family firm, what else happened today?" Sierra asked brightly.

He smiled, appreciating her attempt to lift the mood. "Sorry for dumping all this on you. I seem to be making a habit of spilling my guts at this kitchen counter."

"That's why they make these surfaces food-friendly," she said, rapping her knuckles against the marble. "So you can wash off all the guts." She swept her hair over her shoulder. "And I don't mind listening."

Her green eyes met his. Her cheeks were a little flushed from the wine, and she had a smear of pizza sauce on her chin.

All of it looked pretty good to him. Too good.

He returned his focus to his food and wine.

"Got any big plans for the weekend?" he asked, switching the topic to something nice and safe and neutral.

"I don't, but I'm betting Jed will have some chores lined up for me."

"Think you're going to miss doing ranch work?" he asked, curious.

She was lean and strong from working the land, her face and arms lightly tanned. He bet she had callouses on her hands, and that she was used to waking early and doing whatever it took to ensure the ranch remained viable.

Covering for Jack must be a big change for her.

"Probably. But like Jed said this morning, it's only six weeks, and no one is going anywhere."

Her glass was empty and he picked up the wine bottle. "Gotta get our money's worth."

"Oh, for sure. God forbid that we waste a single drop of this crazy wine," she said, holding her glass while he poured for her. "What about you? You got big plans for the weekend?"

"Work. Figure it's going to be that way for a while," he said with a shrug.

"You've got to have downtime or you'll go crazy," she said. "Casey's band is playing in Bozeman Saturday night. You should go check him out. The Whiskey Shots are pretty amazing."

"I've heard good things. I'll keep it in mind." He hesitated, then asked the question that was suddenly burning in his mind. "Will you be there?"

He knew he shouldn't have asked, that the question veered into territory he'd told himself he was going to avoid, but she was easily the most appealing, funny, smart, accomplished, sexy woman he'd met in years and suddenly that seemed far more important than anything else.

Sierra took her time answering, shifting her glass on the countertop, and he could feel his pulse thrumming in his throat as he waited for her response.

"Probably not," she finally said, and he could feel how carefully she was weighing her words. "I mean, I probably shouldn't."

Her gaze lifted to his, and he saw the conflict in her. Like him, she felt the pull of the mutual attraction between them, but like him, she was also knew it was a dumb idea to give in to it.

Thank god one of them was thinking straight.

"Yeah," he said, nodding. "That makes sense. It's probably not a good idea."

"Any other time, I'd be up for it," she said, and he had a sudden flash of what Sierra being up for something might look like.

This was a woman who hadn't hesitated to get between two raging men armed with nothing but a garden hose. If she chose to do something, she wouldn't hold anything back.

He could feel himself growing hard at the thought, and he reached for his wine, swallowing it in one long gulp.

"Good to know," he said. "I'd better get back to that work."

"Sure," she said. "Don't worry about all this. My turn to do the dishes."

"Thanks, Sierra."

He left her in the kitchen, walking away while he still could.

It wasn't until he was in the study, the door closed, his laptop open, that he felt a sense of relief. Up until that moment, all he'd felt was regret.

Because he wanted to know what Sierra Carmody tasted like. He wanted to run his hands along her lean, smooth thighs. He wanted to see if she was as brave and bold in bed as she was out of it.

But that would be a mistake, and he didn't have room for mistakes in his life right now.

So, yeah, thank god sanity had prevailed.

Chapter Nine

THE SECOND GARRET disappeared down the hall, Sierra scooped up her phone and got the hell out of the kitchen. She strode through the house at a pace just short of a run and didn't stop until she was safely in her room, the door closed between her and temptation.

That had been so, so close.

And she'd been so, so tempted.

One moment they'd been talking innocuously about Casey's band, the next they'd been neck-deep in dangerous waters. All it had taken was four words.

Will you be there?

Such innocent words but, coupled with the heat in his gaze and what had happened by the pool, they'd taken on a whole new meaning. There wasn't a doubt in her mind that if she'd said yes, she and Garret Tate would be tearing each other's clothes off right now.

Just as well she'd said no.

Actually, technically you said "probably not." So don't pat yourself on the back too hard.

If Garret was a different kind of man, he'd have picked up on the ambivalence in her response. He would have recognized how torn and tempted she was and charmed and cajoled her into changing her mind—and she was afraid she would have been very susceptible to his charm because barely an hour ago she'd returned from a long hike to find him rising out of the pool like a mythical god and her panties had all but spontaneously combusted.

One minute she'd been thinking about how hungry she was and what to have for dinner and the next she'd been frozen in her tracks as she watched him stride to where he'd left his towel, a very different kind of hunger consuming her.

She only had to close her eyes and there he was again, filling her mind's eye.

Tight, wet boxer-briefs . . . Muscular thighs and broad shoulders . . . The ripple and bulge of his strong arms as he reached for his towel . . .

He'd moved with an unconscious animal grace, his wet skin combining with the warm glow of the house lights to give the impression he'd been gilded, and she'd honestly never seen anything more beautiful or desirable in her life.

Then he'd shaken his head playfully, sending droplets flying like tiny diamonds and setting off a chain reaction of muscular ripples across his chest and torso, and she'd forgotten her own name, how to breathe, what year it was, and everything else that wasn't Garret Tate.

She'd been literally transfixed by his male perfection, unable to look away.

As though he'd sensed her heated regard, he'd looked over his shoulder and their gazes had locked. Twenty feet had separated them but she'd felt the flare of need in him, just as he'd recognized the desire in her. For long seconds that recognition had burned bright between them, filled with heated possibility.

If that dog hadn't barked . . . But it had, and reality had slammed her hard enough to send her racing up the stairs as quickly as humanly possible.

Which made this latest retreat the second time she'd run from her own desire this evening. Not exactly the greatest stats, given this was only her first week on the job.

He's just a man. It's just sex. Just because you think it might be good with him, it's not worth compromising the job over. It just isn't. And let's not even get into how Jack would feel if he learned you'd crossed the line while covering for him.

The voice in her head was absolutely right, and the rational part of her brain was utterly convinced by it. But that didn't account for the way her heart was still racing even though she'd been pacing her room for nearly five minutes now. It definitely didn't account for the fact that her panties were wet with need for Garret Tate.

Despite all of the good and rational and smart reasons for keeping her distance, she wanted him. God, she wanted him. And it wasn't just because he had the body of a mythical hero. That was definitely a huge part of it, but he was also *nice*. It was a much-maligned word in today's cynical world, but that was exactly what he was—a nice, good person. He was also thoughtful, and clever, and conscientious. He was literally working himself into the ground to support his parents while simultaneously dealing with deeply heavy crap of his father's making.

If they'd met and gotten to know each other under different circumstances, if he wasn't her boss . . . But what was the point of playing what-ifs? This was the hand she'd been dealt, and all she could do was play it as well as she knew how.

"Which means keeping it in your pants," she told herself.

She dropped onto the bed, exhausted after the battle of wills with herself. How many more of these self-talks was she going to have to have before she could trust herself to be around Garret? Ten? Twenty?

As many as it takes for as long as it takes.

Well, that was a cheery thought.

It was only nine, but an early night wouldn't hurt her. She'd scheduled the maintenance on the Bell for tomorrow and she needed to be at the airport by seven. She went to brush her teeth before stripping down to her panties and pulling on a tank top and pajama pants. Then she climbed into bed and opened up the e-book she'd been reading on her phone, intending to read for twenty minutes or so until she felt dozy enough to fall asleep.

Twenty minutes turned into an hour, which turned into two, and she was still too wired to sleep. So much for having an early night. Then an alert popped up to let her know her battery was running low and she decided the universe was telling her to put the device down and try falling asleep the old-fashioned way.

First, however, she needed to put her phone on the charger. She got out of bed to grab the cable from her bag, only to swear softly when she remembered she'd taken it down to the kitchen earlier, intending to charge her phone down there, and then had taken it off again when she'd opted to go for a hike.

Which meant her charger was still in the kitchen.

She was a genius, pure and simple.

Annoyed with herself, she slipped out of her bedroom and made her way downstairs. The house was silent and dark and she guessed Garret was either long in bed or still holed up in the study. Either option was good for her—this was going to be a covert op, in and out as quickly as possible.

Moonlight streamed in the kitchen window, turning the world monochrome as she crossed to where her cable snaked from an outlet near the oven. She pulled it free, wrapping the cord around the plug, then pivoted to make the return journey—only to find Garret standing in the doorway wearing nothing but a pair of unfastened jeans.

His hair was rumpled, his beautiful chest bare. At this range she could take in the important little details she hadn't been close enough to see earlier—the dark hair that covered his pecs, the arrowing trail that disappeared beneath the elastic of his boxer-briefs, visible in the open V of his unfastened jeans.

She swallowed, her hand clenching around the charger. "I thought you were in bed."

"I was. Couldn't sleep."

"Me either." She swallowed again, then closed her eyes and very consciously reminded herself why this was a bad idea: he was her boss, and she was filling in for Jack, and this was her first professional pilot gig.

Then she opened her eyes and he was still standing there in all his perfection, and her heart was still banging like crazy in her chest, and she still wanted him.

He wanted her too—she could see it in the way he was

watching her, the still readiness of his body. As if he was just waiting for her to say the word, and anything she wanted was hers.

"This is a really bad idea," she heard herself say.

"I'll go," he said, turning away.

"Don't."

The single word echoed in the space. He stilled. Then he turned to face her. She could hear herself breathing, the sound harsh and fast.

Dear god, she was panting and he hadn't even laid a finger on her.

"Tell me what you want," Garret said.

"I want—" Sierra took a deep breath. "I want you to fuck me."

He flinched, as though her words had hit him with the visceral force of an electric shock. Then he was moving, closing the short distance between them even as she moved toward him.

They met in the middle, his arms coming around her, his head lowering toward hers as she lifted her face. Then his lips were on hers, warm and soft, his tongue sweeping into her mouth, and the world fell away.

He tasted like mint and red wine and his mouth moved over hers with a questing assurance, his hands gliding up her back until he was holding her head in both hands, taking control of the kiss.

She made a small, needy sound, overwhelmed by how good his body felt pressed against her own, how amazing he tasted, how good he smelled, her hands gripping his hard biceps as though her life depended on it. He made an approving sound, and then her back was against the wall, his body pressing into hers even more urgently.

He was so hard, she could feel his erection against her mons. Her inner muscles tightened as she imagined what he was going to feel like inside her.

So good.

She arched her back, rubbing herself against him provocatively. He lifted his head, breaking their kiss.

"You taste so fucking good," he murmured, pressing a kiss to the sensitive skin beneath her ear before trailing more kisses down her neck.

She shifted her grip to his shoulders and then his back as he blazed a sensual path toward her breasts. His body was hard as granite beneath her hands, every muscle straining toward her.

He pressed an open-mouthed kiss to the inner curve of her breast, his tongue hot and wet through the fabric of her top, and it felt so good she almost couldn't bear it. Pushing him away, she grabbed the hem of her tank top and whipped it over her head.

"Oh, fuck," Garret breathed, his tone reverential, then his hands were on her breasts, his thumbs gliding over her nipples.

"Do that again," she demanded, his touch reverberating through her like a plucked violin string, sending jolts of pleasure to her already-aching pussy.

He did better than that and lowered his head. She gasped as one of her nipples was drawn into the shocking wet heat of his mouth. His tongue flicked against her, then he sucked hard, dragging a helpless moan from her throat. Her legs were shaking as he transferred his focus to her other breast, and she wove her fingers into his hair to hold him in place, greedily wanting to ensure her own pleasure.

She could feel how incredibly wet she was, and she squeezed her thighs together to try to relieve the growing ache of desire. Hazy images formed behind her closed eyelids. She needed . . . *more*. She needed him inside her. She need him to touch her. She needed—

As if in answer to her unspoken prayers, he slipped a hand beneath the waistband of her pajamas. She arched her hips forward, silently encouraging his touch, and his fingers skimmed over her mons before delving between her thighs to trace the seam of her pussy.

"Oh, god," she moaned, widening her stance to accommodate him.

He did it again, this time delving deeper and teasing her aching entrance with a brief, shallow dip of his finger.

It felt insanely good—his hands, his mouth, his body, all of it. Need spiraling inside her, she reached for the front of his jeans and slid her hand into his boxer-briefs, her fingers closing around the straining shaft of his erection.

He was very hard and thick and her thumb found a small bead of moisture when she ran it over the head of his cock. He shuddered as she used her thumb to tease his plump head, rubbing his pre-cum into his sensitive flesh before gliding her hand down his shaft in a firm stroke.

And then suddenly he was gone.

"Wha—?" she protested, blinking at the abrupt loss of sensation.

"Put your arms around my neck," he said.

She complied, then followed his urging as he grabbed her ass and boosted her up, wrapping her legs around his waist. Then he was moving through the dark house, somehow kissing her and finding his way at the same time.

She had a vague sense of passing through a doorway, then he dropped her onto his bed, the mattress yielding beneath her. His hands went straight to the waistband of her pajama pants and she lifted her hips as he yanked them off, taking her panties with them. She made equally short work of his jeans, and then he was climbing onto the bed, naked and hard and ready.

She spread her legs as he settled over her, savoring the first press of his entirely naked body against her own.

"Sierra," he said, her name a guttural groan.

He reached between his legs to grip himself, dragging the head of his cock along her pussy, the blunt pressure intense and crazy-making. She pressed her hips forward and up when he did it a second time, hands gripping his smooth, muscular ass as she urged him inside her.

"Wait a second."

He leaned across to open the bedside drawer. She was about to protest when her lust-hazed brain comprehended he was retrieving protection. Seconds later he was tearing a small foil pack open and smoothing a condom over his erection.

He took himself in hand again, taking up where he'd left off with a slow, torturous glide along her needy, slick pussy. This time when he got to her entrance he slid inside, giving her the merest taste of his deliciously hard cock before retreating. She made an impatient noise, her hands curling into the hard muscles of his backside as she tried to drag him back. He ignored her, giving her a little of what she so desperately wanted again, and then again.

"Stop fucking around and fuck me," she growled, wrapping her legs around his hips and locking her ankles behind him.

"Yes, ma'am," he said. Then he thrust inside her in one powerful stroke.

She closed her eyes, awash with pleasure, feeling the stretch, savoring the fullness and heat and hardness of him.

"Where have you been all my life?" he said.

"Waiting for your beautiful cock."

He withdrew almost to the tip, then plunged inside her again and it was just as good as the first time. She forgot to breathe as he found a rhythm, his hips pressing forward to rub the base of his shaft against her swollen clitoris on each down stroke.

It was exactly what she needed—the steady rhythm, the pressure, the feel of his weight bearing down on her, the stretch inside her, the gentle abrasion of his chest hair against her sensitive nipples, his harsh breath against her cheek, his searching, urgent mouth on her own.

Her climax hit her hard, an avalanche of pleasure, and she cried out his name and held on for dear life as her pussy clenched around him again and again. She felt the moment he tipped over, too, his body shuddering into orgasm just as she was coming down off her own climax. She reveled in the hard clench of his ass cheeks as he drove into her and stayed deep, the added pressure wringing the final ripples of pleasure from her own body.

They were both breathing heavily when he lifted his head and braced himself on his elbows to look into her eyes. She wondered if she looked as flushed and spaced-out as he did, his pupils dilated with arousal. The thump of his heartbeat reverberated through his body into her own as she stared into his eyes, her thoughts still oddly detached and disjointed.

He lifted a hand to her face, brushing a strand of hair from her temple. There was a world of gentleness and wonder in his touch, as though he couldn't quite believe what had just happened between them.

That made two of them, because she'd had good sex be-fore—great sex, even—but she'd never had sex like this. He had *owned* her from the moment his lips found hers, and when he'd stroked inside her that first time . . .

Her pussy clenched just thinking about it, and a slow smile curled Garret's mouth.

"Really?" he asked. "Already?"

"Not my fault you're hotter than a bike seat in summer," she said.

He laughed, his eyes warm on her. "I'm going to need a moment or two to catch my breath."

"I can live with that."

She stifled a protest as he withdrew from her, shifting to the edge of the bed and standing. He disappeared in what she assumed was the direction of the bathroom and she took advantage of the small moment of privacy to press her hands over her hot face.

Dear. God.

What the hell had just happened to her? She felt as though her body had been holding out on her. No man had ever made her feel so good so fast. And usually she needed a little extra help to get over the line—more foreplay, a helping hand—but not with Garret.

"Hey. Want a shower?"

She opened her eyes to find Garret standing in the doorway, his tall, muscular body framed by the opening. He looked too good to be true, and she felt a powerful need to pinch herself to prove that yes, this was real, and this gorgeous man had just been inside her.

"You okay?" he asked, moving toward the bed.

"Yes. Just a little . . . I don't know . . ."

"Blown away?" he asked.

"Blown somewhere."

He laughed, then held out his hand. "Come have a shower, and I'll do dirty things to you with the massage nozzle."

She blinked. Then she took his hand and let him pull her up from the bed.

HE COULDN'T GET enough of Sierra.

The moment they stepped into the spacious double shower he kissed her, needing to taste her again, needing to feel her instant, heated response. She gave back as good as she got, her tongue chasing his, her hands smoothing over his chest, shoulders, back. He loved the way she touched him, as though she couldn't quite believe he was real, but he loved touching her more.

Everything about her fascinated and aroused him. Her eyes, so expressive and revealing. Her wild, wavy hair. The lean athleticism of her body. The different textures of her skin—soft and silky here, firm and taut there.

Backing her against the tiled wall, he gave free rein to his curiosity and need. Abandoning her mouth, he kissed his way across her cheek to her ear. He already knew she liked it when he kissed the soft skin there, and he opened his mouth against her neck as he cupped her breasts in his hands.

Her breasts were fuller than he'd expected, heavy and round in his hands, her nipples a dark pinkish brown. When she was turned on they tightened into hard little berries, so fucking sweet to suck on, something he intended to do again very soon.

Now, he swept his thumbs across them, enjoying the way her hips pressed forward in response. Breaking away from her briefly, he reached for the soap. Holding her eyes, he lathered up, then very deliberately reached out to cup her breasts again. She swallowed, her eyes closing briefly. He kept watching her face as he pinched her nipples lightly before soothing them with his palms. She bit her lip, her head dropping back against the tiles.

She looked so decadent, wet hair streaming over her shoulders, skin glistening, her chest rising and falling rapidly, as though she couldn't quite catch her breath.

His cock stirred back to life, eager to join the party, but he ignored his own needs to concentrate on hers, gliding one hand down over her ribs and belly then between her legs.

She was very wet, her delicate flesh plump and swollen with arousal. Watching her face, he slipped two fingers inside her. Then he found her clitoris with his thumb. She gasped, her eyes popping open. He started to fuck her very slowly with his hand, his thumb teasing the stiff little bud of her clitoris, his eyes never leaving hers. He felt every tremor, every shudder, every clench as he played with her pussy, stroking her and teasing her until she was panting, her hands tightening on his shoulders as she fought to keep her knees from buckling.

"Come for me," he told her.

"That's the plan," she said, her mouth curving into a quick, wicked grin.

Then she was gasping, her hips pushing forward, and he felt her pulse around his hand as pleasure took her. She didn't break eye contact the whole time, letting him see what he'd done to her, how crazy he'd made her, how good it was between them.

He was hard again, and all he wanted was to bury himself inside her, but he'd forgotten to bring a condom into the shower. He consoled himself with a deep, long kiss, his hands gliding down her body as he ground his erection against her thigh. It wasn't what he wanted, but it still felt damned good. Everything with Sierra felt damned good.

They kissed deeply for long minutes, water beating down on them, then she slipped a hand between their bodies and started stroking his aching cock. He groaned his approval, and seconds later she sank to her knees, glancing up at him with erotic intent before taking him into her mouth.

"*Oh, man.*"

Her tongue danced across the head of his cock before trailing down his shaft. Then she took him deep, the suction incredible as she slowly drew back before doing it all over again. His eyes nearly rolled back in his head. It felt so good, and it wasn't long before he was ready to lose it a second time. He tightened his grip on her shoulder, gently pushing her away so he could finish like a gentleman, but she simply curled her fingers into his ass cheeks and kept driving him crazy with her mouth. Moments later he came, his body straining. Sierra stayed with him, only relinquishing her claim on his cock when he sighed. One hand still holding his cock, she looked up at him, satisfaction and triumph dancing in her eyes. Then she licked her lips provocatively, making him laugh.

"Come here," he said, drawing her back to her feet.

The rest of the shower passed in a haze of slippery hands and steam. Afterward he dried her off before tumbling her onto his bed again.

"You cannot be serious," she said when she saw he was hard again already.

"Your fault," he said.

She looked a little put out. "I just gave you some of my very best work in the shower."

"And I appreciated it immensely. Couldn't you tell?"

He ran a leisurely hand down her body, stopping at all the good places along the way. By the time he was done, she was smoky-eyed and flushed, her hips moving restlessly.

"Okay, you're talking me around," she said.

"I haven't even started yet."

Pressing a kiss to her left breast, then her right, he slipped farther down in the bed. Her stomach trembled as he tongued her belly button. He glanced up at her and smiled when he saw the anticipation in her eyes. "You like this?"

"Who doesn't?" she asked.

He slipped farther down the bed, nudging her thighs wider. The neat patch of hair on her mons was still damp from the shower and he brushed his cheek against it before pressing a kiss to her inner thigh.

"Feel free to scream," he said as he eyed her plump, pink pussy.

"Is that a threat or a promise?" she asked.

"Both."

Then he lowered his head and began the delicious task of making her come again.

Chapter Ten

I T WAS STILL dark outside when he woke. For a moment he couldn't remember where he was—Marietta, Helena, Seattle. Then his brain kicked in and it all came back to him: Ron, pizza and wine, Sierra.

God, Sierra.

In the kitchen, her hand in his jeans.

In his bed, moaning his name.

In the shower, staring into his eyes as he made her come.

He stretched out a hand, but all he encountered was tangled sheets and an empty bed. She must have slipped out at some point while he slept.

Relief hit him like a sledge hammer, profound and real, closely followed by visceral regret.

He was such a piece of shit.

You know it, buddy. A real chip off the old block.

For years he'd judged his father for his affairs—and it hadn't even taken a week of working with Sierra to prove he was every bit as unethical and self-indulgent as his father.

He sat up, raking his hands through his hair, beyond grateful Sierra wasn't here to witness his regret and shame. She was his freaking *employee*. He owed her so much more than what she'd gotten from him last night.

Angry with himself, he kicked off the sheets and strode into the bathroom. There was no way he was getting more sleep, so he might as well go into work early and get started on what was sure to be yet another life-affirming day of stressful challenges and unpleasant discoveries.

Oh, yeah, now is definitely the time to feel sorry for yourself, sport.

He turned the water on as hard as it would go and stepped beneath the jets. Instantly he was assailed with memories from last night—the feel of Sierra's soapy breasts in his hands, the intense, heated suction of her mouth on his cock, the way she'd licked her lips afterward and given him a saucy, provocative smile.

He was hard in seconds, his erection straining against his belly.

So now he could add that to his list of things that were wrong with his life—he'd broken every tenet of decency in regard to employer/employee relations last night, and even though he was now marinating in guilty regret, he still wanted her.

God, he probably wanted her more now that he knew how good it was between them.

No, *good* didn't even come close. Being skin to skin with her had been *intense*. He'd been so tuned in to her pleasure, and her to his. He'd never felt so connected, so aroused, so *intimate* with another human being.

Well, hey, that makes it okay then. Three cheers for you, man. Collect two hundred dollars and pass Go.

The voice in his head was an asshole, but it was right.

He turned the water to full cold, gritting his teeth and forcing himself to stay beneath the punishing spray. Only when his erection was well and truly banished did he flick the water off and step out of the shower to towel his goose-fleshed body dry.

He dressed with brisk efficiency in the walk-in, only to stop in his tracks when he returned to the bedroom and registered the state of the bed. The duvet was half on the floor, the sheets a tangled mess. He had a sudden flash of Sierra fisting her hands in the sheets as he pressed open-mouthed kisses to her pussy, her needy cries filling the room.

Jesus. He was going to have to move rooms if these crazy flashbacks kept up. Striding forward, he yanked the duvet off the floor. The cleaner was due today, so he stripped the sheets and threw them into the corner. Then he spread the duvet across the bed and stacked the pillows against the headboard.

He felt stupid the moment he was done. As if he could undo last night just by erasing the evidence of their encounter.

He went to brush his teeth and fix his hair, then grabbed his briefcase and headed for the front door. It was only five thirty, and the house was utterly silent as he let himself out.

It wasn't until he was almost at Tate Transport that he realized he was actually looking forward to burying himself in work for the day. Anything to distract him from the tight feeling in his gut.

You're still going to have to look her in the eye tonight.

He was, and he had no idea how he was going to handle the situation, what he should say, if he should say anything.

They'd both agreed last night that sleeping together would be a bad idea. He'd offered to go, but she'd stopped him.

So the bad decision had been mutual. The difference was, he had all the power in this relationship, and therefore the onus had been on him to walk away.

And he hadn't.

Jaw set, he concentrated on the road ahead. He'd be seeing Sierra soon enough. Hopefully by then he'd have worked out what to say to her.

SIERRA WOKE IN lazy degrees. She felt *good.* Loose and relaxed, well rested. Then she stretched and yawned, registering the damp tenderness between her legs, and suddenly she was very wide awake.

Oh, boy.

She'd slept with Garret last night. Not just slept—she'd climbed him like a cat on a curtain.

She stared at the ceiling with wide eyes. So much for being smart. So much for her first job as a private pilot being more important than potent sexual attraction.

It's almost funny, the stories you tell yourself sometimes.

Almost.

Because no matter what had happened last night, no matter how good it had been—and it had been very, very good—she was going to have to meet Garret at the airport this afternoon and be professional and cool and collected. She was going to have to look him in the eye and forget that he'd coaxed her to a scream-inducing climax with his mouth. She was going to have to forget the feel of his lovely cock in her hand and her mouth, and the way he'd brushed the hair from her face so tenderly after their first time.

She rolled onto her stomach and pressed her face into the pillow.

If only she hadn't left that stupid charger in the kitchen.

If only he'd been wearing a shirt.

If only she'd had enough self-control to walk away.

Her phone started to buzz, letting her know it was time to wake up and face the day. She reached out blindly and managed to swipe the screen to silence.

She lay like that for another five minutes, then the knowledge that she was going to be late to meet the mechanic spurred her into action.

It wasn't until she was pulling on her socks and tying her boots that it occurred to her that in all likelihood, Garret was probably feeling equally awkward this morning too. After all, neither of them had planned to get hot and heavy in the middle of the night. It had just happened, and they had both been equal participants. Very eager, very enthusiastic, insatiable, equal participants.

So this feeling she was experiencing—this sense of exposure and vulnerability and regret—he was probably feeling the same way.

The realization helped ease the tightness in her shoulders. They'd crossed a line—together. It had been a mutual transgression, and all they needed to do was acknowledge that it had been inappropriate and move on.

Excellent strategy. Because denial worked so well for you before.

Sierra snatched her jacket and headed for the door. She

had a mechanic to meet, and the taxi she'd ordered would be at the door any minute now.

Sure enough, the car was waiting for her, and she locked the house carefully after setting the alarm. She was getting used to the speculative looks she kept receiving from taxi drivers when they saw the Tates' house—apparently she didn't match anyone's idea of the sort of person who lived in a lakeside mega-mansion—but this time she didn't bother explaining she was just the hired help. Instead, she stared out the window and thought about the day ahead, the questions she had for the mechanic, the checks she wanted to run on the Bell.

Anything except last night.

The mechanic was almost half an hour late, but once he got there the day proceeded smoothly enough and all the necessary maintenance tasks and checks were completed by midafternoon. Sierra grabbed a late lunch at the airport coffee shop, sitting outside to eat it in the sun while she watched the fixed-wing planes taxi down the runway.

It was a strange thing, but she'd never been drawn to fixed-wing aircrafts the way she was to helicopters. They just didn't have the same hands-on appeal for her. But that didn't mean she couldn't appreciate the magic moment when the combination of the plane's speed and the shape of the wing resulted in gravity-defying lift. Every time it looked impossible—the plane too cumbersome and heavy, the runway too short—and every time the laws of physics proved themselves as the plane swooped into the air.

The miracle of flight really was a beautiful thing.

The small moment of peace and contemplation helped

calm her nerves as departure time approached. Apart from the first day when he'd been early, Garret typically arrived close to six o'clock, and she made a point of going to the bathroom before he was due. She retied her ponytail and straightened her polo shirt. Then, feeling like a complete dick, she practiced smiling her best friendly-yet-still-professional smile.

Because that was the key here—she needed to let Garret know she was *fine* about last night, that there would be no weirdness, and that they should just continue on as they had in the past. She had no expectations, and she certainly wasn't going to start flirting with him or assuming anything while on the job.

Sure. The guy's just been inside you. You wouldn't want to come across too friendly and give him the wrong idea.

"Oh, shut up," she snapped, turning away from her reflection.

Garret's car was pulling into the Tates' reserved parking spot as she exited the hangar. Sierra wiped her damp palms down the sides of her chinos, then lifted her chin and walked across to the Bell. She checked the time on her phone as Garret approached, just to give herself something to do, then pasted on a smile and steeled herself to meet his eyes.

"Mr. Tate. Hope you had a good day. We'll have a tailwind on the way home, so it should be a nice fast flight," she said.

This was the moment where he would hopefully say something to make last night okay. Maybe some kind of self-deprecating joke, or some other acknowledgment that even though they'd made a mutual mistake, it was not big deal and nothing needed to change between them.

Garret's face was unreadable as he glanced at her. "That's good. I need to be at an appointment at the hospital by seven thirty."

"Not a problem. You'll make it with time to spare."

She moved ahead of him to open the passenger cabin door, then stepped well back so there would be no chance of them accidentally brushing against one another. He climbed into the passenger cabin, and she secured the door behind him.

She pressed her hand against her stomach as she turned away, willing the sick, nervous feeling away. So what if he was distant? It wasn't as though she knew how to handle this situation either. She clung to the belief that all they had to do was get through this first, awkward flight and they'd be back on track. Last night would be forgotten, an aberration never to be repeated.

She wouldn't have messed up irreversibly, and no one ever needed to mention it again.

She climbed into the pilot's seat, fastening her own seat belt. Then she went through her preflight routine. Collective and throttle friction off, check the range of the cyclic, fuel valve open . . . Once the overhead rotor was whirring and she was satisfied with all her instrument readings, she checked to ensure Garret was seated and belted in before she took off. Their gazes clashed in the mirror, and she realized he'd been watching her. He quickly looked away, but not before she'd seen the coolness in his eyes. The discomfort.

Heat climbed into her face as she lifted the collective and opened up the throttle. The Bell lifted into a hover and she automatically went through her hover check.

It was one thing to recognize that what she and Garret had done last night was both foolish and inappropriate, but it was another thing to look into his eyes and see nothing but regret.

This is why people don't sleep with their bosses. Just a little note for future reference.

Sierra spent the next few moments doing everything by the book as she asked for clearance from the tower, did another visual check, and then opened up the throttle. Only when the prickly-hot feeling of embarrassment had dissipated did she let herself think of anything other than the job at hand.

It didn't take long to come to the conclusion that there was nothing she could do if Garret chose to view last night's encounter as a big mistake. He felt the way he felt. Did it sting a little that he felt that way? Oh, yes. But she'd been wallowing in regret today too. For some reason it was so much easier to remember all the reasons why sleeping with each other was a bad idea *after* the event.

Genius, really. She blamed the fog of hormones, which was only marginally less dangerous than the fog of war, apparently.

As she'd promised, the tailwind gave them a helpful boost and they arrived at the Tate ranch five minutes ahead of schedule. Sierra set the Bell down and switched the engine off. Then she braced herself for more cool politeness before climbing out of the helicopter.

Garret was gathering papers together and putting them back into his briefcase when she opened the door to the passenger cabin. She kept her face as neutral as she could while she waited, every muscle in her body tense with the awkwardness of the situation. Then one of the documents Garret was wrangling slipped free, gliding across the cabin to land near the door. Wanting to be helpful, she immediately leaned in to collect it.

"I got it," Garret said, his tone crisp.

Feeling as though she'd just had her hand slapped, she moved back as far as she could and still hold the door open. Seconds later Garret exited the Bell, offering her a brusque "thanks" accompanied by zero eye contact as he headed for the house. Sierra stared after him for a beat, almost wishing she'd stayed in her room last night.

She turned to give the cabin her usual scan to make sure everything was in order before hangaring the Bell. The glint of light bouncing off something shiny caught her eye where Garret had been sitting. His phone must have slipped from his pocket.

She climbed in quickly and grabbed it. Garret was almost at the front door, and she took off after him at a jog.

"Garret."

He stilled and turned toward her, and she held his phone up to let him know he'd left it behind. He watched her jog the remaining few feet, his face even tighter and more closed off than before.

"Found it down the side of the—"

"Thanks," he said, holding out his hand.

Sierra blinked at his abrupt rudeness. Then she handed the phone over.

"I'll see you tomorrow, the usual time," he said, turning

away.

"Am I going to lose my job?" The words popped out before she could stop them.

He froze, then turned back toward her. "Of course not."

"Are you angry with me? Is this a blame thing we've got going on right now?" She was already knee-deep in this, might as well go for broke. If she'd been cast as the seductive vixen in this little drama, she wanted to know about it.

He frowned. "Why would I blame you for something I did?"

Her shoulders relaxed fractionally at his words. "So this is a guilt thing? We both got naked last night, Garret. Neither of us is married. At least, I'm not and I figured you would have mentioned it at some point if you were . . ."

"I'm not married, but I employ you. I shouldn't have crossed the line." He said it so sternly, his body rigid with the strength of his conviction.

"I crossed the line too. And I've got more to lose than you. If you're worried that I felt coerced in any way, shape, or form, get that idea out of your head. I wanted what happened just as much as you did. In case that wasn't obvious."

They stared at each other, and it was impossible not to think about the way he'd held her gaze last night while he fucked her with his hand.

She pushed the memory away.

"Look, I had a really good time, and I think you did too," she said. "We obviously had some pent-up sexual tension to deal with. But we've dealt with it, right? It's gone now. We don't need to walk around wearing matching hair shirts and whipping ourselves." She paused. "Unless you're into that, of course."

His mouth twitched, just enough to let her know her words had gotten through.

"Sorry for being an asshole," he said after a moment.

"You need a little work before you reach asshole status," she said lightly. "You were borderline douchey, at best. Perfectly acceptable for most captain of industry types."

He smiled for real then, his face lighting up momentarily. "My apology still stands."

"Accepted."

His eyes were warm as they scanned her face. "I feel like you're giving me a free pass here, but I'm going to take it."

"Frame it and hang it on the wall. It's all yours." She took a step backward. "Have a good night. I'll see you tomorrow."

She made herself turn and walk away then, because she could feel herself looking for excuses to stay and keep him talking. That wasn't going to happen. They'd made their one, glorious mistake, and they weren't going to go there again.

Her stride long and sure, she headed back to the hangar put the Bell to bed for the weekend.

GARRET LET HIMSELF into his parents' house and dumped his keys and phone on the hall table. He called out but wasn't surprised when no one answered—his mother spent every spare second she had by his father's side these days.

He loosened his tie as he made his way to his bedroom.

He had time to change before driving in to the hospital, but instead of stripping his clothes he sank onto the end of the bed.

He'd handled everything with Sierra really badly, snapping at her, avoiding unnecessary eye contact. As though she'd done something wrong.

Was it any wonder she'd confronted him and asked what was going on?

If you're worried that I felt coerced in any way, shape, or form, get that idea out of your head. I wanted what happened just as much as you did.

Her bold, up-front declaration had gone a long way toward making him feel less guilty about last night, but he still wasn't ready to let himself off the hook. In many ways, it didn't matter that she'd wanted him as much as he'd wanted her. He should have known better.

He did know better.

But maybe continuing to give himself a hard time over it wasn't the most productive thing he could be doing right now. Maybe he needed to cut himself a little slack. His life had just imploded, and Sierra was off-the-charts sexy. Was it that big of a surprise that he'd given in to instinct where she was concerned?

Either way, he couldn't undo it, so there was no point wasting any more energy on regretting what had happened. He'd simply have to take her at her word and make sure he never went there again.

He surged to his feet on the thought and toed off his shoes. Five minutes later he was letting himself out the door and striding to the garage. He was about to climb behind the wheel of his father's SUV when he spotted the dust-covered shape of his motorcycle against the far wall.

The thought of taking the Ducati into town, blowing the cobwebs away, was hugely appealing. He crossed to the bike and pulled the dustcover off, then deftly reconnected the battery. The keys were in the cabinet built into the wall, and he threw a leg over the bike before holding his breath and starting the motor. It had been five months since he'd ridden the bike—hence the battery being disconnected—but it started on the first try, the engine thrumming to life between his legs. Gratified, he swapped his casual jacket for the leather bike jacket hanging on a hook on the wall, then donned his helmet.

He coasted down the drive in second gear. The road was clear in both directions when he reached it, and he opened up the throttle. The Ducati took off with a feline snarl, inertia tugging him backward as he shot down the road.

He indulged his need for speed for a minute or two, then throttled back to the legal limit. The few minutes of intense focus and adrenaline had done the trick, however, and he felt more clear-headed when he arrived at the hospital.

He stowed his helmet on the bike, then went into the hospital and asked for directions to the rehabilitation unit. His mother was waiting already when he arrived at the rehabilitation director's office, sitting with a sporty-looking redhead in her late thirties.

"Garret," his mother said chidingly when she took in his motorcycle jacket. "I thought you'd given up on that death machine."

"Nope," he said, then addressed himself to the woman.

"I'm Garret. Good to meet you."

"Kathleen," she said with a smile. "Grab a seat."

He didn't miss the quick, appraising head to toe she gave him as he settled into the remaining guest chair. She was an attractive woman, but nowhere near as sexy and appealing as Sierra.

It was a dumb comparison, and he kept a careful rein on his wandering thoughts for the next forty minutes as they went through the arrangements his mother had put in place to facilitate his father continuing his rehabilitation at home. He'd done his best to stay abreast of the constant stream of emails his mother had shot him during the week, but he was impressed by how on top of it all she was, spouting off acronyms and discussing the merits of various pieces of equipment and therapies with Kathleen as though she was an old hand.

"I'll come out and take a look at your setup once you've had the bathroom altered, but it sounds like you've got a really good grip on it," Kathleen said. "I do want to warn you that I really want Gideon to reach certain markers before we send him home. I know you want to have him home with you as soon as possible, but I would be doing him a disservice if we discharged him too early."

"I understand. Gideon might not, but I'll tell him he's just going to have to suck it up," his mother said with a determined smile.

Afterward, he waited in the corridor while his mom said her goodbyes to Kathleen, who she'd obviously struck up a friendship with.

"Look at you, winning over hearts and minds," he said as

his mother joined him.

"You get more flies with honey than vinegar," his mother said. "And she's a smart lady. We need all the smart people we can get on our side."

"How's Dad today?"

"Tired. They did a double therapy session, and it took a lot out of him. He was already drifting off when I left him to come here. I'm just going to pop my head in to check with his nurses and then head home. So don't feel as though you need to hang around."

Garret frowned, caught short by the announcement. He'd mentally allocated his evening to visiting his father.

"Why don't you catch up with a friend? You've been working nonstop. Take some time for yourself."

"I might just crash, actually," he said.

It wasn't as though he'd gotten a lot of sleep last night.

"How are things at the business?" his mother asked. "It must be hectic, with Ron walking out the way he did."

He paused, but the corridor of a busy hospital wasn't the place to disclose what he'd uncovered. And his suspicions hadn't been confirmed yet. He'd already decided there was no point adding to his mother's burdens until he fully understood what he was dealing with and nothing had changed to make him revise that decision. "I'm getting there. Slowly."

"Ron called again this morning, but I just let it go through to message bank like all of his other calls."

"Good. The lawyers are handling everything, and you don't need him raging at you right now," Garret said.

"I still can't believe he walked out like that. It's so out of character for him."

"I'm sure he had his reasons," he said.

"Well, I'll see you back at the house later."

He kissed her goodbye and walked slowly through the hospital to the main entrance. He wasn't surprised Ron was still trying to find a way to talk to his father. The other man was deluded in the extreme and didn't seem to understand that even if Gideon wanted to overrule Garret, he couldn't right now. Not when Garret's mother had used her medical power of attorney to appoint Garret as Gideon's replacement.

Twilight had fallen while he was in the hospital, the air soft and warm on his face as he exited. He shrugged into his leather jacket, then threw his leg over the bike. The sounds of the world deadened as he pulled on his helmet and started up the engine.

His stomach rumbled, reminding him he hadn't had dinner yet, and he decided to grab something from the diner rather than defrost yet another meal at home. He was lucky enough to score a spot right out front and he parked and went inside.

The Main Street Diner never seemed to change—it had had the same exposed brick walls and red vinyl booths since he was a kid, the same music playing on the jukebox.

Hokey, maybe, but there was something reassuring about its dependable consistency, especially when the rest of his life was in the toilet.

There was an empty stool at the end of the counter and he slid onto it and reached for a menu, even though he was pretty sure he was going to go for a cheeseburger. He was trying to decide between a chocolate shake or a soda with his meal when a sense of being watched had him lifting his head.

A slim woman with a blond pixie cut was staring at him with blatant interest from the booth in the far corner, looking him over like he was a side of prime beef. She was pretty cute, and the colorful, abstract tattoo on her forearm gave her an edgy, artsy vibe, but—again—she was no Sierra.

Really gotta stop doing the Sierra comparison thing, man.

He returned his attention to the menu, but the sense of being watched was like an itch on the back of his neck and he found himself glancing toward the far booth again—just in time to see Sierra's head duck back behind the booth wall.

Speak of the devil.

The blonde woman was laughing, and it wasn't hard to work out that she was teasing Sierra for getting busted. She glanced toward him again, her gaze speculative, and he shifted his focus back to the menu.

Sierra was over there, just a few feet away. Under any other circumstances—say, if he hadn't slept with her last night—he'd go over and say hi. Hell, he might even join her and her friend if they invited him to eat with them. Sharing another meal with her would hands down be the highlight of his day.

But that wasn't going to happen. Not now.

"Evening. What can I get you?" the waitress asked, a young woman he guessed was not long out of high school.

"I'll grab a cheeseburger to go, thanks."

"Any fries with that?"

"Just the burger, thanks."

"Coffee while you wait?" she asked, jug poised above the

mug at his place setting.

"Thanks. That'd be great."

She poured, then moved off to serve other customers, and Garret pulled out his phone to try to stop himself from checking on Sierra and her friend again. It didn't stop him from wondering who the blonde was as he stared blankly at his email inbox. She didn't look familiar, but then he hadn't lived in Marietta for years now, so he was woefully out of touch.

He drank his coffee, then the waitress delivered a paper bag to him along with the bill. Garret had just enough self-control to get through paying for his meal before he glanced toward the corner booth again.

The blonde woman was leaning forward, talking intently to Sierra, who remained out of sight, hidden by the high booth side.

He told himself it was just as well, then grabbed his meal and headed for the door.

Chapter Eleven

"**H**AS HE GONE?" Sierra asked.

Eva's gaze flicked over Sierra's shoulder. "Yep. Leaving now. Very nice caboose, by the way."

Sierra relaxed, ignoring Eva's verdict on Garret's ass. Her friend had been ogling him shamelessly ever since he'd arrived and Sierra had made Eva swap with her to avoid a potentially awkward situation.

Not that she had needed to bother, it turned out, since he'd busted her checking him out anyway and clearly hadn't felt the need to come over just to be polite.

She told herself that was a good thing, but it was a big fat lie.

Before last night, he would have come over. They'd been well on the way to becoming friends before they'd torn each other's clothes off.

"You can relax now," Eva told her. "No need to wrestle with your unprofessional lust anymore."

Sierra gave her a look.

"Hey, I completely understand where you're coming from," Eva said. "He's a hottie, just like you said. I give him a solid nine."

"Nine? Are you blind? The man is clearly a seventeen. Maybe an eighteen." Sierra clenched her jaw but it was too late, she'd already given herself away.

"Gotcha." Eva laughed. "You are so into him, Sierra, it's not funny. I've never seen you like this around a guy. Remind me again why it would be so bad if you had your wicked way with him."

"Because he's my boss. That's about one hundred reasons under one heading." She craned her neck. "Why's our food taking so long, anyway? The kitchen is really slow tonight."

She could feel Eva studying her and was powerless to stop the tide of heat creeping up her chest and into her face.

"Oh my god," Eva said. "You totally did him, didn't you?" Delight sparkled in her blue eyes.

Sierra opened her mouth to deny it, but Eva beat her to it. "Before you say anything, you need to know that you're a terrible, terrible liar. All Carmodys are. It's your family's weakness."

Sierra stared at the woman who had started out as her brother's girlfriend and had quickly become one of her closest friends.

"I don't want to talk about it yet," she said.

Eva's face went from amused to concerned in a heartbeat. "Why? Did something bad happen?"

"No."

"Don't tell me the sex was terrible?"

"The sex was fine. But it was awkward afterward, and I'm pissed with myself for not having enough willpower or common sense to keep my hands off him."

"Only fine?" Eva gave an annoyed little huff. "Major disappointment, especially after seeing him in person. Talk about false advertising."

"That's the part you want to focus on, of all the things I just said?" Sierra asked.

"Don't get me wrong. I'm not happy about the morning-after awkwardness and your guilt, but I was really hoping you were in for a wild ride with a hottie. Every woman deserves a wild ride with a hottie on a regular basis."

Sierra toyed with the serviette dispenser and told herself it didn't matter that Eva had the wrong end of the stick regarding the quality of her indiscretion with Garret. There was absolutely no onus on her to correct her friend. The fact that the sex had been off-the-charts good was irrelevant. Immaterial. And it wasn't as though word was going to get back to Garret that she'd given him a C+ in the bedroom department.

"I guess you just can't tell, can you?" Eva mused. "I mean, the flirt factor can be awesome with some dudes, and then the buzz just isn't there when you get your clothes off. But at least you know now, though, right? You won't be tempted to go there again when you know it's just going to leave you yawning."

There was a devilish glint in Eva's eyes and Sierra's mouth twisted into a reluctant smile.

"You are such a smart-ass."

"I told you Carmodys are terrible liars. It was amazing, wasn't it?" Eva asked, one elbow on the table as she rested her chin in her hand.

"He totally blew my mind," Sierra admitted.

Eva clapped her hands together in triumph. "Yessss!

That's what I like to hear."

"It doesn't matter if it was good or bad," Sierra said. "The important part is that it was freaking dumb. This is my first ever professional piloting gig and I couldn't even last a week before jumping my boss. Jack would be so pissed with me if he found out."

The smile faded from Eva's lips as she scanned Sierra's face. She reached out to take Sierra's hand. "Sorry. I didn't mean to joke around when you were hurting."

"You don't need to apologize."

"Yeah, I do. I was teasing you but you're really upset about this, aren't you?" Her face was creased with worry and sympathy.

"I just don't understand why I was so self-destructive," Sierra said quietly. "I don't normally do dumb stuff. Well, not when I know going in that it's dumb. Usually the dumb realization doesn't come until later. But this time, it was there in hot-pink neon and I just did it anyway."

"There's a reason the human species has managed to survive for centuries," Eva said. "Men and women like sex. It feels good. And sometimes you meet someone you just know it's going to be amazing with, for whatever reason, and the primitive monkey part of your brain takes over. Pink neon signs don't work against monkey brain."

"I can't afford to let my monkey brain take over. And neither can Garret. His whole life just imploded. I can't even begin to tell you how much he's got on his shoulders right now. So much pressure, and it's only going to get worse."

"Worse how?" Eva asked, head tilted.

Sierra shook her head. "It's business stuff." And potentially legal stuff, but she was hardly going to say that. Everything Garret had shared with her about Tate Transport was in the vault, under lock and key. "He's working around the clock, juggling a million things. I need to be the easy part of his life right now, not another problem."

"What about your feelings? What about what you want?" Eva asked.

Their food arrived then and Sierra busied herself squirting ketchup on her fries and sucking the froth off her milkshake, hoping Eva would take the hint and drop the subject because she honestly had no idea what she wanted right now.

Once the waitress had moved off, Eva gave her a sympathetic look.

"I won't keep pushing, but I'm just going to point out—again—that you sound very concerned about the feelings of this guy you just happened to have crazy-good sex with. And that's okay, sweetie. You're allowed to have feelings for the sex god hottie that you really like. That's kind of the way it's supposed to work."

Sierra sighed. There was no way of explaining how not-on-the-market Garret was for anything romantic without explaining everything.

"Trust me, there is no future with this man. Not right now, anyway."

Eva fell silent, and Sierra guessed her friend was biting her tongue, trying to honor her promise not to push. Sierra racked her brain for a change of subject then gasped as she remembered the very juicy news she had to report. "I keep forgetting to tell you. You know how I'm always trying to get

Jed to let me set him up with one of my friends?"

"Yeah."

"He finally said yes."

Eva's eyes widened. Then she put down her hamburger, a sure sign she was shook—generally speaking, no one got between Eva and food.

"Shut the front door," Eva said. "Are you dicking with me?"

"No dicks were harmed during the making of this news item."

"Were you holding a gun to his head?"

"Nope. In fact, he kind of asked me to do it," Sierra said.

"Oh my god. This is because this Mae woman he used to see is getting married, isn't it?" Eva said.

Sierra nodded. Even though it made her sad to have confirmation that Jed had been pining after his first love all these years.

"She's finally out of reach. I think maybe it's really hit home for him now."

They were both silent for a beat. Then Eva sat up straighter, a determined light coming into her eyes.

"So our mission is clear, then," she said, rubbing her hands together. "Operation Hookup is officially launched. We need to find Jed a woman who can make him fall in love again."

"No, we need to find a woman who can make him fall *out* of love with Mae, and *in* love with her," Sierra corrected.

"So, what are our options? Who is on the table?" Eva asked, all business.

"I've narrowed it down to Carrie Hunter, my friend Ashley, and Jane Bianco."

Eva frowned. "Jane is the short one with the dark hair, right? Kind of serious and quiet?"

Sierra nodded. "She's really sweet and super smart."

"Hmm. I don't know. Jed's on the quiet side. Until he gets comfortable, anyway."

"Sure, but he can handle himself. He doesn't clam up like Casey can sometimes."

"I just think he might need someone who will make a real impact, to give him a kind of cosmic jolt. You know?" Eva said.

Sierra understood where she was coming from. She ate a couple of fries, pondering. "Okay. So Ashley, then?"

"She's the one who dances on the bar sometimes when the Shots have gigs at Grey's, yeah?" Eva asked, her tone doubtful.

"Too much impact?" Sierra asked.

"Didn't she also have a huge crush on Casey?"

Sierra pulled a face. "That was mostly just a running-joke type thing. I think."

"Let's come at this from a different angle. What was Mae like?" Eva asked.

Sierra frowned, casting her mind back. Jed and Mae had fallen for each other in high school and had gone off to college together, living off-campus in an apartment. Through those years Mae had become a mainstay at the Carmody house, practically a member of the family.

"She's really smart. I think she was even valedictorian for their year, but don't quote me on that. She was a bit goofy and nerdy. Loved *Star Trek* and *Star Wars*, and I remember she was obsessed with the *Lord of the Rings* movies and Jed used to tease her by calling them 'Bored of the Rings.' But he went with her to see all of them, because he knew she loved them. I think he even read the books for her."

Eva's gaze softened. "Aww. They sound so cute."

"They were. She grew up on a ranch, too, so she knew how to work hard. She and Jed had all these plans to start up their own place and specialize in niche horse and cattle breeds. Kind of a boutique operation, I guess. Jed was studying animal husbandry and she was studying business, and they used to joke that together they were undefeatable. It was true too. They filled in each other's gaps. She was smart and analytical, and he was practical and down to earth. And they were awesome at making each other laugh, even if the rest of us sometimes didn't get the joke."

Sierra fell silent as sadness washed over her. Jed had cut Mae loose when their parents died, refusing to let her give up her dreams and ambitions just because his life had gone up in flames.

"She sounds awesome," Eva said solemnly.

"She was. We were so messed up after the accident, I don't think it really registered that we'd lost her too. Not until later, when I realized how much Jed had changed, how much he'd given up."

"Maybe it's wishful thinking, but he feels . . . lighter lately," Eva said.

"Yeah. Hashing things out with Jesse took a weight off, I think. And letting us all take on some of the management burden of the ranch. There's no reason in the world for Jed to carry it all on his own, and I think he's starting to see that now."

Eva demolished what was left of her hamburger, a thoughtful expression on her face. "I have a feeling this isn't going to be as easy as it first sounded," she finally said.

Sierra sighed. "I know. I was so excited when he said yes, but then I started thinking about who I should set him up with and freaked out."

"With great power comes great responsibility."

"Did you just quote *Spider-Man* to me?" Sierra raised her eyebrows.

"I did. You got a problem with that?" Eva asked with a grin.

"Yeah. Next time make it *Wonder Woman*."

Eva laughed. Then she reached out to catch Sierra's hand. "That was some high-level distraction bait you just threw me with the whole Jed-dating situation, but I want you to know that if you need or want to talk about Garret, I'm your girl. Okay?"

"Okay," Sierra said, returning Eva's hand-squeeze.

She didn't bother saying that she really hoped it wouldn't be necessary. She figured she'd made that plenty clear enough already.

Now she just had to make it reality.

GARRET SPENT THE weekend trawling through Ron's and his father's email archives, looking for any emails that rang alarm bells. There was nothing overtly shady—kudos to his father and Ron for not being *that* obvious—but by Sunday evening he'd flagged a series of opaquely worded exchanges that needed a closer look. The next step was to create a spread-sheet detailing client names and dates so he could pass the information on to Mae, but that was a task that was going to have to wait for tomorrow because he was heartily sick of thinking about Tate Transport.

Because it had worked so well last time, he took the Ducati for a spin to clear his mind. It did the trick, except that the moment he stopped thinking about work, Sierra slipped into his thoughts to take its place.

He was going to see her again tomorrow and he needed to put some strategies in place so he could do better where she was concerned, like avoiding overnighters in Helena unless they were absolutely necessary.

The less time the two of them spent under one roof, the better, because willpower alone was clearly not enough to keep him in check. A galling and humbling admission.

To think he'd once judged his father for not having any self-control when it came to women. Obviously, Garret's situation was different, in that he didn't have a wife and child at home, but that didn't mean he had a free pass.

Having a plan in place helped him feel more relaxed as he left the house at seven the next morning. As usual, Sierra was busy preparing the Bell for takeoff when he arrived at the helipad. She had her sunglasses hanging by an arm in the open neck of her polo shirt, and while she offered him a friendly smile as he approached, he detected a certain measure of wariness too.

Not surprising, given how douchey he'd been last time they'd spoken.

"Morning," she said.

"Morning."

She looked good—bright-eyed, shiny dark hair pulled up in her usual high ponytail, legs going on forever in her neatly pressed chinos. When she turned to open the door to the passenger cabin for him he remembered the way she'd locked her ankles behind his back as he'd carried her to his bedroom that first time.

Not helpful, thanks.

He batted the memory away and climbed into the helicopter. Minutes later they were rising into the sky, the now-familiar *whop-whop* of the rotor blades made bearable by his headset.

He spent the flight compiling the data from his email trawl into a spreadsheet for Mae. There were more than twenty entries, referencing ten companies. Three of those were from what he considered their core client base—the big hitters who kept the lights on at Tate Transport.

He really, really hoped that most of the emails he'd flagged were innocuous. Because if they weren't . . .

But there was no point borrowing trouble. Not when it was headed his way, anyway.

The wind came up when they were twenty minutes out of Helena, and his headset came to life as Sierra checked to make sure he was still buckled in before warning him there would be some turbulence. She sounded so calm and matter-of-fact that it didn't occur to him to be worried until they'd battled their way through nausea-inducing winds to land at the airport.

Some instinct made him glance at the mirror as the sound of the rotors died and he saw the relief on Sierra's face that they were safely down. By the time she'd exited the cockpit to come let him out, however, her professional mask was back in place.

"Hope that wasn't too rough for you," she said as he climbed out of the Bell.

"Let's just say it made me appreciate the smooth runs we've been having."

"Should be okay this evening. I checked the forecast this morning, and they're predicting these winds will die down after midday," she said.

"Something to look forward to. I'll see you this afternoon," he said.

She nodded, and he had to fight the deeply inappropriate urge to rest a hand on her shoulder, just to touch her and convey his faith in her.

Instead, he headed for his father's Lincoln.

He sent his spreadsheet off to Mae the moment he hit the office, then got lost in the myriad moving parts that made up Tate Transport. It was midafternoon when it hit him that if it hadn't been for the background buzz of anxiety over what Mae might find, he might be in danger of actually *enjoying* the breakneck pace of it all. He wasn't sure if that made him a glutton for punishment or an adrenaline junkie.

Maybe a bit of both.

It was nearly six when he left the building and made the short run out to the airport. Sierra was exiting the hangar as he pulled into his parking spot, pulling her ball cap down over her forehead. Safely hidden in the privacy of the car, he allowed himself a small moment of indulgence as he watched her walk to the Bell.

He was almost certain she had no idea how sexy her long, confident stride was. Some men—insecure morons—might be put off by her take-no-prisoners competency and capability, but he liked it. A lot.

Enough. Get your head back in the game.

He made an exasperated noise, then leaned into the back seat to grab his briefcase and suit jacket.

"No strong winds, as promised," Sierra said as he approached the helicopter. "Should be a nice boring flight home."

"Having experienced the other kind, I am up for that," he said.

"I'll do my best."

His phone rang as he climbed into the passenger cabin. He pulled it from his pocket and checked the screen, ready to send it to voice mail if it wasn't important.

He frowned when he saw it was Mae. She'd indicated he shouldn't expect to hear from him until sometime next week, and he braced himself for more bad news as he took the call.

"Garret. Are you in Helena or Marietta today?" she asked, not bothering with any of the usual polite niceties.

"Just about to take off for Marietta from Helena airport. Why?"

"Can you delay your departure?"

He glanced to the cockpit where Sierra was going through her preflight routine. He knew they only had a half-hour window before nightfall made it impossible for them to fly back to Marietta, but Mae was clearly keen to talk to him.

"I take it this isn't something we can handle over the phone?"

"I've got a lot of detail I need to talk you through. I'd prefer to do it in person," Mae said.

There was something about the careful away she worded her response that pushed his spider senses into the red zone.

"All right. I can head back into the city or come to you."

"How about I come to your place?"

"Okay, sure." He rattled off the lake house address. "It'll take me twenty minutes to get there."

"I need to finish up a few things here in the office so I might be half an hour or so. See you soon."

She ended the call, and he registered for the first time that Sierra had twisted in her seat so she could see him instead of simply using the mirror.

"Everything okay?"

"We're going to have to stay overnight," he said. "Something urgent has come up."

"Not a problem."

"How long will it take you to put the helicopter away from the night?"

"Ten minutes, maybe fifteen. You go ahead if you need to, I'll catch a cab."

He checked his watch. "I can wait. Anything I can do to help?"

"Stay out of the way," she said with a quick, cheeky smile.

He did as instructed, watching from the sidelines as she positioned the tow cart beneath the helicopter and maneuvered it smoothly into the hangar. Even as he was admiring her quiet skill, a part of his brain was fretting over Mae's phone call, playing the what-if game.

He could feel his shoulders creeping higher and higher as he shuffled through potential scenarios, each more catastrophic than the last. One thing was absolutely certain—Mae was not rushing out to the lake house to tell him good news, which meant she must have found something damning.

It was what he was paying her for, but that didn't make it any easier to face.

He rubbed the back of his neck, then made his way to the car. Tossing his suitcase into the back seat, he shed his suit jacket. Then he pulled his tie off as well. By the time he was closing the door Sierra was walking toward him, a small duffel bag over her shoulder.

"All tucked away for the night."

"Sorry about the change of plans."

"No biggie. It was my turn to cook dinner, so you actually did me a favor because I didn't have a clue what I was going to make," she said.

"What's your specialty?" he asked as she settled into the passenger seat.

Her arm brushed his as she secured her seat belt, and it occurred to him that it was the first time he'd shared the close quarters of a car with her.

"I make a mean meatloaf, mostly because it's my mom's recipe and she was a genius in the kitchen. If I'm being honest, I'd have to class myself as a passable cook. Nothing fancy, but mostly it tastes like it's meant to."

"Now, there's a marketing campaign just waiting to happen," he said as he put the car into gear.

"Right? People would be unable to resist the siren's call

of that faint praise," she said, her tone bone dry.

They both fell silent, the only sound the motor and the whir of the tires on the road.

"Would you mind if I make a quick call?" she asked.

"Go for it."

He tried not to listen as she called home, letting whoever was on the other end know she'd be staying overnight in Helena again. She laughed a couple of times in response to whatever the other person was saying, and each time he glanced across at her, drawn to the sound.

Drawn to her.

So much for his grand plan to avoid overnight stays as much as possible. But it wasn't as though there was much he could do about it this time.

A shiny red Mercedes coupe was waiting in the driveway when he arrived at the house. He parked in the garage, and by the time he and Sierra were heading for the front door Mae was waiting for them beneath the portico.

Sierra's step faltered when she saw the other woman.

"Mae?" she asked, her voice high with surprise.

Belatedly he remembered the old connection between Mae and the Carmodys. Mae was looking surprised, too, a smile curving her mouth. "Sierra. How are you?"

"I'm good. I can't believe this." Sierra made a jerky motion with her arms, almost as though she wanted to hug Mae but wasn't sure if the gesture would be welcome.

Mae solved the problem by stepping forward and kissing Sierra's cheek.

"I always knew you'd wind up as tall as your brothers," Mae said.

"They're all still taller than me, but I got close," Sierra said. "You look so good."

She was openly appraising the other woman, and he remembered his own surprise when he'd first met with Mae during the week.

"Amazing what a good hairdresser and decent credit card limit can get you." Mae shot a glance at him, her gaze curious. "How long have you two been together?"

"What? Oh, no," Sierra said, and he could hear the embarrassment in her sharp laugh.

"Sierra's a helicopter pilot. She shuttles me between Marietta and Helena," he explained.

"Sorry. I just assumed, because you were here together . . ." Mae shook her head, embarrassed by her mistaken assumption.

Garret punched in the security code and unlocked the front door. "Come in," he said.

He led the way inside, conscious of Mae taking in the grand scale of the foyer as she followed him. The sooner he could convince his parents to sell this place, the better.

"You guys obviously have business to discuss, so I'll leave you to it," Sierra said. "But before I do, I hear you're getting married soon, Mae. Congratulations."

Mae blinked. "Wow. I see the old Marietta whisper network is still alive and well."

"I think you can blame Facebook for that one," Sierra responded.

"Ah, right. Mom does like to post her whole life on there," Mae said, her expression rueful. "Don't know how many times I've tried to get her to adjust her privacy settings."

Maybe it was Garret's imagination, but it seemed to him that there was an undercurrent beneath their words, as though there was a whole world of unasked questions lurking beneath the surface of their conversation.

This time Sierra was the one who initiated a cheek kiss. "It was great to see you."

"You too."

Sierra slipped away then, shoulders very straight as she strode toward the kitchen.

"Study is this way," Garret said, gesturing to his left.

Mae gave him a distracted nod, following him up the hall. He didn't know her very well, but his gut told him she'd been thrown by the encounter with Sierra.

"All good?" he asked as he waved her into one of the leather chairs in front of the fireplace.

"Yes. Sorry. It's just I haven't seen Sierra for years. She was just a kid back then." She smoothed her hands down her skirt. It was the first time in any of his interactions with her that she'd seemed anything less than coolly professional.

"Can I get you a drink?"

"No, I'm okay. Thank you. I'm really sorry for springing this on you at the last minute, but I figured this was something you'd want to know."

Garret braced himself. "I take it you've found some anomalies."

Mae surprised him by shaking her head. "I'm still working my way through the records. This isn't about the slush fund. I didn't want to get into it on the phone, just in case there's an issue."

He frowned. "What kind of an issue?"

Her gaze held his, steady and serious. "This may or may not be something we need to worry about, but I had coffee with an old friend from college this afternoon. He works for the DA, and he mentioned he's been working on a big commercial bribery case in the transport industry."

Chapter Twelve

H E WAS GLAD he was sitting down, because his legs suddenly felt as heavy as lead.

"Commercial bribery?"

"Look, this may not be about Tate Transport. There are three major transport companies in the state. It could be any one of them. Or even smaller players."

"But we already know my father and Ron were up to something," Garret said. "What are the odds?"

Mae didn't say anything, her expression grave.

Fuck.

He shot to his feet and went to the sideboard, yanking open the cupboard that held his father's liquor supply. He sloshed whiskey into two glasses with a visibly shaking hand and took one of them back to Mae. Then he knocked his back in one big swallow, welcoming the sharp, almost painful burn at the back of his throat.

Mae watched him, her mouth an unhappy straight line. "Are you okay?"

"Yep." He resumed his seat, trying to triage his panicky thoughts. "What do I do? How do I get ahead of this?"

Because surely that was the most important question. For

now.

"You're already doing it. We follow the money, find out the scope of what we're up against. We create a paper trail that shows you are doing everything in your power to come to grips with a situation that was not of your making. And we cross our fingers and hope that my friend was talking about another transport company."

"What if it's us? What if it's us, and you find evidence that Tate Transport has been involved in commercial bribery? What are the likely charges?"

"Montana didn't even have legislation covering commercial bribery until last year. And I'm no lawyer."

"But?"

Mae licked her lips, clearly not enjoying being the bearer of bad news. "If the bribe value is higher than a thousand dollars, jail time is on the cards. Up to five years. And there are fines, up to fifty thousand dollars per offense. Also, there's precedent for anyone harmed by the bribery to file a civil suit. Your competitors, that sort of thing. Given you weren't an officer of the company at the time these offenses occurred, it's unlikely they'd come after you for any of this, but Ron and your father will definitely be in the line of fire. My best advice is that you retain a lawyer to make some discreet inquiries on your behalf. Someone outside of the business, given our current suspicions. In the same way that you brought me in, it's good to start with a clean slate."

Garret thought of the string of email exchanges he'd flagged over the weekend. Ten companies had been referenced. If he was right on every count . . . Tate Transport was in big trouble and his father and Ron were in worse trouble.

The kind that ended with wearing a bright orange jumpsuit. "Can you recommend a good law firm? Someone you've worked with and trust?"

"I'll forward you some names. But let's not get ahead of ourselves," Mae said. "Like I said, this may be a completely false alarm."

"I can't afford to operate on that principle," Garret said, his mind suddenly crystal-sharp and clear. "I need you to move faster. I need to know what I'm dealing with, how exposed we are. What's it going to take to get you working on our issues full-time?"

"Funny you should ask that. I've already reached out to a colleague and asked if she has the capacity to take over my other clients. Most of them are cases that are winding down now, anyway, and she's indicated she'd be happy to take over for me. I'll hand everything off to her next tomorrow and then me and my team are all yours."

"Good. Thank you. I appreciate you going the extra mile."

Mae's professional mask slipped as she eyed him with compassion. "Garret, you have been handed a flaming paper bag full of crap. I just hope I can help you put the fire out without everyone getting shit all over them."

Garret smiled grimly at her analogy. "You and me both."

She pushed to her feet. "I'll call you tomorrow, but I'd like to suggest that maybe it's time to come out of stealth mode on this and go nuclear. That means giving my team an office and access to anything and everyone, along with letting your staff know that anyone on my team is god as far as they're concerned for the duration."

"Done. I'll get Mandy to sort out a space for you first thing."

Ron's office was empty—it seemed appropriate that Mae set up camp in there.

"Also, you've mentioned your coffee machine business in Seattle a few times. Can I assume you're still a partner?" Mae asked.

Garret blinked, surprised by the question. "I am. It's all on hold until I find my feet, but as of today I'm still an equal partner."

"Might be time to think about how this might affect that business if things blow up."

Garret nodded. Jesus, yet another angle to consider. "Good thought, thanks."

"I'll see you tomorrow as soon as I've finished handing over my clients," Mae said.

He stood to escort her back to the front door. "I hope this didn't mess up your plans for the evening."

"Nope. Sam is in California right now at a conference, so it's Netflix and pizza for me."

Garret opened the door for her. "Sounds good."

Mae hesitated on the threshold. "Would you mind if I had a quick word with Sierra before I go?"

"Of course." Garret was so preoccupied, it took him a moment to shift gears. "She's, uh, probably in the kitchen or her room."

He led the way to the kitchen, but there was no sign of Sierra.

"Her room is this way. He stopped at the foot of the stairs in the modern wing of the house. "She's in one of the bedrooms off the landing."

"Thanks. And don't worry too much, okay? We can get on top of this. Some of these investigations take months. With a bit of luck, we'll have scoped out your vulnerabilities and come up with a game plan well before the DA makes a move. If she even does."

Garret really, really wanted to take her assurance at face value, but nothing in his life had felt lucky lately.

"Did your friend say how long he'd been working on the commercial bribery investigation?"

Mae's expression clouded. "No. Sorry."

Garret nodded, then took a step backward. "See you tomorrow."

He headed down the hallway, his chest tight, his gut an acid bath.

What a mess. What a stinking, rancid, colossal mess. No doubt his father had justified his and Ron's actions over the years, characterizing any kickbacks they'd paid as the cost of doing business, the price of getting ahead and being the best. And for a long time, it had paid off and they'd reaped the benefits—Tate Transport was a multimillion-dollar operation. Both his father and Ron had lived very comfortable lives as a result of its success. A thousand people put food on their families' tables and paid their mortgages because of what Gideon and Ron had built.

And now there was a good chance it was all going to come tumbling down.

By the time he was entering the study again he was so angry he wanted to smash something. He stood in the middle of the book-lined space, vibrating with a potent mix of rage and shame.

Then, just as quickly as it had swept over him, his anger drained away and he dropped into a chair, gutted and shaken.

Please let Mae be wrong.

Because he had no idea if he was equipped to handle what might happen if she wasn't.

SIERRA WAS DOING some yoga in her room, still processing running into Mae after all these years, when a tentative tap sounded on her door.

"It's open," she called.

The door swung open, revealing Mae standing there, looking uncertain.

"Hi," Sierra said, getting up off the floor and dusting off her backside.

"Sorry to interrupt. I just felt like . . . It's been so long. I wanted to catch up a little. If that's okay?" Mae asked.

"Of course. I was thinking the same thing. Come in." She'd changed into leggings and a tank top when she'd come up to her room and she scooped her discarded work clothes off the chair in the corner. "Grab a seat. Or we could go down to the kitchen?"

"This is fine," Mae said, sitting in the chair.

She looked so polished, so chic with her perfect hair and tailored suit, Sierra couldn't help but smile and shake her head. "You know, I think I would have walked past you on the street," she admitted. "You look so different."

"I would have recognized you. Those Carmody eyes are

pretty hard to miss," Mae said. "And I always knew you'd grow up to be stunning."

Sierra made a rude noise. "Hardly."

"You can be modest all you like, it doesn't change reality," Mae said. She crossed one smooth leg over the other and Sierra noted the flash of red on the soles of her shoes.

Even living in small-town Montana, Sierra knew that meant they were Louboutins.

"So what do you do now? I know you were studying business at college," Sierra asked, genuinely interested in the path her brother's ex had taken.

"I'm a specialist accountant. I help untangle messes, follow the money. That sort of thing."

Sierra remembered the things Garret had told her about his father's business dealings. Clearly Mae had been brought in to help Garret get on top of the situation but was being super discreet about it.

"Do you love it?" Sierra asked.

"Are you asking if I'm still a massive nerd?" Mae asked with a laugh.

"I thought *geek* was the preferred term these days?"

"Either way, the answer is yes. I like solving problems and tracking things down. How about you? How long have you been flying? I have to admit, I always imagined you working on the ranch with you brothers. Which is probably dumb."

"Actually, you're not far wrong . . ." Sierra filled Mae in on her recent history, then answered her questions about Jesse and Casey and the ranch. All the while, they both avoided talking about the cowboy in the room: Jed.

Finally Mae smiled and titled her head. "And how's Jed? Is he well?"

Sierra hesitated, unsure how to respond. Health-wise, Jed was well. But there was no denying he'd lost a part of himself when he'd given Mae up. Sierra couldn't just blurt that out, though. For starters, Jed would flip out if he ever learned she'd exposed him like that, and Mae was getting married to another guy. She didn't need or want to be dragged back into the past.

"He's good. We've had a few problems at the ranch, so he's been a bit stressed, handling all that. But things are improving now, so . . ." Sierra shrugged.

Mae nodded. "Well . . . good."

Sierra could feel that Mae had more questions, and she made an educated guess what they might be. "He's single. Claims he's too busy to date."

Sierra watched in fascination as color crept up Mae's chest and into her face.

"Hey, none of that is any of my business," Mae said. "Although I want him to be happy, obviously. Like I am. It would be nice for him to find someone. I always thought he'd make a great husband."

"He's been an amazing stand-in for Mom and Dad over the years," Sierra agreed.

Mae stood and adjusted the front of her suit jacket. "I should go. But thanks for catching up with me. It's good to know you're all doing so well. I'll keep an ear out for Casey's songs on the radio."

Sierra stepped forward and wrapped her arms around the other woman, giving her the hug she'd never had the chance to give her thirteen years ago. "I'm really sorry we never got to say goodbye properly. Everything was so messed up back then, but I want you to know we all missed you so much. Especially Jed. It was just a really horrible situation."

Mae's arms were tight around her, and Sierra felt her suck in a shaky breath.

"Thank you. That's really nice to hear. I missed you guys too. Mom used to keep me updated. But then I asked her to stop." Mae gave a wry, self-deprecating smile as they stepped back from their embrace.

"Can I grab your number? Maybe we could have coffee or lunch sometime?" Sierra asked.

"I'd love that."

They exchanged numbers, then Sierra walked Mae to the front door.

"Before I go . . . I don't know how well you and Garret know each other, but he's had some shitty news tonight . . ."

Sierra understood what she was asking. "I'll check on him. Thanks."

Mae smiled, then gave her a final hug. Sierra watched her walk to her shiny Mercedes and waited until she'd driven down the drive before closing the door.

She paused for a moment, gathering her thoughts, then she went in search of Garret.

She found him in the study, nursing a glass of whiskey, his face gray. He glanced across at her when he registered her standing there, and the bleak flatness behind his eyes made her take an involuntary step forward.

"Are you okay?"

It took him a moment to respond. "Sure. Mae gone?"

"Yes." She frowned at him, not sure what to do. She'd never seen him like this, tight and closed off. What exactly was the shitty news Mae had just delivered?

"It's okay, Sierra," Garret said, reading her concern.

"Is it? You look like someone just died."

He smiled, although it was more like a show of teeth. "Yeah, well."

He tossed back the last of his whiskey and stood, dropping the heavy crystal glass onto the side table with a noisy thunk. He went to the desk where his briefcase lay on its side and pulled out his laptop. When she didn't move or say anything, he glanced at her. "Did you want something?"

Sierra debated whether she should push the issue, then decided against it. If he didn't want to confide in her, that was his business. Just because they'd slept together didn't change the essential nature of their relationship.

"I'm ordering dinner. What would you prefer, pizza or Chinese?" she asked instead.

"I don't want anything. But thanks for asking."

Sierra's gaze went to the whiskey bottle sitting on the side board. Without saying a word, she turned on her heel and made her way to the kitchen. Sitting on a stool, she called up the menu for the Chinese place on her phone and put through an order for way too much food.

Then she helped herself to one of the beers she'd bought last week and killed time checking out the news headlines on her phone until the doorbell rang. She took delivery of two bulging bags' worth of food and ferried them to the kitchen. She piled two bowls high, then tucked a bottle of soda water under her arm, picked up the bowls, and made her way to the study.

Garret was sitting behind the desk, tapping away at his computer at an almost violent pace. Sierra slid one of the bowls in front him, and he stopped working to glance at her.

"What's this?" he asked tersely.

Sierra calmly sat on the corner of the desk and dug into her own bowl. "Dinner. Whatever else is going on, you need to eat. Even if it just means you can drink a larger quantity of whiskey before you pass out."

"Passing out is not on the agenda."

"Great. Mmm. This lemon chicken is *good.*"

He was silent for a moment, staring at her, his jaw set. Then he reached for his bowl, the gesture almost grudging. They ate in silence for a few minutes and she watched out of the corners of her eyes as the harsh, tight look left his face.

"Bet you drive your brothers crazy," he said.

"Because I can read their tiny minds? Or because I'm right all the time?"

He laughed, and it felt like an achievement. The best thing she'd done all day.

"For the record, the lemon chicken is not that good," he said.

"Hell, no. I was just selling it to you," she admitted, and he barked out another laugh.

She'd piled the bowls so high she had to set hers down when it was still half full.

Garret shot her an appraising glance. "Admitting defeat?"

"A girl has to know her limits."

It wasn't long before he was following suit.

"I may have been a little overambitious with the ordering," she admitted. "On the plus side, lunch is taken care of tomorrow."

He was watching her, his expression serious. "Thank you."

"It's just food. And I was eating anyway."

"It's more than that."

She looked away, unable to hold his eye. Afraid that if she did, he'd see exactly how often she thought of him, how much real estate he occupied in her mind.

"What do I owe you?" he asked.

She snapped her focus back to him. "Nothing. It's all good."

She slipped off his desk and grabbed both bowls.

"You can't keep buying me dinner."

"You paid for the pizzas last week," she pointed out.

"You know what I mean."

"Just think of it as a friend looking out for a friend."

"So we're friends now?" He was frowning, almost as though he was offended by the notion.

"You don't want to be my friend?" she asked.

"That's not what I meant."

They stared at each other, and she could see the desire in his eyes, could see him fighting himself, trying to hold back. She reminded herself of what she'd said to Eva about not becoming another problem for him.

He wanted her, but he didn't want to want her. That much was obvious.

And she liked him enough, cared for him enough, to do the thing that had to be done. The hard thing. The right thing.

"Don't work too late," she said. Then she walked away, leaving him to deal with whatever crisis Mae had brought to his doorstep.

GARRET SAT AND listened to the soft scuff of Sierra's bare feet on the floorboards as she walked away. He told himself that it was a good thing she was putting some distance between them. He'd made a promise to himself that there wasn't going to be a repeat of the other night. She worked for him. She needed to be able to do that without her boss fantasizing about spreading her across his desk and losing himself in her sexy body.

He dropped his head back against the chair, trying to cool his heated thoughts, willing himself to not be an asshole. He refused to take advantage of Sierra, to use her instinctive generosity and kindness against her. Right now he was a drowning man, and the need to reach out for something good and real and solid was profound.

His life was turning to shit, and she was amazing, and the way she made him feel was nothing short of nuclear. The temptation to indulge in the potent distraction of their chemistry was real.

So real.

But it was also more than that. If this was any other time or place or situation, he'd be moving heaven and earth to make her a part of his life for more than one night.

He liked her that much. He wanted her that much.

She was smart and sweet, sexy and strong. She didn't take crap from anyone, and she'd survived immeasurable loss and come out the other side resilient and generous.

She was fucking incredible.

Which was exactly why he should stay away from her.

He closed his eyes, trying to find the strength to deny the need thrumming through his body.

Images from the other night flashed across his mind and his fingers curled around the armrests as he remembered the smoothness of her skin, the silk of her hair, the warm, wet welcome of her body as he slid inside her.

She had been so responsive, so daring, and yet so vulnerable and accepting at the same time.

He'd never felt more connected to another person. Ever.

Who the fuck are you kidding here?

The question was like a bolt from the blue, delivering a moment of piercing clarity.

Because, really, who the fuck was he kidding? There was no way he was going to be able to keep his hands off Sierra. Pretending he wasn't crazy for her was a pointless, stupid exercise in self-deception. Even if he won the battle of wills he was waging against himself now, he was still bound to fail another night—be it this week, or the next, or the one after that.

Why wait when he wanted her now? Why deny both of them the magic that happened when they were skin to skin?

He stood, his heart pounding in his chest. He felt weirdly detached from his body as he made his way to the kitchen. It was empty, the surfaces pristine. He walked through it, heading for the modern wing. Then he climbed the staircase and stepped onto the landing.

The door to her bedroom was open. Sierra stood next to

the bed, folding clothes into her duffel bag. She froze when she saw him standing there, her eyes wide.

For a long beat they stared at one another, potential ricocheting between them. Then her expression shifted, her eyes warming, her mouth softening. She reached for the hem of her T-shirt, pulling it over her head. She tossed it into the corner and faced him wearing nothing but a black lace bra and yoga leggings. She lifted an eyebrow, tilted her head.

"What are you waiting for? A written invitation?"

Everything in him wanted to close the distance between them. The need to have her body pressed against his own was visceral and urgent. But he planted his feet, refusing to give in until he'd been plain with her. "This isn't just about sex for me."

"I know. Me either."

Her words set him free, and he moved toward her, hands lifting to the collar of his shirt. She tucked her fingers into the waistband of her yoga pants and pushed them down in one smooth motion. He got stuck on the third button down and lost patience, grabbing either side of his shirt and yanking until the remaining buttons popped free. He tossed his shirt into the corner as she retrieved a condom from the bedside drawer before pulling back the covers on the bed and lying down. He fumbled with his belt, then his fly, kicking his pants free before toeing off his shoes.

Then he was naked, and the mattress was giving beneath him as he climbed onto the bed, and her arms were coming around him. Her breasts were warm against his chest as she wrapped her legs around him. The sensation of being close to her again, of being one with her again, stole his breath away.

For a long moment they simply held each other, arms tight with unspoken words and unacknowledged emotion. Then she smoothed a hand down his side and onto his ass, and he lifted his head so he could kiss her. She opened to him, giving him everything he wanted and more, and even though he wanted—needed—to take it slowly tonight, to stay with her and inside her for as long as he could, to take solace and shelter and comfort from her lean, strong body, her amazing green eyes, and her clever mind, he was powerless against the rising tide of desire building between them.

Within minutes they were both shaking and panting as he guided his cock to her entrance. He slid inside her with a satisfied, earthy groan of appreciation, overwhelmed by how hot and wet she was, how tight and perfect. A shiver rippled through her, and he withdrew almost all the way before sliding inside her again, just to see if he could make her shiver a second time. He could and she did, and it wasn't long before he was nothing but sensation, his body racked with almost painful pleasure. Sierra's face was flushed, her nipples tight and pink and wet from his mouth, her legs locked around his hips as she urged him to go harder, faster, deeper.

And then she arched off the bed, her hips lifting with a jerk, her eyes closed as she said his name over and over as she pulsed around his cock. He loved watching her come, so much so that he pushed back on his own need and reached between them to find the swollen bud of her clitoris. Her eyes popped open as he circled his finger, sliding over and over that taut little bead as he continued to pump into her.

"Again," he said, his voice low and demanding. "Come for me again."

"Can't. Not yet," she said, trying to push his hand away.

"Dare you," he said, and he saw the flash of amusement and appreciation in her eyes.

He slid deeper, his finger still plucking away at that needy little bead, and she bit her lip, her eyes fluttering closed.

"That's right," he said, because he could feel her muscles clenching tighter, could feel the way her fingers were curling into his ass cheeks with new urgency now. "Come hard for me, baby."

And then she was there again, her head falling back on her neck, her body grasping his, and he was gone, too, light exploding behind his eyes as he lost himself and the world and everything except Sierra and the way she made him feel and the exquisite pleasure of being inside her.

They lay tangled together afterward, breathing heavily, the smell of sex and sweat and Sierra's perfume in the air. Her eyes were closed, and he turned his head so he could catalogue her face, admiring the arch of her eyebrows, the slope of her nose, the fineness of her skin. Finally she opened her eyes and turned her head so she could look at him. After a second or two her mouth curved into a small smile.

"They should take a photo of your face right now and put it under the definition for *smug* in the dictionary," she said.

He held up two fingers. She laughed.

"Not that anyone's counting," she said.

"I'm getting a T-shirt made," he said.

She rolled onto her stomach, offering him an unimpeded view of the long line of her back and legs. In the not too distant future, he planned to kiss every inch of that smooth, tanned skin.

But first he needed a few minutes to catch his breath.

Sierra pushed her hair over her shoulder, then propped her chin on her hand. She considered him for a long moment before speaking. "I don't want to bring down the mood, and you don't have to tell me what's going on, but I want you to know that I'm happy to listen if you need to unload. Well, unload in a different way," she said with a suggestive wiggle of her eyebrows.

He looked away from her searching gaze, suddenly aware of the cool air on his naked body.

"Give me a second." He rolled off the bed and stepped into the en suite bathroom to dispose of the condom.

He glanced at the mirror and recognized the unease in his eyes. The truth was, he didn't want the ugliness of what he might be facing at Tate Transport to intrude on what was happening between them, but Sierra was clearly worried on his behalf and he'd confided in her enough over the past week to feel as though he owed her an explanation.

Taking a deep breath, he turned his back on his reflection and exited the bathroom to go bare his soul.

Chapter Thirteen

S IERRA GAVE HIM a searching look as he climbed back into bed and pulled the duvet over both of them.

"Thanks," she said as he settled the duvet around her shoulders, but he knew she was waiting for him to respond to her offer.

He sighed heavily. "Mae's gotten wind that the DA is working on a commercial bribery case in the transport industry."

Sierra's face went stiff and blank with shock. "So . . . does that mean Tate Transport is in trouble? Has Mae confirmed that your dad and Ron were doing sketchy deals with that slush fund?"

"Nothing is confirmed yet." He tucked his hands behind his head and stared at the ceiling, his mind once again whirling with anxiety and half-formed thoughts. Even the best sex in the world could only keep the Tate Transport shitstorm at bay for so long.

"What does your gut say?" she asked, her hand sliding onto his chest and coming to rest over his heart.

"That we're in trouble." He wondered if she could feel the way his heart rate ratcheted up as he said the words.

"What does Mae say?"

"That we need to know what we're dealing with before we start freaking out."

"She's one of the smartest people I've ever met, so if she's not freaking out yet, you shouldn't either," Sierra said.

"Easier said than done. She said if they come after us, if they can prove kickbacks took place, Ron and my father could be looking at prison time. And the fines could cripple the business."

She was silent for a moment, her hand still and warm on his chest.

"All that effort they put into building the business, and it might be the very thing that destroys it," she said.

"Yeah. The irony is not lost on me."

She shifted so she was lying on her side now, then pressed a kiss to his shoulder and rested her cheek there. It felt like the most natural thing in the world to slip his arm around her shoulders and hold her close. He loved the way her body fit alongside his, shoulder to shoulder, hip to hip.

"What's your mom saying about all of this?" she asked.

He shrugged uneasily. She pulled away so she could look him in the eye.

"You haven't told her?"

"I was waiting for Mae to confirm my suspicions. Figured there was no point getting everyone worked up until they needed to be. Now . . ."

"She needs to know."

"Yeah." He sighed heavily, dreading the conversation that lay ahead.

Sierra was silent for a long moment, her expression troubled. He could practically hear the wheels turning in her mind, and he suspected he knew what she was thinking.

"Whatever it is you're trying to be diplomatic about, just say it. God knows, I'd like for one part of my life to be honest, at least."

"She's been married to him for decades. Surely there's a strong chance she already knows about the slush fund. Isn't there? I mean, she must know her own husband, how he operates. What he's capable of. So maybe you're trying to protect her from something she already knows."

"It's a possibility." One that had been lurking in the back of his mind for a few days now. "It's just . . . hard to let go of the habit of looking out for her. Protecting her."

It wasn't until the words were out of his mouth that he realized how they might be interpreted. Sure enough, Sierra frowned, her body tensing alongside his. "Protecting her from who? Not your father?"

"Not in the way you're thinking," he reassured her quickly.

Not surprisingly, she was still frowning. It was tempting to just say something generic and soothing and move the conversation on, but he'd meant what he'd said—he didn't want to taint what was happening between them with lies and half-truths.

If Sierra was going to be a part of his life, she needed to know the grubby secret he'd kept on his father's behalf all these years. No one deserved the truth more—except maybe his mom.

The thought of sharing his father's shameful actions with Sierra made him go both hot and cold at the same time. He pushed himself higher against the pillows, pulling his arm from around her shoulders. He'd never told anyone the truth of that night, and of course it meant so much more to her. Because of her parents.

"Garret?" she asked uncertainly.

"There's something I need to tell you. And it might be hard to hear. Not that it changes anything, but . . ." He realized he was building it up into something it wasn't, and shook his head. "It's about the night your parents died."

She blinked. Then she followed his lead and sat up so she was leaning against the headboard beside him, the duvet pulled over her breasts. "Okay."

For a moment he stalled, not sure where to start. Then he realized there was no point finessing the story. "My father wasn't alone in the car when the accident happened. He had his office manager with him. Lucy."

Sierra cocked her head, confusion in her eyes. "But . . . that can't be right. I've read the police report. He was alone, heading north on the state highway. My parents were heading south."

"That's because he was alone by the time the ambulance and the police got there. After the accident, after he dialed 911, he called me. Told me to come to the nearest crossroad and pick Lucy up because he didn't want Mom knowing he'd been with her."

The bitter taste of shame filled his mouth. His father's actions had been so selfish and calculated. And Sierra's parents had died that night.

"Jesus Christ, Garret. Are you fucking kidding me?" Sierra said, her palm slamming down onto the bed between them emphatically. "How old were you? Sixteen? And he called you to cover up an affair? What the hell?"

It said a lot about the sort of person Sierra was that her first thought was for him and the position his father had put him in. Later, he suspected she'd get to thinking about what kind of man was so self-interested, so self-preserving, that he could orchestrate a plan like that when there were two people—neighbors—crushed in their car nearby.

"Lucy was pretty upset when I got there. Not a scratch on her, but bruised and cold. He'd made her walk a mile in the snow. She kept telling me she'd checked the other car to make sure there was nothing she could do to help before agreeing to walk to the crossroad. So I drove her to her place, then I went home and waited for Dad to come home and break the news of the accident, like I didn't know about it already." He stared at the backs of his hands, rubbing the spot over his left index knuckle where an old football scar dimpled the flesh. "He hadn't thought about that part for himself. That was my contribution—the acting surprised part. As soon as I could get him alone, I told him he had to tell Mom. That I wouldn't cover for him. That it was wrong."

"I bet that went over well," Sierra said.

He glanced at her, saw the tight, angry look on her face. He refocused on his hands. He couldn't get the rest of this story out while he looked at her. It was too fucking ugly.

"He flat-out refused to come clean. Kept talking about the police report and causing trouble for Lucy and hurting Mom. When I threatened to tell Mom myself, he looked me in the eye and told me it would ruin her life. But if I wanted to be responsible for that, if I wanted to rip away her happiness and destroy our family, then I should go right ahead. So I decided I'd do it, because she deserved to know. But then I saw the way she fussed over him, telling him how lucky we'd all been that he'd survived the accident, how much she loved him . . ."

"You couldn't do it."

He shook his head. He still struggled with the shame of that moment—that he'd chosen cowardice over what his mother was owed.

"Garret . . ." Sierra's hand slid into his, warm and strong. "Your father put you in an impossible position."

"I know. I've had plenty of time to parse the situation from every conceivable angle and I know he made me responsible for his bad behavior. I know it was on him. *Is* on him. I didn't want to be the keeper of his secret, but that's what happened." He shrugged. "It changed everything for me. I was so angry with him afterward. And I didn't trust him."

"Of course you didn't. You didn't respect him anymore. How could you, after what he'd done, the position he'd put you in? That's some serious shit to be dealing with when you're sixteen." Sierra pulled her knees up and twisted toward him. "That's why you went to Seattle after college, isn't it, instead of working for Tate?"

"Pretty much. Up until then, I'd been all about joining the business. Dad and I had all these plans, like him wanting me to do a double major in business and marketing, so I could bring that expertise back into the business. But I didn't want any of it, not after what he'd done. What he'd made me do. Then I found out that Lucy wasn't even the first woman from Tate he'd had an affair with, and that sealed the deal for me."

Sierra squeezed his hand. "And then he had a stroke, and it felt like all bets were off because he might have died. So you stepped up to do whatever had to be done. And now he's fucked you over again. You get to carry the can for his bullshit yet again."

It was ridiculous how grateful he felt that she'd connected the dots and understood so quickly. Just hearing someone else give voice to the frustrated outrage and anger that had been simmering inside him ever since he'd learned about the slush fund was a relief. "Yeah. That pretty much sums it up."

"You must be so angry," she said. "How can you not be hulking out? There must be a part of you that just wants to dump it all in his lap and let him deal with the crap he's created."

"Believe me, I'm angry. Getting angrier by the day. But it's not just about me. It's about my mom, and it's about all the people who rely on Tate Transport to keep the lights on. My job right now is to find a way through this. And to hope like hell that the DA is going after someone else."

Sierra shook her head, her expression bleak. "You're a better person than me."

"Oh, yeah, I'm a saint." He was confused, stressed, frustrated and, yeah, scared. He didn't feel better than anyone right now. He felt as though he was barely keeping his head above dark, murky water.

"You didn't ask to be put in this situation, Garret. And you definitely didn't ask to be put in a position where you had to choose between two horrible options. Your father is an asshole. Honestly, I don't think I could look him in the eye again without wanting to punch him in the dick."

She surprised a laugh out of him with her bold announcement, loosening the band of tension binding his chest and shoulders. Suddenly he felt lighter. Better than he had in days. Nothing had been resolved, but he felt understood. He felt *known*, and it was a little shocking how much that meant to him.

"Come here," he said, pulling her closer, and she slipped a leg over both of his and shifted so she was straddling him, her hands resting on his shoulders. "You're an excellent listener." He combed his fingers through the long length of hair that trailed over her shoulders.

"When you live with a bunch of taciturn cowboys, you learn to pay attention when they finally open their mouths."

His gaze swept over her pretty face. Her mouth quirked into a small smile, and her eyes were warmly sympathetic as she watched him. Fuck, he liked her so much. "I feel like I owe you an apology for how much Tate family crap you've had to deal with since you took this job."

"Don't apologize for things you can't control. Save it for when you mess up on your own account. Because it'll happen eventually, and trust me, you are going to want to keep your powder dry."

He laughed. "So pragmatic."

"Yep. Unapologetically so."

He laughed again at her play on words. "I see what you did there."

"Do you?" She smoothed her hand down his shoulder

and along his arm until she was holding his hand. She lifted it to her breast, encouraging him to cup her there. "Do you see what I did here too?"

Her breast was warm and heavy and smooth in his hand and they both watched as he ran his thumb across her nipple, back and forth, teasing it to hardness.

"Hell, yes," he said, lifting his other hand to cup her right breast.

She took a deep, shuddery breath as he toyed with her, her breasts rising and falling in his hands, her eyes bright with renewed desire.

"About how wet are you right now, do you think?" he asked conversationally, his cock growing harder by the second beneath the weight of her perfect ass.

"I'd hate to say without checking first."

Holding his gaze, she made a show of gliding her hand down her belly and between her legs to where she was spread wide across his lap. He watched as she stroked herself as though she had all the time in the world before slipping a finger inside her pussy.

"Feel good?" he asked.

"Oh, yeah."

"I can make you feel better."

Holding her hips, he urged her up on to her knees as he shifted down in the bed. She gave a shaky sigh as he encouraged her to settle over his mouth, and when he licked along the seam of her sex she reached out and gripped the top of the headboard, as if she understood she was going to need support to survive what came next.

He lost track of time as he feasted on her most delicate

flesh, pulling her clit into his mouth to trill it with his tongue and then shocking her by sucking on it until her hips started to buck and shake. Pulling back, he soothed her with long, luscious licks, toying with her inner lips before making his way back to that sensitive little bud where he knew she needed him the most. She was quivering, her breath coming in desperate pants now, and he smiled against her pussy as she pleaded with him to give her what she wanted.

"Patience, baby," he murmured, then he set about torturing her some more.

She came minutes later, her body arching above him as she gripped the headboard, riding out the storm he'd created inside her.

It was the sexiest thing he'd seen in his entire life and all he could think about was being inside her again as quickly as was humanly possible. As if she'd read his mind, Sierra shifted backward, reaching for his already-straining cock. Then she was lowering herself onto him, and the heat and tightness was almost too much.

"Baby, you feel so fucking good," he said.

"You feel good. Oh my god, your cock is so fucking hot. I can't stand it."

She started to move, her top lip curling with pleasure-pain as she rode him. Everything about her pressed his buttons, from her rounded hard-nippled breasts to the quivering muscles in her belly to the way her hair swished across her shoulders as she stroked him with her body.

"So . . . fucking . . . amazing," he gasped, and then he was beyond words, his climax squeezing his balls in a pleasurable vise as he lost track of the world for a few glorious seconds.

He felt her climax again seconds later, then she was a rag doll in his arms, flopping onto his chest, panting and damp and lax. He wrapped his arms around her and curved a hand around the back of her head, holding her close, not wanting to let go of this moment of unity and connection.

No other woman had ever rocked his world the way she did. No other woman had ever inspired him to be so honest, to share so much, to want so much. His life might be a dumpster fire right now, but Sierra was the one good thing that made all of it worthwhile. If he could survive the next few weeks and months and come out of this mess with her still by his side, in his bed, a part of his life . . . Right this second, it felt like it was the only thing that mattered. Everything else could go fuck itself, as long as he got to have her in his life.

She stirred, sliding off him, and it wasn't until she was curling into his side that he realized they'd forgotten to use a condom in the heat of the moment.

"Whoa," he said quietly, his eyes popping open.

"Relax," Sierra said, her hand patting his chest reassuringly. "I'm on the pill. So we don't have to worry about *that.*"

He heard the unasked part of her question and was quick to reassure her.

"I'm always careful. And I had a checkup recently."

"Me too," she said. "So I guess that means no more interruptions. Hallelujah."

Her head was on his shoulder and he couldn't see her face, but he knew she was smiling. He pressed a kiss to the top of her head, then pulled the duvet up to cover both of them. "Get some sleep. We've got an early start."

"Do you still need to—oh."

"Exactly. I don't like to be rushed in the morning," he said, reaching out to turn off the light.

"Well, then. I guess we'd better make sure we leave ourselves plenty of time," she said, her voice a suggestive husk in the dark.

His body felt warm and heavy and satisfied and he closed his eyes, giving himself up to sleep. No way had he imagined that such a shitty day could end this well.

But Sierra made everything better. He was starting to understand that now.

Chapter Fourteen

S IERRA COULDN'T REMEMBER the last time she'd shared a bed overnight with a man. It had been a while, she knew that for certain, and she'd forgotten what it was like to wake up with a hard male body pressed against her own. She'd forgotten the warmth of it, the quiet companionship of it.

And she'd forgotten how freaking hot it could be, two sleepy bodies exploring each other under the covers until suddenly everything was urgent and necessary and unstoppable.

Afterward, she shared the shower with Garret, groaning with pleasure as he massaged first shampoo then conditioner through her hair.

"I love your hair," he said as he helped her rinse it off. "I love the way it covers your pretty tits when we're fucking. I love feeling it on my chest when you're on top."

"Well, now you've gone and done it, haven't you?" she told him. Reaching out to flick off the water, she led him back into the bedroom and had her wicked way with him yet again.

Somehow they managed to keep their hands off each other long enough to get dressed and make it to the kitchen.

There, Garret unearthed some bread from the freezer and put it on to toast before making her a coffee with a complicated-looking machine hidden behind one of the many cupboards.

"Wow. I didn't know this was here. Not that I would know what to do with it, but still."

"I'll show you," he said, smiling at her briefly before concentrating on pouring expertly steamed milk into a mug.

When he passed it to her, she saw he'd created a little smiley face in the foam.

"Look at you, with your fancy foam art," she said. "Are these your beans?"

"Nothing but the best. Stick with me, and I'll hook you up with the good stuff."

"For the record, I don't need an incentive. I'm more than happy to use you for your skills in bed. But if it's a package deal . . . I'm not gonna say no," she said.

"Drink your coffee, Carmody," he said, smiling at her over the top of his mug.

She did as instructed and closed her eyes with bliss. "Oh, wow. That's about a million times better than what I usually drink in the morning."

"I believe you."

She laughed, then the toast popped and she got busy with butter and raspberry jam.

They sat side by side at the counter, alternating between sips of coffee and mouthfuls of toast. When she was done, Sierra gave a happy sigh. "That was so good. Can we do it all over again? I have no idea why I'm so hungry this morning."

She deliberately didn't look at him directly as she spoke,

but she could see his slow smile out of the corners of her eyes.

"Maybe you had really active dreams," Garret said. "Now that I think about it, I think you might even have been talking in your sleep."

"Really? Interesting. What was I saying?" she asked, using the tip of her index finger to collect the final few crumbs of toast off her plate.

"It was pretty incoherent. The only thing that was really clear was something like 'Garret is a sex god.'"

He said it with an admirably straight face and Sierra burst out laughing.

"Pretty sure I didn't say that in my sleep," she said.

"I'm an ear witness, so I think my version of events is more credible."

An ear witness. This man was both gorgeous and a goof ball. No wonder she couldn't resist him. "Well, then, I stand corrected."

She leaned over and kissed him, her mouth still curved into a smile. The morning after had never felt so natural, so *easy* before.

"I can drop you at the airport on the way to the office if you want," he said when they finally came up for air.

"Okay, thanks. That'd be great."

They talked casually on the way to the airport, and when they got there Garret spent nearly five minutes kissing her goodbye.

"You're going to be so late for work," she said when she finally opened the door and slipped out of the car.

"Totally worth it. I'll see you later, okay?"

"Have a good day."

"I will. I'll be thinking about you."

Sierra stood next to the hangar and waited until he'd driven out of sight before turning away, aware she was probably wearing the biggest, goofiest smile on her face.

But so what? She liked the man. She loved the things he did to her when they were both naked, and she enjoyed spending time with him when they were clothed. He was special.

A keeper, some people might say.

But not you because you're not the stupid sort of woman who goes racing ahead of the current state of play and sets herself up for an almighty fall. Am I right?

Sierra made an impatient noise. She wasn't going to make apologies for the way she was feeling right now. She hadn't felt this way about a man since . . . Well, she'd never felt this way about a man before. Garret was smart and funny, his body was crazy hot, he was a ridiculously generous lover, and he had a huge heart.

Just look at the burden he'd carried for thirteen years because he couldn't bear to break his mother's heart.

Thinking about their conversation last night and the invidious position Gideon Tate had put his sixteen-year-old son in all those years ago made Sierra's blood boil over again. She'd been so angry on his behalf last night, so righteously outraged, she'd been hard-pressed not to get out of the bed and pace and rant and rave. But she'd seen how hard it was for Garret to share his father's betrayal with her. She'd felt the tension in him, had noted the way he stayed focused on his hands rather than her face while he filled in the details for her.

He'd been embarrassed—ashamed—for his father, and it had broken her heart a little to see it. Even after all the shitty things Gideon had done, Garret still loved his father.

What a pity Gideon Tate was so terribly unworthy of Garret's love and loyalty.

She'd always had a bit of a soft spot for the man, despite her brothers' oft-stated dislike. He'd been good to her, graciously allowing Jack access to the Bell so he could teach her to fly in his spare time. She'd always known he was most likely motivated by guilt, but she was pragmatic enough—and desperate to fly enough—to accept the help he'd offered. As she'd said to Casey when he'd balked at the prospect of her working for the Tates, surely it was better that the man felt some sense of responsibility than nothing at all?

But now she knew Gideon's first thought after the accident that killed her parents was for himself, and the cold-hearted, bone-deep self-interest inherent in that action made her feel queasy.

The night of the accident, one of the local policemen had been tasked with the grim duty of driving to the Carmody ranch and breaking the news to the family. She and Casey had been home alone, and she could still remember the way the police officer's hands had shaken, the tremble in his voice, the paleness of his face as he'd explained the situation to her and Casey. He'd come directly from the accident site and the trauma of what he'd witnessed had been plain to see.

Yet Gideon Tate, who had endured the visceral shock of a head-on collision—explosive air bag deployment, glass shattering, metal tearing, the knowledge that two people had died, all of it—had such a powerfully developed instinct for self-preservation that his first act after notifying the authorities was to take action to save his reputation.

No shaking hands for him. He'd been all about damage control and covering his ass.

No wonder Garret was ashamed. She'd be ashamed, too, if one of her parents had been revealed to be so calculating and manipulative. It made her feel a little dirty that she'd allowed Gideon to salve his conscience by being generous toward her.

But none of that had anything to do with Garret, or how she felt about him. He was a very separate, distinct person from his father. A whole different type of man altogether.

Her thoughts kept circling around the subject throughout the day as she gave the Bell a deep clean, going over both the interior and exterior of the helicopter until it gleamed. She'd come to a few conclusions by the time Garret's car pulled into the reserved spot behind the hangar late in the afternoon.

Shutting the cockpit door, she adjusted the brim on her ball cap as she watched Garret lock up the car. She couldn't keep the smile off her face when he walked toward her, his eyes alight with pleasure at seeing her. At being with her again.

As if just being near her was enough to make him happy.

It was the way she felt, too, and when he reached the Bell they both simply stood and looked at each other, matching smiles on their faces.

"Good day?" she asked.

"Hell, no. It sucked big hairy ones. How about you?"

"I washed the Bell. Prepare yourself for a new level of excellence as you enter the passenger cabin."

"Actually, I was thinking I might ride up front with you. If that's okay?"

She blinked, thrown by the request. "Um, sure. If you like. It's nowhere near as comfortable, though."

"It has other attractions."

She gave him a mock-stern look. "I'm on the clock right now, Mr. Tate. I'm going to ask you to remember that for the duration of our flight this afternoon."

She said it lightly, but there was a thread of seriousness beneath her words and she knew Garret had received her message when he gave her a small, decisive nod.

"Totally understood."

"It's just I take the notion of having your life in my hands very seriously," she explained.

Also, right at this moment, she was his employee, not his . . . whatever she was to him when she wasn't on the job. It was important to her that they both understood there needed to be a firewall between the two relationships.

"Let me assure you, I wholeheartedly respect and support that commitment," he said.

"Then I'll just stow your briefcase for you, since there's no room for it up front."

She held out her hand and he relinquished his bag to her. She made short work of securing it on the cargo hold, then opened the passenger door to the cockpit. "Make yourself at home," she said, waving him onboard.

"Dangerous invitation, Ms. Carmody."

She smiled and waited till he was seated and pulling on

his seat belt before shutting the door. She was aware of him watching her as she slipped into the pilot's seat, deftly maneuvering to accommodate the cyclic between her knees.

"Just need to run through a few checks before we start the engine," she told him.

She went through her preflight routine, forcing herself to concentrate despite the potent distraction of having Garret close by, his amazing aftershave wrapping itself around her. Later, when she wasn't in pilot-mode, she needed to ask him what it was called because it was fast becoming her kryptonite.

She collected her headset and Garret followed suit, picking up on her cue. Then she fired up the engine, and they both glanced overhead as the main rotor began to turn.

She checked with the control tower and received the all clear to take off. Then she glanced across at Garret, only to find him watching her with a decidedly wicked glint in his eye.

She didn't need to ask to know what he was thinking, and it made her feel more than a little hot to know he was turned on by watching her work. Competency porn, she guessed. Whatever it was, she planned to exploit it at the first non-work-associated opportunity.

For now, they needed to get airborne.

She opened up the collective, and the Bell rose nose first. Once she was high enough, she hovered a moment and glanced back at the pad, then found her heading and opened up the throttle to her preset flight speed.

"That little hover back there. You always do that. What are you checking for?" Garret asked.

"Anything that shouldn't be there, basically. Oil or fuel leaks. The engine's under a lot of pressure when it starts up. Better to know early if there's something not quite right."

"Again, I applaud your commitment to safety," Garret said.

"You ever been up front before?"

"Not since I was a kid."

"Want me to walk you through it?"

"Only if it doesn't interfere with anything."

"I can chew gum and walk, don't worry," she said, shooting him an amused look.

She spent the next ten minutes giving him a tour of the cockpit, explaining the various instruments and displays and demonstrating how the cyclic and foot pedals worked. He asked smart questions and listened attentively to her answers, and when she was done he gave a small shake of his head.

"Honestly? It's still completely baffling and damned intimidating. Can't imagine having to keep it all straight." There was admiration in his voice and the look he gave her, and she was powerless to control the flush that warmed her cheeks.

"Tell me about your day," she said, wanting to distract them both from how self-conscious she was feeling.

"Pass. Next topic."

The only other topic on her mind was the thing she'd been brooding over all day. "I've been thinking about what you told me last night," she said, glancing across to catch his reaction.

"Thought you might have been."

His smile dimmed a little, and she adjusted her grip on

the cyclic.

"We don't have to talk about that, either, if you don't want to."

"We can talk. What's on your mind?"

"Your mom. I was thinking about what you said, about not wanting to be responsible for blowing everything up after the accident. You said it yourself last night—you're in the habit of protecting her."

He was frowning, but he nodded. "Yeah. I guess I am."

"The thing is, she's not your responsibility. You know that, right?" His frown deepened, and she rushed back into speech. "I don't mean that you don't owe her care and consideration, but she's an adult. She married your father. She's lived with him for, what? Thirty years?"

"Something like that. And I know what you're saying— Shit. Is that a hawk?" Garret's voice was sharp with surprise, and she followed his sightline and spotted the bird riding a thermal fifty feet or so to their right.

"Cooper's hawk. Female by the wingspan," she said.

"Which has got to be at least forty inches," he said, awestruck. "Amazing. How big do the males get?"

Sierra's mouth twitched into a smile. "Believe it or not, the females are larger than the males."

He laughed. "Of course they are. She's beautiful."

Neither of them spoke for a few seconds as they watched the hawk glide. Then, with an abruptness that stole Sierra's breath, the hawk tucked her wings tight to her body and dived out of sight with ferocious speed.

"Something is about to become dinner," Garret said.

She adjusted their heading minutely, conscious they'd

need to start ascending soon to take their usual route through the mountains. After a moment or two, Garret picked up the conversational thread again.

"I appreciate what you're saying about my mom. It's a good point. She's not stupid. You should see the way she's pulled everything together so Dad can do his rehab at home. I just don't want to add to her burdens."

"Because thirteen years ago your father put her happiness in your hands, and you're still holding it," Sierra pointed out. "Let me put this another way—she's part owner of the business, right? She needs to know what you're dealing with. If shit gets real with the DA, she needs to be prepared."

"Don't even say that out loud," Garret said, the frown back on his face.

"Sorry."

"It's not your fault. And I appreciate you being in my corner."

He sounded tense and unhappy and Sierra regretted bringing the subject up. He had so much going on. He didn't need her second-guessing him and offering coaching from the sidelines.

"The thing is, I'm not sure how I'm going to tell her without letting it all out. You know?" Garret said suddenly, as though he couldn't hold the words in any longer. "The way I feel about the mess I've uncovered at the company is all mixed up with the stuff from the accident. It's the same arrogant, the-rules-don't-apply-to-me bullshit from my father all over again, and I'm afraid I'm just gonna spray it all around like a fire hose once I get started."

"Okay. Little thought experiment here—would that be

such a bad thing? Haven't you kept that secret long enough?"

Garret was already shaking his head. "I can't. The way she is with Dad right now . . . She's literally living for him, Sierra. It's like she's breathing every breath *with* him. If he makes any kind of recovery, it's going to be because of her. Because she willed him to do it. If I tell her what he did, what he made me do . . ." He broke off, shaking his head, his gaze distant.

She opened her mouth to apologize again and he held up a hand, shooting her a warm but firm look. "Don't apologize again. I'm the luckiest bastard in the world that you're prepared to put up with all my drama right now."

"It's only because you're so good in bed," she said because she wanted to make him smile again.

"You've mentioned that a couple of times now. I'm starting to feel like I've got a reputation to live up to."

"God, yes. I've been conditioned to expect multiple orgasms now. There's no turning back."

He laughed, and she shifted the subject, pointing out that they were about to start their run through the mountain pass. By mutual unspoken agreement they kept the conversation light for the rest of the flight. They touched down at the Tate ranch right on schedule and Sierra went through the shutdown procedure, flicking off switches and checking gauges. When she was done, and the main rotor was slowing overhead, she slipped her headset off.

Garret followed suit, running a hand over his hair where the headband had flattened it.

"Nice landing," he said.

"What was it you said this morning? Nothing but the

best?"

"Are you off the clock yet?" he asked, his gaze dropping to her mouth.

"Nope. Not until this baby is in the hangar." She smiled at him, loving that he wanted her so badly.

"I can wait."

He did, too, leaning against the frame of the hangar door and watching while she towed the Bell inside and tied the rotor down for the night. Once she was done she put the tow cart back on its charger and walked across to the beaten-up old desk, putting as much sass in her strut as she could. Parking her butt on the desk, she crossed her arms over her chest and smiled her best come-hither smile at Garret.

He pushed away from the open doorway and moved toward her with the focused intensity of a lion on the hunt. She spread her legs and he stepped between them, his head lowering toward hers. And then his mouth was on hers and she was being pushed back onto the desk with the ferocity of his need. Everything in her turned to molten liquid, her mind filling with erotic images as she imagined what might come next—him stripping off her shirt, her pulling at his belt and his fly, all the pesky pieces of clothing they needed to dispose of to get what they both so desperately wanted.

She was sliding her hands onto his belt buckle when he tensed and lifted his head. Which was when she heard the sound of a car engine.

"Pretty sure that's Mom," he said regretfully.

"Well . . . damn," Sierra sighed.

He laughed, reaching out to run his thumb across her pouting bottom lip. "I'll make it up to you tomorrow night.

Pack to stay in Helena again, okay? How does two nights sound?"

"You sure you're up to that?" she asked, lifting an eyebrow.

"You just worry about your pretty little self." Then he kissed her once, hard, and stepped away. She could see the frustration in him, in the way he smoothed his shirt over his flat belly and adjusted himself.

"Feeling is mutual," she told him.

"I know. See you tomorrow, Sierra Carmody."

She watched wistfully as he made his way out of the hangar. Then she let out a shaky sigh and dropped her head back for a moment, conscious of all the places her body was still hot and ready for him.

After a minute, she pushed herself upright and palmed her car keys.

Tomorrow was another day. And then she would have Garret to herself again for two whole nights.

Delayed gratification. She could live with that.

Chapter Fifteen

GARRET COULD HEAR his mother moving around in the kitchen when he entered the house, and he dumped his bag in the study and went to join her.

"Hello. I was wondering if you were back already," she said brightly, pausing in the midst of unpacking groceries.

"Just got here."

"I thought I'd make some grilled chicken with a nice salad for dinner. And how do you feel about an apple pie?" she asked.

"That all sounds great. What can I do to help?" he asked.

His mother waved a hand. "Nothing. You've been working all day."

"I can still help. Why don't I peel the apples?"

"Oh, all right. If you're going to be pushy about it." His mother gave him a playful smile to let him know she wasn't serious.

Garret cocked his head. "You've had some good news."

Her smile widened. "I have. Your father might be home by the end of the week. I've found a physical therapist who can come in daily, and the hospital is happy with his progress. If he keeps on the same trajectory, he'll be all ours by

Friday."

Her eyes were suddenly glassy with unshed tears and Garret put down the soup cans he was about to transfer to the pantry and gave her a hug.

"I'm not upset," she said as he rubbed her back soothingly.

"I know. But it's a big deal. I get it," he said.

"I'm just so grateful he's coming home," she said as she pulled away. "When I got that call from Jack telling me what had happened, that he'd collapsed . . . I thought we were going to lose him, Garret."

"I know."

She put her hand on his forearm and gave it a little squeeze. "But we made it. Still a long way to go, but the only way is up from here."

She turned to put the milk in the fridge and Garret collected the cans of soup and ferried them to the pantry. His mother was talking as though they'd turned a corner and the worst was over, when in fact this could be the calm before the storm. If Mae's tip-off was accurate, their lives could be about to implode.

She's not your responsibility.

Sierra's words circled his mind, but even though he knew she was right, the thought of crapping all over his mother's good mood soured his stomach. He'd wait for a better moment, when he had more information to share with her.

He was shutting the pantry door when it occurred to him that there would probably always be an excuse for him not to tell his mother what was going on. With news like this, there was never going to be a good time to come clean.

If shit gets real with the DA, she needs to be prepared.

Sierra's words again, haunting him. Because they were true and real. He needed to man up and do this. Get his mom up to speed so she could prepare herself for a potential nightmare.

Taking a deep breath, he slid onto one of the stools at the counter. His mother had set out a cutting board for him, along with a peeler and half a dozen apples. He picked up an apple and squeezed it, feeling his hand stretch around the fruit. "Mom. There's something I need to tell you about the business. I've been holding off, waiting to get more information, but you need to know what's going down."

His mother was pulling herbs and spices from the custom drawer in the island counter and she glanced up at him. "Does this have something to do with the fight with Ron?"

"That's part of it." He set down the apple, then realized he missed the weight of it in his hand and picked it up again. "One of the first things I asked for when I started was a report from each department so I could get up to date on operations. Ron intervened to stop me from getting the financials from sales. When I asked why he'd do that, he went ballistic and stormed out. Then he called his secretary and asked her to bring his laptop and a bunch of files down to the parking garage."

His mother frowned. "All because you asked to see the financials for the sales department?"

"Bear with me. When I spoke to the guy in charge of sales, he explained that Ron and Dad had an 'executive account' in the sales budget that they administered personally. The story was that it was for promotions and incentives, wining and dining influential account managers, that sort of thing. Nearly half a million dollars."

His mother set both hands flat on the counter as though she was steadying herself. "I take it you think this account is a slush fund? Is that what you're trying to say? You think your father and Ron were paying people off to get business?"

He'd been expecting more shock from his mother, maybe even a vociferous defense of her husband, but there was a measured calmness behind her words.

"Pretty much. I don't know for sure yet who was being paid for what. Ron took any records that existed when he took his laptop and those files. I've got a forensic accountant looking into things, trying to work out what money went to whom and why. Hopefully we'll know more soon."

"Why on earth would you do that?" his mother asked, her voice sharp.

Garret stared at her, wrong-footed. "So I know where the bodies are buried. So I can understand how exposed we are and take steps to put things right."

She shook her head, her smooth blond bob swinging around her shoulders. "No, Garret. There's no need to go kicking up a hornet's nest when you don't have to. Ron is gone now, and you're in charge. That's the important part. You can clean things up, draw a line under whatever Ron was up to and make sure this never happens again."

It took a few seconds for Garret to process his mother's words and what they meant.

"You knew already, didn't you?" he said slowly. Another realization hit him. "That's why you were so insistent on me taking over Tate instead of leaving Ron to run things."

He could still remember how insistent she'd been. At the time, he'd just assumed she was stressed, looking for ways to secure her world. But apparently she'd had another agenda.

His mother blinked a couple of times. Then she took a deep breath and looked down at the counter, moving a few spice bottles around pointlessly. "I didn't *know*. I *suspected*. Your father has always been a law unto himself. You know that. He and Ron were always strategizing about ways to get ahead."

"Okay, so you *suspected*. And you didn't give me a heads-up?" Because *what the fuck?* Why on earth would she send him in blind like that?

"I didn't know anything for certain. I didn't want to prejudice you."

"Mom . . ." He swallowed a four-letter word, sliding off the stool so he could take a few steps away to try and keep a grip on his temper. "If I'd known what you suspected going in, I would have done everything differently. Ron wouldn't have been able to walk with the files. I'd have known what I was up against."

His mother did the blinking thing again. Then she licked her lips nervously. "I'm sorry. In my defense, I was hoping I was wrong."

Garret made himself count to five. There were a lot of things he could say right now, but none of them were kind or constructive.

"Garret. Please. I was just trying to make the best of a bad situation. But the good thing is that you're in a position to make sure it never happens again. You can ensure that everything is aboveboard from now on."

"It's not as simple as that, Mom."

"I know it probably goes against the grain for you to look the other way in regard to Ron, but isn't it worth it to just be done with it all and protect your father's legacy? Talk to Ron, pay him out whatever he wants, and we can put it all behind us."

It was his turn to blink. "You want me to hand over a fat payout to the crooked asshole who colluded with Dad to game the system?"

"If that's what it takes to make this go away and protect your father's legacy, then yes. We have to be practical, Garret."

"There's a good chance the DA is investigating Tate Transport for commercial bribery." He hadn't meant to say it so bluntly, but his mother had left him with no choice. "The only way for us to get through this is to do everything by the book, and that means pursuing Ron and finding out the extent of the problem, not just covering it up and hoping for the best."

His mother's face was pale with shock as she stared at him. "How do you know we're being investigated?"

"A well-connected friend dropped a word in my ear. Apparently the DA is investigating commercial bribery in the transport industry in Montana."

"So it might not be Tate Transport," his mother said, hope flaring in her eyes.

"Come on, Mom. Tate Transport is one of the biggest players in the state. And we know we've got a huge fucking slush fund hidden on the books. What are the odds it's not about us? You really want to take that risk?"

She flinched. "There's no need for that kind of language."

"I happen to think there is, but fine. I'm sorry for expressing my sincere outrage at the stinking cesspit Dad has left on our doorstep. My bad." The words were out Garret's mouth before he could stop them, laced with fury, underscored with frustration.

"You're angry."

He laughed, the sound ugly and hard. "Yeah, I am. Just a little bit. You let me walk into this, Mom. And Dad dug this hole for everyone. If this hits the fan, Tate Transport could go under. All the people who rely on us will be out on the street." He waved a hand around the spacious designer kitchen. "All of this could be gone."

"I'd appreciate it if you didn't raise your voice," his mother said with stiff dignity.

Garret closed his eyes for a beat, then took a slow, deep breath. "I'm sorry. But I have been living with this for over a week now. I didn't want to dump it on you when you've got so much on your hands with Dad, but you need to know what could be coming our way."

"I appreciate that. And I know you've been under a lot of pressure."

He nodded and pushed his hair back off his forehead. "Anyway. That's where we're at. The accountant has promised a report by the end of the week, so we'll know more then."

"I see." His mother crossed to the wine rack next the pantry and pulled out a bottle of wine. She glanced at Garret and he nodded to indicate that yes, please, he would really frickin' love a glass of wine right now.

She poured and pushed a glass his way, then took a big gulp from her own. "What exactly is this accountant advising?" she asked when they'd both been fortified with alcohol.

"We haven't talked specifics yet. I suspect it depends on what she finds."

"And if the DA is investigating Tate Transport?"

"Then we get great lawyers and start praying."

"Couldn't you do some kind of deal with them? Don't companies do that all the time? Give them some kind of undertaking, pay a fine, whatever they want to make it go away?"

"I don't know. Maybe. I've got an appointment to brief a new lawyer tomorrow. He might have some ideas."

"What's wrong with using David? Your father's used him for years."

"That's exactly why I can't use him. I have no idea how deep the rot goes."

She took another big gulp of wine.

"I'm going to speak frankly, Garret." She held his eye, her jaw set. "Tate Transport is your father's life's work. He gave up everything to build that business, to protect and provide for us. And now it's our turn to protect and provide for him. I want you to promise me you'll do *everything in your power* to make this go away. Whatever it takes, even if it might seem unpalatable. The end result is all that matters."

Garret glanced down into the dark red wine in his glass, needing a moment to recover from the psychic gut punch his mother had just delivered. After a moment he lifted his head. "Just so we're on the same page here—you're asking me break the law if necessary to save Dad's ass. Have I got that right?"

His mother's eyes were flinty as they met his. "I'm asking you to remember that everything you are and everything you have came out of your father's sacrifices and hard work. And before you read me a lecture on Business Ethics 101, let me remind you that we're talking about a few kickbacks here. No one was hurt. Yes, your father has his excesses, but he's not a monster. Far from it. He's a good man, and we need to protect him, Garret. I need you to help me protect him."

Garret's stomach churned with acid as he absorbed his mother's words.

Holy fucking hell.

For a moment, he didn't know what to do. What to think.

And then he did.

"Good to know where you stand," he said. "Thanks for the TED Talk."

His glass clinked against the marble countertop as he set it down. Then the only sound was the rapid percussion of his shoes on the polished parquet floor as he made his way to the front door.

Night had fallen while he'd been having all his illusions destroyed over a nice glass of merlot. He walked into the dim coolness, away from the house, away from his mother.

Away.

He didn't stop until he was halfway down the driveway. Then he simply stood there, the sky a dark void overhead, hands hanging by his sides, and tried to deny the sting of angry emotion burning at the back of his eyes.

All these years, he'd kept his father's shitty, sordid little secret to protect his mother. For thirteen years it had chafed at him, kept him from home, pushed him to build his life thousands of miles away.

And it turned out she probably hadn't needed protecting at all. Turned out she was a deeply practical, pragmatic woman. He laughed, the sound rough in his throat. What had she said? *Yes, your father has his excesses.*

She knew about the affairs. Suddenly there wasn't a doubt in his mind.

"Jesus motherfucking Christ."

He was so stupid. He'd whipped himself for years over covering for his father. He'd put his mother on a pedestal, driven by guilt—and now she wanted him to compromise himself in order to save his father's ass. God, she hadn't even hesitated to ask. It had been her default, automatic position. Her first line of defense.

He shook his head, trying to imagine what she thought he could do against the power of the DA. Was he supposed to bribe someone? Or maybe he was just supposed to do some creative accounting, whatever it took to destroy all traces of his father's crimes.

That's what a good, loyal son would do, no matter the potential cost and risk to himself and his future.

He let his head fall back. The sky was blue-black above him, the stars distant pinpricks of light. So much emptiness. So much coldness.

He stood like that for as long as his neck would allow, then he turned and trudged back up to the house. His mother had switched the outside lights on—so thoughtful—

and he paused in the shadows, unwilling to go inside just yet.

Instead, he moved toward the garage, letting himself in via the side door. He grabbed his bike helmet, then strode across to punch the button to lift the roller door. He cranked up the Ducati inside the garage, the roar of the motor ricocheting off the walls. Then he took off, shooting down the driveway, uncaring that he was still in his work shirt and pants.

Right now, he just wanted to turn his brain off and stop thinking.

Leaning over the handlebars, he opened the throttle.

SIERRA AGONIZED OVER whether to tell Jed about running into Mae all through dinner. As her family bickered and laughed around her, she batted the pros and cons back and forth in her mind.

Pro: she didn't like keeping things from Jed. Con: he'd just reached a point where it felt like he might be open to getting out there again, and news of Mae might throw him off balance. Pro: maybe hearing about her and her life now would help give him some closure. Con: maybe hearing about her and her life now would send him into retreat.

In the end, the habit of honesty and the knowledge that Jed would hate to think she was coddling or protecting him in some way won out. She waited until he'd slipped out of the house for his nightly check on the horses to follow him to the barn.

She found him talking softly to Pedro, promising him a good long run tomorrow. He'd been stuck inside making calls and chasing up parts for their busted tractor all day, so she figured Pedro wasn't the only one suffering from cabin fever.

"Let me know if he ever answers back, and we'll alert the mental health team at the hospital," she said, resting her forearms on the top of the stall gate.

"Don't try to shame a man for communing with his horse," Jed said.

"I believe the word you're looking for is *mock*, not *shame*."

He snorted out a laugh. "How are things going with the defying-gravity business? You enjoying the job?"

"I am," Sierra said. "It's ridiculous that someone is paying me good money to live my dream."

Jed's smile was warm and she could tell he was genuinely happy for her. "You getting along okay with Garret?"

The memory of Garret below her on the bed, his eyes smoky with lust, flashed across her mind. "Um, yeah. He's pretty easygoing. We get on well." She shrugged and gave thanks for the dim lighting, hoping it hid her blush. At some point she would have to tell her family about what was happening between her and Garret, but not yet.

She watched as he checked the water trough then stepped back to allow him to exit the stall. He was about to head inside, which meant she was about to lose her chance to have this conversation privately.

Spit it out, Carmody. Get it over with.

"So, a weird thing happened last night." Her voice sounded odd—stilted—and Jed threw her a look.

"Okay?"

"Garret had a meeting with his accountant at the house and—huge coincidence—it was Mae. As in Barringer. Mae Barringer."

Jed's face went blank, all expression disappearing behind the wall of taciturn neutrality he was so good at projecting. "That is a coincidence. How is she?"

"Good. Really busy with work. Successful, if being able to afford Louboutins is anything to go by."

Jed frowned and she realized he probably wasn't up on the nuances of women's fashion footwear.

"They're shoes. Expensive ones," she explained.

"Sounds like she's doing really well for herself, then."

"She asked about you. Wanted to know you were okay. I told her you were great, focusing on the ranch."

He went very still and she swore she could see the flicker of something behind his eyes.

God, please don't let it be hope.

Because then she really had made a huge mistake telling him about Mae.

She held her breath, waiting for Jed to ask more, but he turned toward the house.

"Good to know."

Sierra stared at his retreating back. What the hell? If their positions were reversed, she'd be holding him by the scruff of the neck right now and shaking him until every last tiny detail had been offered up.

But Jed would never reveal himself like that. He was the ultimate poker player, never giving anything away.

She let out a small sigh. Maybe she should have kept it to herself after all. She turned off the lights and shut the barn door, then walked across the yard to the house. Surprise, surprise, there was no sign of Jed when she entered, just the blare of the TV as Casey and Eva watched a music documentary, the two of them tangled together on the couch.

"Hey," she said, touching Eva's shoulder to get her attention. "We need to get that short list happening for Operation Hookup. Strike while the iron is hot."

Eva frowned, confused, and Sierra rolled her eyes.

"Seriously?" Eva was the one who'd come up with the stupid name for their mission to find the perfect date for Jed, after all.

"Oh. Right. A hottie for Jed. I'm with you now," Eva said, her expression clearing.

"What's this?" Casey asked, dragging his focus from the TV.

"Jed's finally going to let Sierra hook him up with one of her friends," Eva explained.

Casey's mouth dropped open. "Bullshit."

"He said it," Sierra confirmed. "And I'm holding him to it."

Especially now, after the whole seeing-Mae-and-telling-him-about-it thing.

"Good luck," Casey said, tone doubtful.

"We don't need luck. We have feminine cunning," Eva said, twirling an invisible mustache.

"Sure. But what we don't have is a short list, so you need to put your thinking cap on, okay? Let's come up with some more prospects and compare lists," Sierra said.

"On it," Eva said, giving Sierra a salute, her gaze already sliding back to the documentary.

Sierra ruffled her short hair fondly before heading for the kitchen to make herself a hot chocolate to take to bed. She had big, decadent plans to finish the book she was reading before falling asleep to dream about Garret doing dirty, beautiful things to her.

It was easier to zap milk in the microwave, but Sierra was old school with her hot chocolate—she liked to make it in a saucepan on the stove, and she liked to use real cocoa and sugar, not some premade packet mix. And if she was feeling super indulgent, there might even be some cream involved.

She collected all the necessary ingredients and was about to pour milk into the pan when she heard the distinctive sound of a motorcycle engine. One of Casey's bandmates, Danny, rode a motorcycle, and Sierra waited for the engine to switch off and the inevitable knock at the front door. She poured the milk and returned the carton to the fridge but hesitated before lighting the burner beneath the saucepan.

Danny still hadn't turned off his bike. Which was strange—if it was actually Danny out there.

Instinct drew her to the kitchen window. All she could see was the shape of a man on a motorcycle, his features obscured by his helmet, but the dress shirt and suit pants told her who it was—that, and her the way her pulse leapt.

Garret.

The instinctive thrill of knowing he was close was quickly replaced with alarm. There was no way he'd seek her out like this unless something bad had happened.

Abandoning her hot chocolate, she slipped out of the house through the kitchen door.

Chapter Sixteen

THE TEMPERATURE HAD dropped in the short time Sierra had been inside, and she crossed her arms over her chest as she walked to where Garret sat on the idling bike. He turned his head when he registered her approach, pushing up the visor on his helmet, and the bleak devastation in his eyes made her heart stutter in her chest.

"What happened?" she asked.

"I shouldn't have come. Sorry. I just . . . I'll talk to you tomorrow," he said, lifting a hand to push his visor back down.

Sierra reached out and turned the ignition off. The sudden silence was deafening. "What happened?"

Garret stared at her, then focused on something in the middle distance over her shoulder. "I told my mother about everything. And she—"

He swallowed noisily, his brow furrowed deeply as he struggled to get a grip on his emotions. Sierra reached out and put her hand on his chest, needing to do something to support him, to let him know she was there for him.

"Everything all right out here?"

Sierra looked over her shoulder to find Casey standing in

the doorway, Eva at his side.

"Everything's fine," Sierra said, waving him off impatiently.

She loved her brothers dearly, but it drove her crazy when they tried to protect her.

"We can do this tomorrow," Garret said, his hand already on the ignition key, ready to take off.

Sierra was aware of Eva encouraging Casey back inside as she reached out and tugged Garret's helmet off his head. His hair was flattened, and there were red pressure marks on his cheeks where the padding had rested, which she guessed meant he'd been riding around on his bike for a while. His eyes were so sad and he looked so wounded she slipped her arms around him and pressed her cheek against his own. His skin felt cool, and the cotton of his shirt was icy from the night air.

His arms came around her, tight and strong, holding her with an urgency that bordered on desperation. After a long beat, she pulled back. "Come on. It's too cold to talk out here."

She waited until he'd dismounted from his bike, then she took his hand and led him through the darkness, past the barn, and around the back to where the old Airstream trailer was situated.

Thirty something years ago, her parents had lived in the streamlined silver trailer while they built the ranch. When it became surplus to requirements, they'd parked it behind the barn and plumbed it in to accommodate guests. Usually no one bothered locking it, but Sierra was still grateful when she felt the latch give beneath her hand—the last thing she wanted to do right now was have to go inside for the key.

Leaning in, she flicked the light on, then climbed the two steps and entered. Garret followed her, his lean, tall frame eating up the space.

"Sit," Sierra said, pushing him toward the end of the trailer where a bare mattress awaited their next guest.

She turned to rummage in the cupboards, sending up a prayer of thanks when she found a box of tea bags, a lefto-ver—she guessed—from when Eva had been living here when she first came to town. She filled the kettle and set it to boil. Then she went and sat beside Garret on the bed.

"You don't need to make me tea," he said.

"You don't have to drink it either," she said. "But in case you hadn't noticed it's fifty degrees outside and you've be riding around like this." She reached out to pinch the thin fabric of his shirt. "Tell me what happened."

Because something had sent him out in the night in his work clothes.

Garret looked down at his hands. She watched as he flexed them, turning them over to study his palms. He'd done the same thing last night when he was telling her about his father and the accident, and she understood it was his way of buying himself some thinking time, some distance from what he was about to say.

"She already knew about the slush fund." He glanced up at her.

Her eyes widened. "And she didn't warn you?"

He shook his head, his expression tight, and she realized she hadn't heard the worst of it yet.

"There's more, isn't there?" she guessed.

He flexed his hands again, then clasped them together. "When I told her about the DA's investigation, she told me I needed to do everything I could to make this go away and preserve my father's legacy. Even if it was—direct quote—*unpalatable*."

Sierra gasped, pressing a hand to her chest. *What. The. Fuck?* "She wants you to put yourself on the line to cover for him?"

He gave the briefest of nods and she could see the hurt in him, and the shame.

Because he was their son, he wanted to love and respect them, but they both kept making asshole choices that he couldn't live with. Unethical, ugly, selfish choices, even if that meant sacrificing his happiness and well-being and—potentially—his freedom.

For a moment Sierra was so filled with rage on his behalf she couldn't see. Then she blinked and realized it was because her eyes were filled with angry tears. "Garret . . ."

There were no words, so she simply scrambled into his lap and wrapped her arms around him. These people were supposed to love and protect him. That was their one fucking job as parents. "I'm so sorry. And so angry for you. This is bullshit. And you deserve so much better."

His face was pressed against her neck and she felt him suck in a shuddery breath.

"I just . . . I'm their only kid. And I knew Dad was . . . I had a grip on him. I understood how it was with him, who he was. But Mom's always been the one—"

His shoulders shuddered again and Sierra cradled the back of his head in her hand, her chest aching for him. She understood what he was dealing with right now was primal parent/child stuff, the kind of connections and beliefs that transcend adulthood, rational thought and experience. His mother had just betrayed him, compounding his father's earlier betrayal, and he was shattered.

She had no idea what to say. Sure, she could rail against his parents, call them every name under the sun, but at the end of the day they were still his parents. He was bound to them with ties of blood and obligation and love.

Look at the way he'd dropped everything to come to his father's bedside the moment he'd heard about Gideon's stroke. He'd abandoned his business start-up, his friends, his whole life so he could support his parents. He'd taken on the burden of a multimillion-dollar business without a blink, wading in to do whatever had to be done, putting in ridiculous hours.

He was a good son—a good man—and they didn't deserve him, not for a second. But they were stuck with each other. Garret would never walk away in his parents' hour of need. He simply didn't have it in him, even though they'd been utterly dismissive of his feelings, his ethics, his happiness.

She could feel herself getting angry all over again and had to take deep breaths and remind herself she could kick something later.

Right now, Garret was all that mattered.

She felt the shift in his body as he pulled back enough to look in her face. Her heart twisted when she saw his spiky lashes and flushed cheeks.

"Told you I shouldn't have come," he said, and she knew

he was feeling self-conscious and exposed now that the storm had passed.

It killed her to see him so vulnerable, but she understood the trust he'd put in her was a gift, too, and everything in her wanted to be worthy of it. "I'm so glad you did." She pressed a firm kiss to his mouth. "No, I'm honored you did. Because you're an amazing human being, Garret Tate. You are thoroughly decent and true and loyal. And you have a huge heart. What your mother asked of you tonight . . ."

She shook her head, biting back a string of four-letter words, stalling once again because she still didn't know what to say, how to help him make sense of his mother's selfishness.

"Yeah. It's a little bit fucked up."

"Just a little," she said, smiling faintly at his understatement. She brushed a hand gently over his hair. "What are you going to do?"

He shrugged a shoulder. "What I was always going to do. Keep working with Mae, and when I know what I'm dealing with, I'll get the best legal advice my father's money can buy and see if I can pull this thing out of the fire. Or not."

She nodded, noting how tired he suddenly looked.

"How long have you been riding around?" she asked.

"I don't know. Couple of hours, I guess. Didn't even realize I was coming here until I turned into the driveway."

He gave her a sheepish look and she kissed him again. "I'm going to keep saying it till you believe me—I'm glad you're here. I wouldn't have it any other way. The thought of you driving around out there, hurting like that . . . Yeah. That doesn't work for me."

He lifted a hand to cup her jaw, his thumb sweeping across her cheekbone. "I got so fucking lucky the day you became my pilot."

"We both did," she said.

He pulled her close, his mouth soft on hers as he kissed her with a sweet tenderness that made her breath catch for completely noncarnal reasons.

This man was very quickly becoming the center of her universe. The way he looked at her, the way he made her feel, the ache she felt for him . . . She was so far gone, so committed, it was scary.

But also not, because she knew she wasn't alone in this. She knew in her bones that Garret was falling just as hard as she was. This wasn't one of those mismatched situations where one of them was about to get a cold bucket of reality and rejection straight to the face.

This was real and big and brave. And they were in it together.

Garret lifted his head and she could see he was more himself now, the shock of his mother's betrayal having worn off a little. She smiled at him, then frowned as something occurred to her.

"I don't want you going back there tonight," she said.

He shrugged, a resigned heaviness coming into his face. "Unavoidable. Unfortunately."

"Not necessarily." She slipped off his lap. "Don't go anywhere, okay? Promise I won't be long."

His brow wrinkled with bemusement but he gave her a small nod and she let herself out of the trailer. She jogged back to the house, letting herself in through the kitchen door and heading straight to the laundry room to find some clean sheets. She was adding a couple of pillowcases to her haul when she became aware of Casey standing in the doorway.

"What's going on?" he asked.

"Garret's staying the night," she said.

"Are you two . . . ?"

"Yep. And if you've got a problem with it, you're going to have to suck it up because I don't have time to argue with you tonight," she said, her chin coming up.

Casey held up a hand. "Cool your jets, Feisty McFeisty. I was just asking."

She narrowed her eyes, waiting for the sting in the tail. When it didn't come, she shook her head and picked up the stack of bedlinen. "Do you mind?" she asked, shooing him out of the way.

He moved back into the kitchen and watched as she dumped the sheets on the table before turning to the stove. She set the milk she'd poured earlier onto heat, then added more to the saucepan before whirling toward the pantry to extract a loaf of bread.

"You're feeding him too?" Casey asked.

"Yep," Sierra said as she pulled slices of cheese and deli meat from the fridge.

"So this is serious, then?" he asked, a small furrow between his brows.

"Did I hassle you about how you felt about Eva?" she asked as she made two cheese and ham sandwiches with brisk efficiency. "Could I have a little privacy?"

Casey let out a bark of laughter. "Come on, Sierra. You were so far up in my business it wasn't funny, giving me lectures about her not sticking around and whatnot."

Sierra tossed her hair over her shoulder. "What's your point?"

"My point is that privacy is thin on the ground around here since we all live in each other's pockets. And I care about your happiness just as much as you care about mine."

She froze, shamed by the sincerity in his voice. She flicked him an apologetic look. "Sorry. I'm just . . . He's got some heavy stuff weighing on him and I'm worried. And I know you hate even hearing the word *Tate*."

"I get it. I didn't exactly roll out the red carpet when you told me you were going to work for them. But Garret is a good guy. He used to be, anyway."

"He still is," Sierra said, and she could hear the ring of fervency in her own voice. Just a little bit revealing.

To his credit, Casey simply nodded. "All right. Me and Eva are going to turn in if everything is good here."

"It is. Thanks."

Casey gave her a one of his sweet smiles and stopped to give her an affectionate squeeze on the shoulder on his way out the door.

Sierra smiled to herself. Sometimes they drove her crazy, but she loved her brothers with everything she had.

It took her another five minutes to make the hot chocolate and pour it into a thermos. Then she tucked it under her arm, grabbed the rest of her supplies, and hotfooted it back to the trailer.

"Sorry it took so long—" Sierra ran out of words as she pushed open the door and registered the empty trailer.

Then she heard the toilet flush, followed by the sound of

the tap running. Seconds later Garret emerged from the bathroom at the far end of the trailer.

"Hey. I made sandwiches and hot chocolate, in case you were hungry," she said.

"I skipped dinner," he admitted.

She shoved the plate at him. "Start eating. I'll make the bed."

Garret being Garret, he insisted on helping her, and within minutes they'd create a cozy nest. Sierra kicked of her shoes and sat cross-legged beside Garret as he ate his sandwiches, then they took turns passing the thermos back and forth.

"This is good hot chocolate," he said.

"I know."

His eyes crinkled into a smile as he looked at her. "I love the way you claim the shit you're good at."

"Do I?"

"Yeah."

"Huh." She'd just been joking about the hot chocolate, but she was prepared to believe in this superconfident version of herself if he did.

"It's like the way you are when you're flying. The way you handle yourself. The look on your face. You're a good pilot, and you know you're a good pilot."

"There's always more to learn."

His smile widened. "Don't get all modest on me now, Carmody."

"No danger of that if you keep talking me up." She kissed him, savoring the taste of chocolate on his lips. Then she rolled off the bed and put the plate and thermos in the small sink.

"I forgot to bring my toothbrush, but we might get lucky . . ." She did another forage in the cupboards and drawers and hooted in triumph when she spotted what she was looking for.

"Ta-da," she said, holding up a fistful of disposable toothbrushes, complete with tiny toothpaste tubes. "Courtesy of CJ and Jesse, who have raided more motel bathrooms than you and I have had hot meals."

They took turns brushing their teeth, then they stripped and crawled beneath the covers. The sheets were cool, and she shivered a little as she pressed her body against his.

"You need me to warm you up, baby?" he asked, his tone all dirty innuendo.

"Yes, please."

He ran his warm hands languorously down her side, swooping over her hip, then down the outside of her thigh. She slung a leg over his hip, pressing her mouth to his. The hair on his chest was silky-rough against her breasts and she made a satisfied sound as she felt him growing hard against her belly.

His hand found her breast then, stroking her nipple to arousal. She made another needy sound, conscious of the empty ache between her thighs. He moved closer, rolling her onto her back and coming over her. She closed her eyes in appreciation as his weight settled over her, her legs spread wide to accommodate him.

Amazing that letting another person this close could feel so right. So inevitable.

When he nudged at her entrance she lifted her hips and

clawed at his back as he filled her with his cock.

"Feels so good," she whispered.

"Fuck, yes," he said.

They moved together, finding a rhythm that was all their own, the perfect mix of friction and slide. She pressed her knees against his sides and lifted her hips as her climax took her, clinging to him as she lost touch with reality for a few precious seconds. Then it was his turn, his body shuddering with pleasure and release above hers.

She wrapped her legs around his back afterward, her hands spread wide on his back. He was inside her still, but she wanted him even closer, if that were humanly possible.

"I love you," he said.

She was so glad and relieved he'd been brave enough to say it first, to give voice to what was happening between them, she closed her eyes and let out her breath on a grateful sigh. "I love you too."

Even though it felt precipitous and a little crazy to be at this place so quickly, there was simply no denying the strength and depth of their connection.

He was the man she'd been waiting for her entire life. The man who filled all her empty places. The man she could imagine tomorrow with, and all the tomorrows after that.

And, yeah, things weren't great in his life right now, but that just meant they'd found each other at the right time. She was going to help him get through this. No matter what.

He lifted himself up on his forearms so he could see her face, and they smiled at each other. She saw the gentleness and wonder and gratitude in his eyes and hoped he understood she felt the same.

He kissed her, then they shared a fierce hug as they both absorbed their new normal. Because they were a *they* now. An *us*. A couple. This was a partnership, and whatever came next, they were in it together.

He kissed her one last time then rolled away to reach out and flick off the light. They shuffled into new positions in the darkness, his arm around her shoulders, her head on his chest, their legs tangled. Sierra sat with the peace and comfort of the moment for as long as she could. Then she shifted her head minutely on his chest, signaling she had something to say.

"Whatever happens, there's no shame in protecting yourself. Okay? I know you love them. I know you feel you owe them. But you have to be able to live with the decisions you make."

"Yeah, I know. I've spent thirteen years maintaining a lie already. I'm not built for bullshit. Which is pretty funny, given who my parents are." There was a bitter note beneath his words. He was entitled to it. He'd had a shitty evening. And his parents were assholes. Big, selfish assholes.

She turned her head and pressed a kiss to his chest. Then she nuzzled closer and closed her eyes. The last thought she had as she fell asleep was that tonight changed everything, for both of them.

Chapter Seventeen

G ARRET WOKE WITH a start, one hand groping for his
phone to check the time. Instead he encountered
warm, smooth skin and a tangle of silky hair.

"What's wrong?" Sierra asked, her voice slurred with
sleep.

"Forgot to set the alarm."

"Oh. Shit." She sat up and leaned over to collect her
phone from the counter at the end of the bed. She showed
him the screen—just past six. They hadn't overslept after all.

"Can't beat the old body clock," she said.

If he got moving now, he'd be able to get home, shower,
and change in time to be ready for their usual seven o'clock
departure.

But first, he had something much more important to do.
Reaching out, he filled his arms with warm, willing woman
and pulled her close. She had a crease on her face, and her
hair was all mussed on one side. Her eyes were still soft and
sleepy, her body languorous against his.

"Morning," he said.

She smiled. "Morning."

He could see the echo of last night's conversation in her

eyes—her sadness on his behalf, the new warmth and depth now they'd both acknowledged their feelings.

Sierra Carmody was his.

It was such an extraordinary thing, having her love him and want to be part of his life. It was going to take him some time to get his head around it.

Her smile faded, and she leaned forward to kiss him. He felt his cock stir, eager to be closer to her. He was pretty sure he'd have to be dead before he stopped wanting her. He smoothed a hand over her ass, loving the contrast between smooth skin, toned muscle, and feminine softness.

"Gonna have to be fast," he warned her.

"I can do fast."

She wrapped a hand around his erection, stroking firmly up and down, up and down. He dipped a hand between her legs, sliding into the slick warmth of her arousal. Knowing she was already wet and ready for him, that she wanted him, was the ultimate turn-on. Within seconds he was inside her, stroking them both toward fulfillment.

"Oh, god. Yes. That's it. Ohhhh," Sierra breathed, her fingers digging into his ass with mindless intensity.

The sheets were a binding tangle around them when they were done. He fought his way free and started dressing, his gaze taking in her sprawled form.

"Man . . . If I had ten more minutes . . ." he said.

She wiggled her eyebrows, then stretched into a yawn and sat up. "Put it in the vault for later, and you can pay for that promise with interest."

He laughed and tossed her T-shirt to her before sitting on the edge of the bed to pull on his socks and pants. He felt faintly ridiculous, heading home in yesterday's work clothes on the back of his bike. But it wasn't as though the world was watching.

Sierra shimmied into her jeans and pushed her feet into her sneakers, then they both exited the trailer together.

"You want me to grab one of Jed's jackets for the ride home? It's cold out, and I don't like the thought of you only having that shirt between you and the road," she said, combing her fingers through her hair, an adorable concerned furrow between her brows.

He dropped a kiss onto her mouth. "It's five minutes. I'll survive, I promise."

Also, he wasn't sure how Jed would feel about Garret borrowing his clothes. Years ago, they'd known and they'd liked each other. But that had been before the accident. Before guilt had made him keep his distance and grief had sent the Carmodys into retreat.

There were probably a few bridges to rebuild there, but he'd do whatever it took to make things work with Sierra. He knew without asking that her brothers were everything to her. He'd do his damnedest to get their approval.

He caught her hand, and she threw him a small smile as they made their way past the barn and out into the yard, only to pull up sharply at the sight of Casey and Jed inspecting his Ducati with patent masculine curiosity and appreciation.

They glanced in unison toward him and Sierra, taking in their joined hands and mussed hair and general morning-after glow. Then, almost in sync, they each squared their shoulders and tucked their fingers into the front pockets of their jeans, their faces carefully neutral.

It was almost funny.

"Morning," Garret said, dipping his head in a nod.

Jed and Casey responded with their own nods. Garret felt Sierra's shoulders lift as she took a breath, ready to wade in.

"I'm in love with your sister," Garret said. "Figured I'd get that out of the way, if you were wondering what my intentions are."

There was a moment of stunned stillness. Then Casey and Jed both did the nodding thing again. Jed stepped forward, hand extended.

"Good to see you. It's been a while," he said, his calloused hand closing strongly around Garret's.

"It has," Garret said.

Casey was next, his grip just as firm as Jed's. "Nice bike."

"Thanks. Don't get to ride it much these days," Garret said.

"What kind of horsepower do you get out of it?" Casey asked, turning to consider the Ducati.

"Ninety-two at eight thousand."

Both Jed and Casey whistled appreciatively. Sierra made a rude noise.

"Awesome. You guys enjoy your sausage fest. I've got to get ready for work." She turned to Garret. "See you soon."

Garret was conscious of her brothers watching, but it didn't stop him from kissing her goodbye. They all watched as she strode toward the house, her long legs eating up the distance.

"You're welcome to take it for a ride sometime," Garret

said, refocusing on Sierra's brothers.

"You're going to regret that," Jed said.

Casey eyed the bike with new interest. "Definitely gonna take you up on that."

"See what I mean?" Jed said.

"I gotta hustle now, but let Sierra know when you've got some free time and I'll bring it over," Garret said as he collected his helmet from where he'd left it on the bike seat overnight.

"Will do," Casey said.

"See you around," Jed said, stepping back as Garret slung his leg over the seat and put the keys into the ignition.

"You definitely will," Garret said.

The bike started with a throaty roar and he saw Casey's mouth stretch into a smile. No doubt anticipating the buzz of taking the Ducati for a spin. Garret lifted a hand, then put the bike into gear and opened the throttle.

Despite all the shit that had gone down last night, his heart was light as he turned out of the Carmody's driveway. He had Sierra. With her by his side, he could handle whatever else came his way.

The Ducati made short work of the three-mile drive to his parents' place. He left the bike running while he dismounted and went to open the garage door. He'd just switched the engine off and pulled off his helmet when he became aware of his mother standing in the side doorway.

"I was worried about you," she said. Her arms were crossed over her chest, her mouth tight.

Garret pocketed the bike keys and turned to face her. "I needed some space."

"Well, I didn't appreciate you storming off like a teenager when we were in the middle of an important discussion."

Garret lifted his eyebrows, incredulous that she was attempting to claim the moral high ground.

"Let's not fuck around," he said coolly. "You asked me to break the law if I had to in order to cover Dad's ass. That's not going to happen. Ever. Here's what is going to happen—I'm going to keep doing what I planned to do, which is to work with the accountant and our lawyers to find a way through this. I'm well aware, however, that the only authority I have at Tate Transport is through you. So, the ball's in your court, Mom. If you don't want to do it my way, I'll call off the hounds and walk away, and you can let Ron come back in and do whatever slippery, underhanded bullshit thing he usually does to cover his ass."

His mother blinked repeatedly throughout his speech, her shoulders getting tighter and tighter. "Well. That was lovely," she said. "What a charming way to start my day."

Garret counted to ten in his head. There were so many things he could say to her, but none of them were going to make this situation better.

"I need a shower." He headed for the house.

"So you're walking out on me again?" his mother said.

He stopped in his tracks, goaded despite himself. "I figured it was better than pointing out the hypocrisy of you clutching your pearls over a four-letter word while simultaneously asking me to commit corporate fraud. But if you want to have that conversation, I'm more than up for it. Let's go. Your serve."

It took his mother a moment to speak. "I was shocked

last night. I panicked."

He nodded. "Okay. Does that mean you want me to stay on at Tate, or would you like to give Ron a call?"

His mother's chin wobbled. "Garret, please. Don't be like this."

"You made it this way, Mom. I'm just playing by your rules. Think about what you want to do and let me know by the end of the day."

"I don't need to think. There's no way I'm giving Ron control of the business."

Despite everything, her answer made his shoulders drop a notch. As much as he hated being stuck in the middle of the mess his father had made, the thought of handing everything over to Ron the Rat made him want to punch a hole in something.

"All right. I'll keep you posted on whatever comes to light."

"I'd appreciate that." She reached out and touched his forearm, her face furrowed with regret. "I really was worried about you last night."

He softened. "I just needed to let off some steam."

She nodded. "Well, I don't want to hold you up."

Normally he'd kiss his mother at a moment like this, go out of his way to reassure her. This morning, he couldn't do it. Not because he wanted to punish her, but because it wouldn't be sincere. He was still angry and hurt. It would pass, but it was going to take time.

He settled for offering her a small smile before heading to the house for a shower.

Thirty minutes later, he was striding toward the helicopter, his mouth stretching into a smile at the prospect of spending an hour with Sierra.

She wasn't in or around the Bell, so he ducked his head into the hangar and spotted her at the desk, making notes in a large book.

"Please tell me that's your captain's log," he said.

She looked up, her green eyes bright with pleasure. "Just the maintenance log. Nothing very exciting. Sorry."

"Are we on the clock yet?" he asked.

She glanced out the door to where the Bell sat on the landing pad. "Technically, yes."

"I'm sensing there's some wiggle room."

"There may be a small window of opportunity where my willpower is not equal to how hot you look in that suit," she admitted.

That was enough for him. He closed the distance between them and leaned over to kiss her good morning. She tasted of minty toothpaste, and he could smell the lemony freshness of her shampoo. He wanted more, but when he tried to deepen the kiss the wheeled chair she was sitting in started to roll backward, and he felt her lips curve against his as she started to laugh.

"This chair is officially now my enemy," he said, lifting his head.

"It's definitely got strong feelings about public displays of affection." She smiled at him, her cheeks pink, her mouth still damp from his kisses.

"Okay." He took a big step backward. "Time to close the window of opportunity or that chair is going to be really offended by my next move."

"Plus you'll be late for work," she pointed out.

"God forbid."

She stood and returned the maintenance log to the desk drawer. Then she reached up and adjusted the knot on his tie minutely. "Was a little crooked."

"Thank you."

He wanted to kiss her again, but he could see she'd already started thinking about the flight ahead so he simply followed her out to the helicopter and handed her his briefcase to stow.

"You don't have to sit up front if you've got work to do," she said. "I won't be offended."

"I can work anytime. Right now, I'm with you," he said.

She smiled ruefully and shook her head, sending her ponytail swinging. "Stop making it so hard for me to stick to my rules, Garret Tate."

He climbed into the front seat and watched with quiet admiration as she went through her preflight routine and fired the engine up. He waited until her concentration relaxed before asking about her plans for the day and they talked and laughed for the next forty minutes until they were approaching the Helena airport. Again, he fell silent, letting her do her thing. Respecting that this was her workplace.

He waited until she was handing him his briefcase on the tarmac before shifting to the personal again.

"I'd like to take you out for dinner tonight. Someplace nice."

"Oh. Okay." She frowned. "That sounds lovely."

"You don't want to go out for dinner?" he asked, trying to interpret the frown.

"No. I'm just going to have to get creative with my wardrobe. Or do a little shopping. Which, to be fair, is probably well overdue."

"Take the afternoon off. I've stolen enough of your evenings making you pull overnighters. Check out the city."

"I might just do that. Or at least finish an hour or so early. I'm not that big on shopping, but if I go in on a search and destroy mission with a specific goal in mind, I'm good."

"Do I get a vote on what the goal of this mission might be?" he asked.

She tilted her head. "Are you about to make a special request?"

"Not necessarily. But I feel honor bound to point out that you have amazing legs," he said.

She laughed, her eyes very green. "I'll keep that in mind."

"Is seven okay?" he said.

"Seven is perfect," she said.

He took a step backward. "I'll be thinking about you."

"I'll be thinking about you too."

He smiled and shook his head at the look in her eyes, and then he turned and strode toward the car. Given a choice, he'd choose to stay at the airport and flirt with Sierra all day over the many meetings he had today.

Pulling on his seat belt, he started the car and reversed out of the parking bay. Then he drove off to do what he had to do.

SIERRA HADN'T BEEN shopping in months but she knew the

moment she entered the small Macy's store in downtown Helena that they were not going to have the sort of dress she was looking for. Sure enough, a quick tour of the compact womenswear section confirmed her suspicion. She chewed on her bottom lip for a second, then inspiration struck and she pulled out her phone.

She found Mae Barringer's number in her address book and sent her a quick text asking for her best suggestion for shopping for a cocktail dress. She figured anyone who owned a pair of Louboutins must know where to shop in Helena. Two seconds later, her phone lit up with a call from Mae.

"Sorry, I had to call. My texting skills aren't up to this conversation," Mae said.

"As long as I'm not interrupting anything."

"The numbers will wait, trust me. What sort of occasion are we talking here?"

"Dinner at a nice restaurant." Sierra hesitated. "I'm thinking something fun. Maybe even something a bit sexy?"

Tonight would be the first time she and Garret ventured out as a couple, the first night that wasn't about seeking refuge from the stress of what was happening with his family business or wrestling with their doubts about the wisdom of giving in to what they both wanted.

Tonight was just about enjoying each other, and Sierra was determined to do her bit to make that happen because she understood Garret needed a safe place in his life right now. An oasis where he could stop and draw breath and recharge before returning to the field of battle.

"I'm going to text you the address of the best boutique in Helena," Mae said with absolute authority. "The owner,

Chloe, is a friend of mine, and she will hook you up. Trust her. She knows bodies; she knows fabrics; she just *knows*."

"Okay. Happy to put myself in anyone's hands, really. Shopping is the devil's work, and anything that makes it easier can only be a good thing."

"Hush your mouth, Sierra," Mae admonished. "Shopping is a sacred and mysterious art."

"Not when I do it. Thanks for lending me your expertise. I owe you."

"Anytime. And I mean that. I'm a little slammed at the moment, but when I can see some daylight, let's catch up for lunch like we said."

"Definitely. Let me know when you've got a free hour and I'm there," Sierra said.

"I will. You're going to have a good time at my friend's shop, Sierra." Mae made it sound like both a threat and a promise as she ended the call.

Seconds later an address arrived with a bright electronic chime, along with a link to a map. Clearly, Sierra had consulted the right person.

The map app on her phone told her it was a ten-minute walk to Mae's friend's boutique, so she exited Macy's and headed back toward the center of town. She found Little Black Dress down a side street in the historic center of Helena. The window was full of beautiful things artfully arranged, and Sierra squelched a surge of panic as she pushed the door open. Small shops like this were usually her kryptonite. Half the time she wound up buying something she didn't really like or want simply because she didn't want to disappoint the sales assistant.

But Mae had said her friend would hook her up, and Mae was brilliant and beautifully dressed, so Sierra took a deep breath and smiled as the woman behind the counter turned toward her. In her fifties with sleek black hair that fell in a perfect curtain to her shoulders and dark brown eyes lined with black cat's eye eyeliner, she was more striking than beautiful and she lit up when she saw Sierra.

"You're Mae's friend," she said. "I'm Chloe. Pleased to meet you."

She sailed out from behind the counter and Sierra took in her elegant wide-legged black pants paired with towering black ankle boots and a creamy silk blouse. It struck her that despite not being conventionally beautiful, Chloe was *sexy*, and Sierra decided right there and then to let go of her nervousness and put herself in the other woman's hands.

"I'm Sierra, and I apologize in advance for being one of those annoying customers who doesn't really know what she's looking for," she said with a grimace.

Chloe was already studying her with an expert eye, sizing her up. "Darling, I could dress you in a hessian feed sack and you'd still be beautiful. Thankfully, we can do a little bit better than that. Mae said you were looking for a cocktail dress, something suitable for a nice dinner out?"

"That's right. Maybe something above the knee. If you think that would be appropriate?" Sierra asked uncertainly.

Chloe smiled, her deep red lipstick a sharp contrast with her white teeth. "With legs like yours it would be a crime if it wasn't above the knee. Let me pull a few dresses for you."

The next hour passed in a blur. Sierra tried on four dresses before pulling on a deceptively simple halter-neck dress made from a shimmering honey-colored fabric. It felt amazing on her skin as it slithered down her body, ending a good two inches above her knees, and when she turned to check the mirror she literally gasped out loud.

"Now that's the sound I love to hear," Chloe said from the other side of the change room door. "Care to share?"

Sierra pushed the door open and stepped out into the larger dressing area. A huge floor-to-ceiling mirror with a baroque gilt frame leaned against wall and Sierra stared in wonder at the woman reflected there.

"Oh, yes, that's the one," Chloe said with a happy sigh. "This color on your skin tone is sublime. And you have the body to pull it off, if you don't mind me saying so."

Sierra shook her head, still feeling a little dazed. She'd never been self-conscious about her body, but she'd never been the type of woman who held her shoulders back to draw attention to her boobs or bent over in short-shorts either. But this dress . . . this dress was sex in fabric form. This dress made her breasts look perky and round. It draped over her hips, hugged her butt, and slinked around her thighs when she walked. This dress made her feel like a vixen and a sex goddess and an international assassin all at once.

"Okay. Well, I think I have my dress," she said.

"Do we need to talk shoes? And how about lingerie? Because this dress is definitely going to require a thong. And no bra, of course."

"Of course," Sierra agreed, even though she hadn't been out in public without a bra for ten years. "Shoes would be good. And lingerie."

What the hell. It had been months since she bought new

clothes, and it wouldn't hurt to indulge herself a little. Just this once.

By the time she left the store she'd also bought a pair of strappy gold sandals and a tiny scrap of lace that was masquerading as underwear. Really, she couldn't see the difference between wearing it and going commando, but she knew Garret would like it.

She took a cab to the lake house and practiced walking in her strappy new shoes, then soaked in the big tub. She shaved her legs and shampooed her hair, then spent far too long drying and fussing with it until it tumbled in big, loose curls down her back. She heard the front door open and close at around six thirty, and she rubbed moisturizer into her legs, spritzed on perfume, finished her makeup, and shimmied into her new barely there underwear. She checked the effect in the mirror and laughed out loud at how decadent she looked. Yep, Garret was definitely going to love these panties.

She waited until the last possible moment to slip the dress over her head. Chloe had lent her a black cashmere shawl and a small black clutch purse—"just drop them by the store when you can, darling"—and she collected them both before making her way down the stairs, patting herself on the back all the way for having had the foresight to practice in her new shoes.

Garret was waiting in the entrance hall when she arrived, and his reaction to the dress was everything she could have asked for and more. He'd obviously heard the click-clack of her heels and was smiling as she arrived, but the expression froze on his face as he got an eyeful of her dress, to be replaced by a dazed, glazed-eyed look she could only describe as pure lust.

"Sierra." He took a step toward her, both hands out-stretched.

"No," she said, holding up her hand, palm facing him. Because she knew what would happen if he laid a finger on her right now. They'd miss their dinner reservation and wind up eating frozen pizza in their bathrobes. As inviting as that sounded, she'd spent two hours shaving and dicking around with her hair, not to mention the money she'd dropped on the dress.

"I promise you can touch me as much as you want later," she said. "But we will never leave this house if you do what you want to do right now."

Garret shook his head as though he was shaking off the effects of strong drink. "You're right. We need to go. But baby . . . that dress is something else. It ought to come with its own personal defibrillator."

"I thought you'd like it."

"Like doesn't even come close. Can I just touch you here?" He hovered his hand near her hip.

"One little touch," she said.

His warm hand landed on her hip, smoothing down the silk, and she felt the tremor of reaction go through his body.

"Holy shit. I don't think I'm going to be able to make it through dinner."

She laughed. "Be good, and I'll let you touch me again when we reach the restaurant."

"Define *good* for me," he said, taking her shawl and drap-ing it over her shoulders.

"You know what good is," she said, shooting him a look over her shoulder.

She sashayed toward the front door, and Garret made a frustrated animal sound before following her.

"Am I allowed to know where we're going?" she asked as they walked to the car.

Garret moved ahead of her to open the door for her. It had been a long time since she'd been on the kind of date where a man pulled out all the stops, and even though she was essentially a no-fuss, no-muss kind of girl, she had to admit it was nice to feel like a princess for a few hours.

"I asked around and Lucca's came highly recommended. Hope you like Italian."

"I *love* Italian," she said as she climbed into the car, very conscious of the shortness of her dress.

She told him about Chloe and her store and how Mae had hooked her up during the drive to the restaurant and didn't bother hiding her smile every time she felt the heat of his gaze sliding down her legs.

"So, did I pass the test?" Garret asked after he'd pulled into a parking spot near the restaurant and turned off the engine. "Was I good enough?"

"You were *so* good," Sierra said. She reached over to take his hand and brought it back to her thigh. She pressed her own hand over the top and encouraged him to slide higher.

"Baby," he groaned, his fingers digging into her flesh as he battled for self-control.

"Later. I promise," she said.

Garret muttered something under his breath and flung open the car door. Sierra laughed to herself, enjoying the small moment of sexual power.

Turned out it was a lot of fun being a vixen, even if it was just for the night.

Chapter Eighteen

THE RESTAURANT WAS rustic and charming, and their table was tucked into a private corner lit with flickering candlelight. They agreed that garlic bread was a must, then gorged themselves on the best spaghetti carbonara Sierra had ever eaten, laughing as they talked about favorite movies, shared memories from high school, and disaster stories from Garret's college years. At some point he reached across to capture her hand and they wound up eating their food one-handed, unwilling to relinquish each other's touch. For dessert they shared an insanely delicious square of tiramisu, dueling with each other for the final bite.

"No fair," she cried when he finally knocked her spoon away and scooped up the prize.

"To the victor goes the spoils," he said, swallowing the small mouthful with ostentatious relish.

Sierra made a big show out of wiping the corners of her mouth with her napkin before pushing to her feet and collecting her purse. "Well. If you'll excuse me for a moment, Mr. Spoils."

She could feel him watching her as she made her way to the bathroom. Once there, she checked her hair, tucking a few strands behind her ears before wiping away a smudge of mascara beneath her eye. She redid her lipstick, then retreated to a stall to take care of business. She opened her purse while she was sitting there, eyeing the small decorative box she'd slipped inside at the last moment before coming downstairs.

It was the fancy packaging for her barely there underwear, and the idea to reuse it had popped into her head while she was soaking in the bath earlier in the afternoon. At the time she'd laughed out loud at her own audacity. Now, she wondered if she had the courage to go through with her sexy scheme.

Then she remembered the way Garret had shivered when he ran his hand over her hip earlier and knew she had to. It would drive him crazy, in the best possible way, and she wanted to push him, wanted to make him forget all the crappy, stressful things in his life for a few minutes. They deliberately hadn't talked about his family or work over dinner. This bubble they were in—this sensual, love-filled bubble—was the best thing in his life right now, and she was about to take it to the next level.

Business finished, she flushed, then balanced one hand against the wall as she carefully stepped out of her panties. Then she folded them neatly and nestled them back into the hot-pink tissue inside the box. She stifled a nervous laugh as she tucked the box into her purse.

She held her own eyes in the mirror as she washed and dried her hands, daring herself to go through with it. Then she stepped out into the restaurant.

It had been bad enough getting used to being braless for

the evening, but feeling the cool wash of air around her lady parts as she made her way back to the table was more than a little disconcerting. If she tripped, or a rogue breeze suddenly blew up out of nowhere, she wouldn't have many secrets from the other diners in this fancy schmancy restaurant.

It'll be worth it. He'll love it.

The thought kept her head high as she approached the table. Garret's gaze was warm as she slipped back into her seat.

"I ordered coffee," he said.

"It's not like we were planning on sleeping, right?" she said with a smirk.

He laughed, and she reached into her purse and pulled out the box.

"A little something for you," she said, sliding it across the table toward him.

He cocked an eyebrow and tilted his head. "Should I guess or just open it?"

"I don't think you'll be able to guess what it is. But you're welcome to try."

"Now I feel challenged. But just to prove I take instruction well . . ." He lifted the lid on the box and folded back the pink tissue paper inside.

She watched as comprehension dawned on his face.

"Did you just . . ." He made a gesture in the air with his hand, inviting her to fill in the blank.

"I did."

"So you're not wearing anything under that dress right now?" he clarified.

"Does perfume count?"

His hand shot into the air, his gaze searching for the maître d'. "Check, please."

He looked so intense, so urgent, Sierra had to stifle a laugh behind her fingers.

"Laugh it up. Wait till we get to the car," he said, his gaze flicking down her body with hungry intent.

Sierra shifted on the seat, conscious of her own rising desire. She loved how much he wanted her. Loved that he was just as obsessed with the magic they created when they were skin to skin as she was.

And he loved her.

He *loved* her, this kind, thoughtful, funny, sexy, strong, compelling man.

If that wasn't like winning the lottery times a million, she didn't know what was.

The check arrived in a discreet leather folder and minutes later they were headed for the door, Garret's hand a burning brand on her lower back as he guided her onto the street.

He held the car door open for her, his gaze avid as she slid into the seat.

"See anything you like?" she asked.

"You're in so much trouble, Carmody," was his reply.

He didn't say anything as he got into the driver's seat, just put his seat belt on, started the car, and pulled away from the curb. She could feel the tension in him and she wasn't surprised when he turned down a side road once they'd left the bright lights of Helena. He drove for a minute or so, then turned again into a small parking area in what she guessed was some sort of nature reserve.

He braked hard enough to generate a spurt of gravel,

then he switched the car off and turned to her.

"Get over here," he said, pushing his seat back as far as it would go.

She didn't need a second invitation, eagerly clambering over the center console and into his lap. She'd barely got a knee either side of him before his hands were sweeping up her thighs and under her dress to cup her bare backside.

"Sierra . . . You drive me crazy," he said, his voice low and needy.

"Same. I've been thinking about you all day. Thinking about your cock. Having you inside me."

His fingers clenched her ass cheeks as he pulled her forward, crushing her mouth in a greedy, take-no-prisoners kiss. She met him tongue stroke for tongue stroke, shivering with delight when he slipped one hand between her thighs to where she needed him the most.

She was so wired, so aroused, it only took a few deft strokes of his clever fingers to send her over the top. She arched into him, shuddering with pleasure, and he swore under his breath. She felt him fumble at his pants, and she lifted helpfully out of the way, wanting his cock desperately now. He was very hard and thick and she took him in hand and slid down over him with a rasping groan.

"How can anything feel this good?" he asked in between trailing kisses down her neck.

"It's a miracle. Or the best trick evolution ever played on us," Sierra said.

He pulled the bodice of her dress out of the way and tongued her nipples, bringing them to hard peaks with teasing licks before sucking with urgent intensity. Sierra closed her eyes and gripped his shoulders as she rode him, reveling in how full she felt, concentrating on the delicious friction of his cock against her swollen flesh. She could tell he was getting closer, could feel the urgency in him, the way his muscles had turned to granite. His hands tilted her hips and guided her up and down, up and down. He did something on each downward stroke, a swivel of his hips—something *extra*—that made it even better for her and suddenly she was there again, coming with his name in her mouth, her breath sawing in and out of her lungs in frantic gusts.

She collapsed against him afterward, floppy and useless, her face pressed into the place where his neck became his shoulder. His hand slid onto the nape of her neck and they simply breathed together for several minutes, their bodies cooling. Finally she lifted her head and smiled at his flushed face and heavy eyes.

"So, I guess I have a new favorite restaurant," she said.

Garret laughed, the sound loose and free and loud, and she couldn't not kiss him. Then she slithered back to her side of the car and put her seat belt on.

"Take me home and let's do that all over again," she said.

"Sierra Carmody, you are full of good ideas tonight."

He took her hand as he pulled back onto the road and Sierra couldn't remember the last time she'd felt so purely, simply happy.

As if he could sense her thoughts, Garret lifted their joined hands and pressed a kiss to the back of her hand.

"How do you feel about putting those panties back on so I can take them off you again? Slowly. With my teeth."

She laughed. "Knew you'd like them."

"Like? They're going to have to invent a new word for how I feel."

He gave her a long, steady look and she shifted in her seat. Lucky they were almost home, and that they had all night, because she could not get enough of this man and the way he made her feel.

SOMETIME AFTER THREE in the morning, Garret wrote a quick email to Mandy on his phone, Sierra curled sleepily against his side, explaining he probably wouldn't land at the office until nine thirty tomorrow morning.

He had no appointments, and he'd been working around the clock since he started. He deserved a few hours of downtime with the woman he loved.

Instead of rushing into work tomorrow, he was going to wake up at a civilized hour and cook Sierra pancakes and make her some kick-ass coffee.

Then he was going to make love to her on the kitchen counter. Or maybe the dining room table. He hadn't decided yet, but he was confident inspiration would strike.

He fell asleep with the tantalizing image of Sierra spread across the dining room table in his mind, his arm wrapped tightly around her torso, breathing in the scent of her shampoo.

He shot awake several hours later, startled out of deep sleep by a sound he couldn't immediately identify. It took him a couple of seconds to recognize the noise echoing through the house as the sound of the doorbell.

Rubbing his eyes, he reached for his phone. Eight in the morning. Who the hell was on his front doorstep at that hour?

"What's going on?" Sierra murmured, pushing her hair out of her eyes.

God, he loved how sleepy and messy she looked in the morning.

He leaned down to kiss her. "Won't be a second. Someone's at the door."

He pulled on last night's pants and zipped up on the way out the door. He ran a hand through his hair and yawned as he entered the entrance hall. Man, last night had been crazy in the best possible way.

Fully expecting to find a lost cab driver or delivery man on the doorstep, he opened the door to find himself facing a phalanx of grim-faced men and women wearing the navy blue of law enforcement. A sandy-haired guy with a goatee and a navy cap featuring a police shield stepped forward.

"Garret Tate?"

It took him a moment to get enough air into his lungs to respond. "Yes."

"Detective Green, DA's office. I have a warrant to search these premises for any business papers or business-related files or computers associated with Tate Transport in relation to an ongoing investigation into charges of commercial bribery under section 15A of the Business Integrity Act."

Garret's mind was completely blank. The cold morning air was like a slap against his exposed skin, but his brain seemed stuck in neutral. There were things a person was supposed to do in circumstances like this, right? Should he call his lawyer?

He stared at the closely typed warrant the man had handed him, then shook his head.

The movement seemed to help, his brain coming sluggishly back online. He didn't have the expertise to challenge or block the warrant. The best thing he could do right now was cooperate.

And, yeah, call his lawyer.

"I'll show you where the study is," he said, stepping back.

"That would be appreciated. I'm going to need you to hand over your laptop computer and phone also."

Garret was acutely aware of his bare chest and feet as the investigators filed into the house, fanning out to inspect the rooms.

"I'm going to need the phone to call my lawyer," he said.

"You'll have to use a landline," Detective Green said, his tone calmly implacable.

Garret was about to say more when he noticed one of the investigators turning into the hallway that led to the bedrooms.

Where Sierra was still lying naked in his bed.

"Hey. Wait a minute," he said, taking off after the guy. "You need you to back up a minute. My girlfriend's in there."

The investigator paused, throwing a look over his shoulder toward Detective Green, clearly checking to see if he should heed Garret's request or not.

"You guys aren't barging in there before she's had a chance to dress," Garret said, ready to go to the mat on the issue. No way was he standing by while a bunch of cops barged in on Sierra.

Detective Green called into the kitchen. "Whitehead. You want to come help us out for a minute?"

Seconds later a young blond-haired policewoman joined them, eyebrows raised in query.

"I'm going to need you to chaperone Mr. Tate's girlfriend while she dresses," Detective Green said.

"Not a problem," the woman said before turning to Garret, her expression expectant.

Garret brushed past the first investigator and strode toward his bedroom, aware of the woman following hard on his heels. He could hear his phone ringing as he entered the room, and was relieved to find Sierra sitting on the bed wearing last night's dress with one of his business shirts buttoned up over the top, her eyes huge with worry.

"Are you okay? What's happening? I heard all the voices . . ."

"It's the DA with a search warrant," he said, and her eyes widened briefly for a moment before shooting across to the silent woman watching them from the doorway.

His phone stopped ringing just as he grabbed it from the bedside table.

"I'm going to need to write down my lawyer's number from the contact list," he told the investigator.

His phone rang again before she could respond. Caller ID told him it was Mandy, and he took the call, whether he was allowed to or not. They could argue the finer points of their search warrant with him afterward.

"Garret, thank god. The place is swarming with DA investigators. They have a warrant, they want access to all the servers, all our files . . ." Mandy's voice was high with panic and urgency.

"They just arrived here at the house. They're about to take my phone, so I'm going to need you to call Alec Stone and fill him in on what's happening. He's a lawyer. His card is in the top left drawer of my desk." He'd only met with the man yesterday. Garret hoped he was as good as Mae claimed he was. "Then I'm going to call you back from the landline in about five minutes, okay?" He was doing his utmost to sound calm even though his heart was going a mile a minute.

"All right. I'll call Mr. Stone now."

He could hear Mandy pulling herself together, making an effort to match his calm.

"Thank you. I'll be there as soon as I can be," he assured her.

"Okay. Good."

Garret ended the call. Out of the corner of his eye, he could see the policewoman stepping forward, her hand extended.

"I'm going to need you to hand your phone over now, sir," she said.

Garret ignored her, toggling to the recent calls menu. The odds were good the call he'd missed as he entered was Mandy and that she'd hit redial immediately when he hadn't answered, but it was better to be safe than sorry.

He stared when he saw the missed call had been from his mother.

It hit him then that the DA had probably raided his parents' home in Marietta this morning, too, as well as the lake house and Tate Transport headquarters.

Of course they had—they couldn't risk missing vital evidence, and the only way to ensure that was simultaneous raids.

Jesus, his mother must be beside herself.

"Sir. You need to hand over your phone," the policewoman demanded.

Garret passed over the phone wordlessly.

"Here, Garret," Sierra said.

He turned and saw she was fumbling in her purse. She pulled out her own phone and handed it to him.

"Thanks."

He dialed and his mother picked up on the second ring.

"Hello?" Her voice sound thin and shaky. Shocked.

"Mom, it's me. I'm calling from Sierra's phone because the police have taken mine."

"Oh, god, Garret. I didn't know what to do. I'm still in my bathrobe. They just pushed their way in . . ."

"I know, Mom. They've got a warrant. There's nothing you could have done to stop them. I assume they're in Dad's study?"

"Yes. I told them he never keeps any work things here. It was all on his laptop, and you've been using that."

"I know. Just stay calm. They'll be gone soon. I'll be talking to the lawyer any minute now, but I need to get into the office. If you need anything, call this number, okay? Or Mandy at the office."

"All right. I will." He heard his mother take a shaky breath. "Garret . . . I'm so sorry. If I had any idea this was going to happen, I wouldn't have landed you in any of this."

He pressed his lips together. She'd had some idea.

Enough of an idea to urge him to step in and take over when Ron was the logical choice of interim CEO in the short term.

But now was not the time to get into any of that.

"I'll call you later, Mom."

He ended the call, very conscious of the silent presence of the policewoman. No doubt she was noting everything he said and did. He had nothing to hide, but that didn't stop him from feeling guilty. Hunted.

"You should get dressed," Sierra said.

It was the logical next step and he shot her a grateful glance.

"You too. Head back to your room and we can meet in the kitchen," he said, taking both her hands in his. They were cold, but she squeezed his hands firmly.

"I won't be a second." She squeezed his hands one last time before letting go and moving toward the door.

"Excuse me, ma'am." The blonde moved to block her path. "I'm going to need to escort you to your room and check to ensure you don't have access to any computers or other devices covered by the warrant."

"Sierra is my pilot," Garret bit out. "She's got nothing to do with any of this."

The woman's face remained stolidly determined, and Sierra caught his eye and gave a minute shake of her head.

"It's okay. I'll be back soon."

She exited, the blonde following her, and he'd barely been alone a second before another investigator stepped through the doorway to take her place.

Of course. He needed to be supervised, too, in case he decided to start trying to destroy all the evidence hidden in his sock drawer.

"Okay with you if I get dressed?" he asked, gesturing toward the walk-in closet.

The investigator moved forward, giving the closet a quick scan before nodding his agreement. "Go right ahead, Mr. Tate." The words were polite, but there was a hard, contemptuous glint in the other man's eyes.

Clearly he thought Garret was the kind of rich corrupt asshole who went around bribing people to get what he wanted and that this morning's raid was the very least of his just deserts.

Get used to that.

Because this was just the tip of the iceberg. There were going to be a lot of people casting a lot of judgments before this was over.

He dressed as calmly as he could, trying to ignore how much his heart was racing, the tightness across his shoulders. When he stepped back into the bedroom he was in full corporate armor, which felt a hell of a lot better than being commando in last night's wrinkled pants.

He headed for the kitchen to find the landline. Sierra joined him just as he picked up the receiver, dressed in her usual navy polo and khakis, her hair pulled into a hasty ponytail.

"What can I do?" she asked.

"I don't know yet. Let me call Mandy. Then I'm probably going to need to head into the office and do what I can in there." He shot a look toward the huddle of investigators conferring with each other in the doorway to the dining room. He had no idea how long they'd be here at the house, and he hated the idea of leaving them to search without being present, but he couldn't be in two places at once.

"I can stay here, keep an eye on all of this," Sierra said, and he slipped his arm around her shoulders and pressed a kiss to her temple.

"Thank you. I'm so fucking sorry you're in the middle of all this." He meant it from the bottom of his soul. Even though having her here helped ground him, he hated that she'd been exposed to all this ugliness.

"You have nothing to apologize for, Garret. Okay?" she said.

Her green eyes were steady and clear as they held his own, and after a second he nodded.

"Sorry, I really need to make this call."

"You do that. I'm going to make us some toast, even though neither of us probably feels very hungry right now, because this might be the only chance you're going to have to eat all day."

She crossed to the freezer to extract a loaf of bread, and he watched her for a moment, seized with a fierce, hot gratitude that he knew her, that she was part of his life. Then he dialed the office and waited until Mandy picked up.

"Tell me where we're at," he said.

He listened as she explained the investigators were concentrating on his and Ron's offices, as well as the IT department. A whole team of investigators were down there, she said, helping themselves to the company's servers.

"What about Alec?" he said.

"I couldn't get a hold of him. His secretary said he had a breakfast meeting, and his calls are going through to voice mail. She's going to get him to call back the second she hears from him."

Garret sighed and rubbed the back of his neck. "Okay. I'm going to be leaving here in ten minutes or so. Call this number if anything comes up before then."

"Sure, like the building collapsing. Something small like that," Mandy said, her tone bone dry.

It took Garret a moment to realize she was joking and he huffed out a surprised laugh. "Yeah, like that."

"Drive carefully."

He set down the receiver just as Sierra handed him a plateful of toast.

"Eat," she encouraged, ushering him onto one of the stools at the island counter.

Garret dutifully took a mouthful of peanut butter toast, chewing mechanically. His thoughts were ricocheting in a million different directions at once. He needed to talk to Mae. He needed to talk to David. He was about to take another bite of toast when another thought occurred to him.

"What?" Sierra asked.

"Just wondering if this is happening at Ron's place too."

"I hope so. Seems only fair."

"Yeah." He finished his first piece of toast and moved on to the second, thinking about how his phone must be blowing up with missed calls and texts.

"I'll call you when they're done here. I'm assuming we're going to be staying the night here again?" Sierra asked.

He finished chewing the last bite of his toast before responding. "We are. Sorry if that screws up your plans."

"You are my plans," she said simply. "Don't worry about

me."

He collected her plate along with his own and put them both in the dishwasher. Then he pulled her into his arms and pressed his cheek against hers. She smelled like last night's perfume and peanut butter, and for just a second the world slowed and he could breathe again.

He forced himself to pull back and kissed her goodbye quickly, resenting the many strangers in his home all over again.

"Call me when you can," she said.

"I will."

Chapter Nineteen

H E LET DETECTIVE Green know he was leaving, then made the twenty-minute drive into work, his body vibrating with adrenaline. The police presence was profound when he turned onto the street where the Tate Transport headquarters was situated—he counted no less than five cars, in addition to a couple of vans.

Belatedly it occurred to him that the press were going to be all over this. There was no way no one had noticed all the unusual police activity.

He parked beneath the building and took the elevator to his office level, walking into an unnaturally hushed atmosphere. The receptionist blinked rapidly when she saw him and he realized her eyes were red from crying. Having a squad full of law enforcement personnel descend on your workplace unexpectedly had to be a pretty upsetting and shocking experience.

He stopped to have a quick, reassuring word, then made his way to his office, where he found Mandy watching two DA investigators sort through files on his desk.

It was hard not to bristle, even harder not to say anything. But the only reason any of this was happening was because of actions his father and Ron had taken. Actions Garret still didn't have a good handle on. There was no merit in getting punchy about anything or pushing back—the sooner these people found what they were looking for, the sooner he could get them off the premises and dive into damage control.

Since his office had been commandeered, he set himself up in the meeting room and had IT bring him a spare laptop to work on. The next few hours of his life were a nightmare of calls from clients, his new lawyer, Mae, his business partners in Seattle, and his mother.

True to form, Jay and Marco rejected his offer to hand back his share in the business, effective immediately, in order to spare them from being dragged into his mess.

"We'll weather the storm. We always do. Call us if you need to scream into the void. And if you need hands on deck, we'll be in Montana ASAP, okay?" Jay had said.

It was a measure of how stressed he was that their unwavering loyalty only made him feel worse. It felt like he was sitting behind the wheel of a runaway bus full of passengers, and he had no idea what was going to be around the next corner.

By lunchtime his head was aching and there was still no sign of the DA's office being done with their very thorough ransacking of the office. Needing to clear his head, he decided to take a five-minute walk around the block. Maybe the exercise and fresh air would loosen the vise gripping his skull.

He was rubbing the back of his neck and circling his shoulders when he exited the building, only to stop in his tracks when a glossy redheaded TV journalist blocked his path, a microphone in her outstretched hand.

"Mr. Tate, do you have any comment on the revelation that the district attorney is investigating Tate Transport for multiple instances of commercial bribery?"

A cameraman loomed over her shoulder, the black eye of a video camera recording his instinctive flinch. The flash of yet another camera drew his attention to half a dozen other journalists waiting to pounce. He recognized insignias from the local paper as well as a cable station and local radio.

He had no idea what to say, how to respond. He felt like a felled wildebeest surrounded by jackals, and every instinct shrieked for him to hold up a hand to block the camera and scuttle back into the building.

Somewhere in the back of his brain, a voice cautioned that running away would only make him look guilty. He knew that voice was right, that he needed to stand his ground. So he willed his feet to stay exactly where they were and lifted his chin to meet the glossy journalist's sharp gaze.

"I have no comment at this time, but Tate Transport will be issuing a statement shortly."

"We understand you've only recently stepped into the business after your father, Gideon Tate, suffered a severe stroke. Has the DA indicated they'll be pushing for charges against your father despite his poor health?"

He blinked, not ready for that one, and forced his face to return to neutral.

"As I said, a statement will be forthcoming as soon as we have more information."

He nodded once, then turned on his heel and walked

back into the building. He didn't breathe again until the elevator doors had closed behind him.

This was a nightmare. Tate Transport was going to be all over the news. Their clients were going to freak, especially once they got wind of the charges the DA was investigating. Every single one of their clients was going to be pulling out their contracts and invoices, going over every line item with a magnifying glass.

For a moment Garret closed his eyes, panic tightening his chest and clamping his throat. His belly felt as though it was full of cement, his legs as heavy as lead. Then he felt the elevator braking as it reached his floor, and he forced his eyes open and sucked in air.

He couldn't afford to freak out. He had people who were looking to him to set an example and lead them through this mess. He had to look as though he knew what he was doing, even if he was really just acting his fucking ass off.

The doors opened with a ping, and he gave the receptionist an acknowledging nod before making his way to the meeting room. Mandy entered seconds later looking relieved. "The lead investigator just told me they're taking a final inventory. They should be leaving in half an hour."

"Good. Call Alec Stone and Mae Barringer and let them know. I want a full roundtable with them as soon as possible. And send an email around to everyone and warn them that if they need to leave the building, they should use the rear exit. There are a bunch of reporters camped on our doorstep."

Mandy's eyes widened. "I'll get right on it."

She hotfooted it back to her office, and Garret hit the space bar to bring his computer back to life. A quick search brought up the first news item about the raid.

It had been filed by the local paper just twenty minutes ago and featured a PR shot of a Tate Transport truck with the familiar red-and-blue logo emblazoned on the side. *Local Transport Business under Investigation for Commercial Bribery.* There wasn't much to the story, just a few paragraphs explaining the DA had raided the building this morning as part of an ongoing corruption inquiry. There were a couple of lines covering his father's stroke and Garret's entry into the business. His coffee start-up in Seattle was referenced in a way that made it sound like a trust fund kid's hobby instead of a genuine, thriving business. He groaned when he saw the photo they'd placed at the end of the story. He was standing next to a bikini-clad model at a crowded party, a cocktail glass in hand, his smile confident and wide. He looked the epitome of a rich, privileged douche. In other words, exactly the kind of guy who'd be involved in sleazy deals to seek advantage for his father's business.

Where the hell had they dug that photo up from? He couldn't even remember when it had been taken. Two years ago? Three? He knew it had been at a supplier's Christmas party in Seattle, and that he'd smiled when it had been his turn to have his photo taken with the bikini girl because he hadn't wanted to offend his host, even though he'd felt sorry for the poor woman, given it had been near freezing outside.

Mandy appeared in the doorway. "Roundtable at two. Mae mentioned she has a friend who works in crisis management. She wondered if you'd like her to bring him along?"

"Great idea. Thanks, Mandy."

He clicked on the next story. This one featured a picture of his father on the golf course, his arm around the shoulders of a local politician. Oh, yeah, that was a *great* look.

For a moment, he wanted nothing more than to punch his father's smugly smiling image. Instead, he shut the browser window. There was going to be a lot of garbage floating around online about his family in the next few days. There would be ample opportunity for him to gnash his teeth and shake his fist at the sky over inaccuracies and slurs and his father's foolhardiness—if he wanted to waste his energy on futile bullshit.

He didn't. He needed to stay focused on the here and now.

The investigators left an hour later. They took the contents of multiple filing cabinets with them, all packed into brown evidence boxes. They also took one of the main servers, utterly unapologetic about the fact that doing so would cripple the business, at least until Garret's IT team could create a work-around or replace it.

The first thing he did was empower his IT manager to do whatever he deemed necessary to get a new server operational. Then he returned to his office and started putting things to rights. Mandy soon joined him, the two of them working side by side in determined silence.

"I'll bring in an extra chair for the meeting," she said when they were done.

"Thanks, Mandy."

Mae arrived ten minutes early, coming into Garret's office and shutting the door. She studied him for a moment before moving forward and taking one of the guest seats.

"You look exhausted."

"Funny, that."

"I'm so sorry, Garret. I had no idea any of this was going to happen. If I had—"

"It wouldn't have made any difference. They had a warrant. And we already agreed the only way out of this is to play it straight."

"Sure, but that doesn't mean we wouldn't have liked to be able to set the agenda a little," Mae said. "If we'd had a couple more weeks, we could have approached them. You wouldn't have the press downstairs panting for juicy tidbits. We could have kept this nice and clean."

"Yeah, well, that's not what happened," Garret said. He didn't have time to mourn what-ifs. "The bigger issue is that right now the DA probably has a better idea of what we're dealing with than we do, thanks to Ron and the magical disappearing laptop."

"My team is making good progress. I'll have a preliminary report for you by next week, I promise."

She sounded utterly certain and Garret nodded. "Good. That's a start."

"My friend Greg should be here any second," Mae said, checking her watch. "He's top-notch. Expensive, but worth every cent, especially given how messy and loud this is already."

"I appreciate you getting him here," Garret said. "I imagine he's a busy guy."

Mae's face creased with sympathy as she looked at him. "You don't deserve to be wading through this."

Garret gave a tight smile. "The music stopped, and I'm

in the chair. It's just the way it is."

The lawyer he'd retained under Mae's advice, Alec Stone, arrived then, followed closely by Greg, the crisis consultant. Garret took one look at his designer suit and doubled his expectations regarding the other man's hourly rate. So be it. Money was not the issue here. Keeping his father out of jail and the business viable was.

Alec dominated the first half hour of the meeting, filling Garret in on the moves he'd made to ascertain what he could about the details of the DA's investigation. The main takeaway was that until the indictment was issued, they were simply going to have to wait to find out what the length and breadth of the charges might be, and who would be swept up in them.

"How long is it going to be before they come up with an indictment?" Garret asked.

Alec pushed his thick-rimmed glasses up his nose. "How long is a piece of string?"

Garret sighed heavily. "Awesome. So we sit around waiting for the axe to fall."

"The other issue we have is funding. Sometimes in cases like these the DA will freeze company assets. In this case, that would mean all private and business funds."

"Is that likely to happen to us?" Garret asked, his mouth suddenly dry. About the only thing they had on their side was access to money to mount a strong defense.

"I can't give you a definitive answer on that yet," Alex said, his expression apologetic. "I've reached out to the DA, though, and if they do go that route I'll negotiate for the business to have funding to remain operational. I'm just mentioning it in case it comes up, so you know we have a plan in place."

Greg shifted in his chair. "This is where I'm going to jump in, if that's okay."

"Please," Garret said, gesturing for him to take the floor.

"By close of business today, Tate Transport is going to be a national talking point. There are going to be think pieces on corruption, analyses of the players, and every bit of public information about you and your family is going to be gone over with a fine-tooth comb. You on Facebook, Garret?"

"I have a profile, but I don't use it regularly."

"As of today, your profile needs to be private only, along with any other social media sites you use. And just to be safe, you're going to remove any images you've uploaded any-where. Your father a big social media user?"

"No. He's old school," Garret said, indicating his father's brag wall.

"So there are going to be photo archives of all this glad-handing then," Greg said, eyeing the many images of a smiling Gideon with a disapproving twist of his mouth. "Not much we can do about that, unfortunately. So, moving on."

For the next twenty minutes, Greg sketched the scale of the crisis Garret was dealing with in blunt, no-nonsense terms. He talked about the press, but mostly he talked about the company's reputation and relationships with its clients.

"You are going to have people cancelling contracts. You are going to have people questioning every invoice Tate has ever issued. This company has broken faith with its custom-ers. And let's not forget that when the indictment comes out, there are going to be red faces among some of your clients when it becomes clear they were involved in these illegal transactions too. Expect mud throwing and blame shifting. Expect civil suits."

The headache gripping Garret's skull ratcheted tighter and tighter as the other man began to detail the kind of exposure Garret could expect personally.

"Expect for some enterprising reporter to dig into every possible angle of your private life. They'll look at your college admission, your grades, your affiliations. They'll look for any dirt they can find on your start-up in Seattle. Ex-girlfriends will be contacted, friends exploited. Any vulnerabilities in your past are going to be weaponized. You got a partner, Garret?" Greg asked, his blue eyes as remorseless as a laser.

"Yes."

"Then she or he needs to be prepared too. This is going to be brutal. Nothing will be sacred."

Greg started on strategy then, talking about getting ahead of the story, issuing statements, and reaching out to clients to offer assurances. He talked about selling Garret as the new sheriff in town, there to clean up any previous improprieties and move on with a clean slate.

Alex stepped back in then to outline the kind of defense that would be required, the additional staff and consultants Garret needed to authorize, and the budget Garret would need to allocate.

By the time they were done and he was alone in his office again, he felt as though he'd spent two hours in a wind tunnel. This day had moved beyond nightmare territory into something else altogether.

He felt annihilated. And angry. And scared, because the hill he was about to climb was steep and dangerous and the climb might go on for years, if Alec's predictions regarding the charges and subsequent court process were accurate. He wasn't just climbing for himself, either—he was climbing on behalf of his employees and his family.

Life as he knew it was over.

The thought echoed in his brain as he gathered the phone Mandy had purchased for him this afternoon and his briefcase. It was barely six, but he needed to decompress. He needed to go somewhere people weren't looking to him to have all the answers. Someplace he could let all his anger and despair loose from the cage he'd confined it in throughout the day.

Sierra. He needed Sierra, the only person he could be totally honest with right now. The only person he fully trusted.

He sent Mandy home on his way out, insisting she walk out with him. Her day had been hellish, too, but she'd been a rock. His father had done one thing right when he hired her, at least.

Then he got in his car and nosed cautiously out of the underground garage, only relaxing when he saw the press were no longer camped out in front of the building. Thank heaven for small mercies.

He was about to turn onto the lakeside road when his phone rang.

"Garret, it's me," Mae said.

"Hey. Everything okay?" he asked, his gut tightening as

he braced himself for yet another shovelful of crap. After all, why should it stop just because business hours were over?

"Nothing new from my end. But I wanted to mention something to you just in case it hadn't occurred to you. This is none of my business, and feel free to tell me to butt out, but you mentioned today in the meeting that you're in a relationship, so I kind of put two and two together . . ."

"If you're asking if Sierra and I are together, the answer is yes," he said.

Mae sighed. "Look, I don't want to rain on your parade, but I can't stop thinking about what Greg said about the amount of scrutiny you're going to be under in your professional and private lives and how that extends to anyone you're involved with. Garret, has it occurred to you that once the press work out who Sierra is, they won't have to dig far to find out about the accident?"

He frowned, his hands tightening on the steering wheel. "No. I hadn't gotten that far."

"That's why I wanted to mention it. Because there is not a journalist alive who wouldn't wet their pants over finding out that the son and heir of the now-infamous Gideon Tate is connected romantically with the daughter of the people Gideon killed in a car accident years ago. You know they would eat that story up with a spoon," Mae said.

"Jesus," he said, because he knew she was right.

Someone would find out about the tragedy that connected their families, and they'd use it generate salacious column inches and clicks. The Carmodys would have to deal with their private loss being commodified into headlines. Their parents' photos would be dug up and recirculated.

It would be awful. Hurtful and grubby and pointless.

"I'm sorry. I wasn't going to say anything, but then I was worried that maybe it hadn't occurred to you."

"I appreciate the call," Garret said, even though a part of him didn't. The part that was exhausted and more than a little overwhelmed by the apparently never-ending shitstorm that had rained down on him all day.

"I'll call tomorrow and give you a progress report. I'm just waiting on a final statement from the bank and we should be able to start pinpointing some areas of concern."

Which was a euphemism, he knew, for being able to finally narrow down which of Tate Transport's clients had received a bribe in order to sway a contract in Tate's favor.

"Thanks, Mae."

Garret let his breath hiss out between his teeth. He didn't know what to do about protecting Sierra from the voracious appetite of the media. Obviously they could be super careful and make sure they were never seen together socially, especially in these early days while the press were still eager to tease out the details of a new story. But would that be enough? Maybe he could talk to Greg, find out what his best advice was for flying under the radar.

He was still pondering the issue when he turned onto the street that led to the lake house. He frowned when he saw the cluster of vans parked around the entrance to his driveway.

More press.

"Fuck me," he muttered under his breath.

He reached for his sunglasses, shoving them on as he slowed to turn into the drive. Camera flashes popped in his peripheral vision as he drove past the huddle of waiting journalists and photographers. What were they hoping for? Some kind of accidental slip of the tongue from him at the end of the day? Maybe they had their fingers crossed he'd get angry and give them footage of a rich angry white guy screaming at journalists through the open window of his luxury car.

He'd never been more grateful for his father's flamboyant taste in real estate than when the curve of the long driveway hid the press huddle from view. At least trespassing laws would keep them at bay and afford him and Sierra some security and privacy.

He parked the car and collected his things before striding toward the house. Sierra rushed out the front door, meeting him halfway and wrapping her arms around him without saying a word. He let himself relax and breathe and made a conscious effort to enjoy the way she felt in his arms.

This was what it was all about. This was real and worthwhile.

Maybe it was because he was still jumpy from all the camera flashes, but some instinct made him lift his head after a few seconds—which was when he registered a low electronic buzz that seemed to be getting louder.

Then he saw it, zooming toward the spot where he and Sierra stood like deer in the headlights, their arms around one another. A drone, hovering maybe fifteen feet off the ground, its camera glinting in the afternoon sun.

He acted without thinking, bringing up his briefcase to block any view of Sierra's face.

"What—"

"Head for the house. Quickly," he said.

He twisted so he could guide them, one hand holding up the case to continue blocking any view the drone might have, the other ensuring Sierra's face was turned toward his chest. Half a dozen steps and they were beneath the portico. Four more and they were inside the house, the door swinging shut behind them with a muted thud.

"Was that a drone? Were they filming us?" Sierra asked, pulling away from him, her eyes wide with outrage. "Can they do that? Isn't that trespassing of some kind?"

"I don't know, but I'm going to find out," he said, pulling out his phone with shaking hands.

Shaking because he was suddenly filled with an almost overwhelming anger.

This was too much, especially today. He'd been pushed too far and too hard and right now a very large part of him wanted to charge down the driveway and find someone to punch in the face. Preferably the piece of crap drone operator who'd just tried to steal his privacy and peace of mind.

Alec answered on the second ring and listened to Garret's terse explanation in silence.

"You can call the police," he said. "I have to admit I'm not up to speed on what the trespassing laws might be in regard to drones. I do know there was a recent Supreme Court ruling that suggests there is no implied promise of privacy in a residential yard. But the cops might still be helpful with moving the press on."

"So these assholes can just harass me at will? No charges have been laid yet, and my every move, my whole freaking life is up for grabs?" Garret vented, stabbing a hand through his hair.

He was conscious of Sierra watching him, her brow furrowed with concern, and he forced himself to take a deep breath. Him flipping out wasn't going to change anything.

"Let me ask around. There might be something we can do," Alec said.

Garret grunted and ended the call. Tomorrow he could feel bad about not being more polite. It wasn't Alec's fault, after all. But right now he was done with courtesy.

He was done. Period.

Sierra's warm hand slipped into his. "It's okay. It's just a stupid drone. So they get a few shots of the exterior of the house and the tops of our heads. Good luck to them."

Her green eyes were steady on his, her mouth slightly curved at the corners as she encouraged him to see the lighter side of the situation.

She didn't understand. But she would soon. She'd read the articles that were popping up online, and she'd turn on the radio and hear Tate Transport's name being dragged through the mud. She'd be identified by some intrepid reporter and all her family history would be spread out for people to pick over. She'd greet him night after night as he came home from days like this, weeks like this, years like this as he dealt with the fallout of his greedy, reckless father's actions, and she'd bear witness to his rage and helplessness and frustration. Over and over.

She'd understand what she'd signed up for then. She'd get the very worst of him and his family. The very worst.

Looking into her beautiful face, seeing the love and concern there, he suddenly understood that he couldn't do that to her.

Even though everything in him wanted to cling to her, to the happiness and joy she brought to him, to the way she made him feel, it would be an act of selfishness of the highest order to subject someone he loved to the ordeal that lay ahead of him.

Only an asshole would do that to someone they loved, and he had a choice. He could save her from all this—if he was man enough to do it.

"Jesus," he said, closing his eyes, his whole body growing heavy with the weight of realization. "*Jesus.*"

"What's wrong?" Sierra said, stepping closer.

He opened his eyes and scanned her face, trying to commit to it to memory. Her dark-fringed eyes, the delicate swoop of her nose, her sun-kissed skin. He reached out and brushed his hand over her hair, feeling the cool silk of it slip through his fingers.

She was so gorgeous. So smart. So funny. So damned brave.

And he had to let her go, because he loved her and it was within his power to prevent her from walking down this dark road at his side.

"Garret, talk to me. What's going on?" she said.

He swallowed and let his hand fall to his side. Then he took a step backward.

"We can't do this anymore," he said. "We can't be together."

She gasped. "*What?* No. What are you talking about?"

"I'm talking about the fact that my life is a dumpster fire, and it's only going to get worse. Once the details of what my father has done get out, this thing is going to be a national scandal. Tate Transport is going to be dragged through the courts. We'll be lucky if the business survives. And god knows what sort of charges my father will be facing."

"None of that has anything to do with us," she said, her gaze intense, as though she could sway him to her way of thinking through sheer willpower.

"I'm not putting you through all that, Sierra. I refuse to drag you down with me."

"You're not dragging me anywhere. I choose to be with you. I choose to help you get through this. I'm not going to just walk away because things are messy."

He laughed, the sound closer to a bark than an expression of amusement. "They're not messy, Sierra. They're *fucked*. Completely screwed. We're already hemorrhaging clients, and it hasn't even been twenty-four hours. My father's probably going to go to jail if the stress doesn't kill him. The Tate name is going to be mud. And I'm going to be neck-deep in all of it and I refuse to inflict that on you. God knows my family is not renowned for doing the right thing, but if I can save you from this nightmare, I'm going to do it. I love you, but we can't be together. That's just the way it has to be."

Sierra was already shaking her head before he'd finished. "No. You can't make that decision for me, Garret. You can't decide what's right for me, how much I can handle. I'm not a child. I know it's not going to be fun, but I don't care. You're the only thing that's important to me."

"I know." And he did. She was the best thing that had ever happened to him, and she would stick by his side through thick and thin. If he let her. If he was willing to do that to her.

Her eyes widened. "No. Don't say it like that, like the decision has already been made, like it's irrevocable. I'm not walking away from you, you idiot. I love you. Don't you get that? Love isn't only about the good times. Love is about the bad times, the sad times, and all the other times in between. I'm not abandoning you because it's going to get hard. I would never do that."

She was breathing fast, her eyes shining with emotion, and she was so beautiful to him, so precious. It would be so easy to cave, to tell himself he'd tried to do the right thing, but she'd overridden him with her loyalty and determination.

But his love for her wouldn't allow him to do that. Because that was the thing about loving someone—he was beginning to understand—suddenly her happiness and well-being were so much more important than his own.

"This isn't a negotiation," he said. "I have a choice here, and I choose to cut you free."

"I don't want to be cut. So fuck that, Garret." Her chin came up and there was a martial, determined light in her eyes. It only made him more determined to stick to his guns. She deserved so much better than what he had to offer her.

"I'll talk to HR tomorrow and arrange a payout for what's left of the time you're supposed to be filling in for Jack," he said. "I'll write a reference recommending you to anyone and everyone. If you'd prefer not to fly the Bell home tomorrow evening, Mandy can arrange for a car to get you home to Marietta."

He headed for the kitchen, not giving her a chance to respond. He knew she wouldn't give up easily, but he loved her too much to back down. This was the one good, decent thing he could do, and even if it killed him, he was going to do it.

Chapter Twenty

SIERRA WHIRLED ON her heel and chased after Garret. He was pulling a bottle of wine from the wine fridge when she entered the kitchen.

"You can't make me stop loving you, Garret. That's not the way this works," she said.

Her shoulders were stiff with righteous indignation, and hot emotion burned at the back of her eyes. Not because she was sad or angry, but because she understood why he was doing this. He wanted to protect her. He was being noble. He was giving her an escape hatch to save her from the future that was bearing down on him.

It was so very Garret to want to do that. His sense of what was right, his essential decency, was part of why she loved him.

But she didn't want an out. She wanted *him*. Whatever he was facing, she would face it with him.

"I know that," he said, pouring wine into two glasses. "The only thing I can control is the degree to which you're exposed to the ugliness my father has created. So that's what I'm going to do, Sierra."

He held her gaze as he spoke, letting her see his determination, how immovable he was, and there was a coolness in his eyes, a distance that stole some of the wind from her sails.

He was so *decided.* Implacable. She'd never seen him like this before, with all his shutters up.

"Garret. Please. You don't need to do this. If you're worried about the media, then we'll be super discreet. If you're worried I'm not up for some tough times, then you don't understand me nearly as well as I thought you did. Carmodys don't quit. This is it for me. I've been waiting twenty-seven years to meet someone I can give my heart to and I met him and it's done. I'm yours now."

"I'm sorry," he said. There was such an air of finality to the two words and the flat determination in his eyes that her stomach lurched.

"No. This isn't happening. You can't do this." Hot tears slid down her face when she blinked. She wiped them away impatiently as she moved closer, grabbing both of his hands in hers.

Somehow she had to make him understand. She had to find the magic words that would break through this shield he'd put between them and make him relent. "Garret, we can do this together. We can. Please, please don't shut me out."

He didn't return the press of her hands. He simply looked into her eyes and she saw that his mind was made up. He'd made his decision. He wasn't going to unmake it. He'd decided this was the best, kindest, most generous thing he could do, and he was going to go through with it even if it killed him.

She opened her mouth to rail at him, her hands clenching around his. Hot, angry, desperate words crowded her throat. She loved him. He loved her. Pushing her away was madness, especially when he needed her so much.

Then she saw tiniest flicker of emotion behind his eyes, the briefest glimpse of what it was costing him to do this, and everything in her went still.

Suddenly she knew that there was nothing she could say to him right now that would get through. He was in lockdown mode, under enormous stress, assailed from all sides. He'd had the day from hell, his picture splashed all over the papers, his home and business raided.

She could argue and plead and beg all she wanted, but he couldn't hear her right now.

A memory came to her then of something she'd said to Eva when she was explaining why she wouldn't let herself give in to the attraction between her and Garret.

I need to be the easy part of his life right now, not another problem.

She closed her eyes for a long beat. Then she released her grip on his hands and took a step backward.

Because that was what he wanted her to do—what he needed right now—and she loved him enough to put his needs above her own. Even though it made her heart twist in her chest to even think of walking away from their brief, precious time together.

It won't come to that. He'll snap out of this and realize he's being crazy, that he needs me. That I need him. He just has to get past this horrible day and get some clear air.

"I'll fly you back to Marietta tomorrow night," she said. Then she turned and left the kitchen.

Every step felt wrong, but she forced herself down the hallway and up the stairs to her room. Then she sat on the bed, gripped her knees, and willed herself not to cry.

Tears were not going to change anything.

After a few minutes the urge passed and she took a deep, shaky breath. Clearly, Garret had a catastrophic day. She'd figured as much when she'd been alerted to the first news stories by her brother Jesse, who had texted her with a big capitalized *WTF* and a link to an article describing the simultaneous raids on the Tates' private residence and business headquarters. It had been accompanied by a photograph of Garret looking about as un-Garret as he could possibly get, posing next to a bikini model with a drink in his hand. She knew him well enough to see the discomfort in his posture, but no one else would. Everyone else would see that photograph and think he was an entitled, spoiled jerk, the perfect heir to his crooked father's business.

She hadn't asked Garret if he'd seen the article. It was safe to assume he had. It was also safe to assume he'd had worse to deal with during the long hours he'd been at the office today.

His life was in free fall, and his knee-jerk response was to try to save her from falling with him. Somehow, she was going to have to convince him that that was not his choice to make.

Not tonight. Possibly not even tomorrow. But this was not over. Not by a long shot. She loved him, and she knew he loved him. The rest was irrelevant.

It was early still, but suddenly she was exhausted. It had been a long, grueling day, and her nerves had been stretched thin even before Garret had made the announcement that they couldn't be together anymore.

She pulled off her clothes, brushed her teeth, and curled up in bed, trying not to remember how good it had felt to fall asleep with Garret's arms around her last night.

How insane that they could go from the fun and sheer *rightness* of last night to today's stark, arid ugliness. A lone tear slid down her cheek in the seconds before she slipped into the oblivion of sleep, the only sign of weakness she would allow herself.

The next day, she waited until Garret had left the house before going downstairs to fix herself breakfast. She found a thermos waiting on the counter for her. He'd made her coffee. The good stuff, because he hated the thought of her making do with anything substandard.

She stared at it, emotion rising up her throat. Then she blinked rapidly and concentrated on making herself a comforting bowl of oatmeal with an extra helping of brown sugar just because.

She caught a cab to the airport midmorning and spent the day finishing up any maintenance issues she'd noted and ensuring the Bell was in pristine condition, ready to fly as needed. At four she towed it out onto the pad and readied everything for departure.

She was conscious of butterflies in her belly as it drew nearer to Garret's usual arrival time. She hadn't seen him all day, had missed him in her bed all night, and she ached to see his face and hear his voice. But she also knew she had to be prepared for him to be cool and reserved with her, like last night. She needed to be braced for that.

She drew in a big, deep breath when she saw the Lincoln driving toward the Tates' reserved parking bay next to the hangar. She set her shoulders and adjusted the bill on her cap and hoped like hell that her inner turmoil and hurt didn't show on her face.

His face was pale and tight as he got out of the car, and her hands twitched by her sides. Despite her resolve to accept his decision, she wanted to go to him. Wanted to put her arms around him and do what she could to soothe the worry marks from his brow and ease the tension from his shoulders.

Just do your job. Make it easy for him. That's the greatest gift you can give him right now.

He was wearing his sunglasses, and he gave her an acknowledging nod before climbing into the passenger cabin. She secured the door and climbed into the cockpit. The preflight check went smoothly, and she took off minutes later after receiving clearance from the tower.

She checked the mirror multiple times during the flight back to Marietta but didn't catch his eye even once. He was buried in his laptop, one hand kneading his forehead as he frowned at the screen, palpable tension rippling off him.

She swallowed her questions about his day and stayed focused on her role as his private pilot, a role she was performing for the final time today. She'd been so busy recovering from the unexpected blow of losing Garret she hadn't had time to process the fact she'd have to explain the situation to Jack too.

She could think about that later, when she didn't have to maintain her best poker face.

For the first time since she'd started flying for Garret, the sight of the helipad beside his parents' house filled her with relief. She was reaching the end of her ability to pretend he was nothing to her and she wasn't hollowed out inside. She needed him to be gone so she could stop swallowing back the tears she refused to cry in front of him.

She touched down and immediately killed the motor. Then she checked her oil levels and went through the rest of her postflight routine before climbing out and releasing the passenger cabin door. Garret stepped out immediately, sunglasses still hiding his eyes.

"Before you go, would you like me to put the word out at the airport that you're looking for a new pilot?" she asked, aiming her gaze somewhere over his shoulder.

He paused. "Mandy's organized someone for me today, but thanks for the offer."

She pressed her back teeth together to stop herself from reacting to how easily she'd been replaced. "All right, then."

She turned to shut the passenger door. She could feel Garret hovering there, waiting for her to turn back, and she willed him to walk away. He was the one who wanted it this way, and she was not going to cry in front of him.

Her phone vibrated in her pocket, giving her the perfect excuse to ignore him, and she pulled it out and checked the screen. It was Casey, and she swallowed a lump of emotion at the thought of being home with her family around her.

She needed that right now, very much. Eva would pass the tissues and say all the right things, and Casey and Jed would be bewildered but kind, doing their best to make her feel better.

"Hey, Case—"

"Where are you? Still in Helena?" Casey asked, his voice sharp and urgent.

"Just landed in Marietta. Why? What's wrong?" she asked, her hand tensing around the phone.

"Jed was out doing a fence repair on the western ridge today, said he'd be back by midafternoon. Figured it was taking longer than he'd thought it would when he didn't show, but I just spotted Pedro hanging around near the main corral."

For a second Sierra forgot to breathe. A horse coming back without its rider was every rancher's nightmare. There was every chance that something might have just happened to spook Pedro, of course, forcing Jed to trudge home on foot. If he was walking all the way from the western ridge, it'd easily take him well into the night.

But there was also every chance that he'd come off and broken something. A leg. His back. His neck.

"Sierra, you still there?" Casey asked.

"I'm here." She whirled to find Garret hovering near the edge of the helipad, a concerned frown on his face.

"I need to borrow the Bell. Garret's horse has come back without him."

Comprehension darkened his eyes. He'd grown up in Marietta. He knew the kind of accidents that befell cowboys. "You got binoculars on board?" he asked.

"There's a pair in the desk in the hangar," she said.

He walked to the hangar in a few long strides, pulling the rolling door open with a single powerful jerk. She returned her attention to the phone.

"I'll be airborne in five," she said, and she heard her

brother sigh with relief.

"Man, you have no idea how much I wanted to hear you say that. Eva and I can go out and start searching, but that's a lot of miles to cover."

"Coverage might be patchy, but I'll call if we can," she said, pulling open the cockpit door and clambering back into her seat.

"He's probably halfway home, cursing Pedro's name," Casey said.

"Yeah. Probably," she agreed. "Any idea what he was wearing so we know what to look for?"

"I don't know. Let me check with Eva, see if she remembers." She heard Eva's voice briefly, then Casey was back on the line. "She said a red shirt and a pair of jeans. She remembers because she gave him crap for looking like the Marlboro man."

"Okay. Good. That ought to make it easier to find him from the air. I'll call you."

"All right."

Garret pulled open the passenger door and climbed in, a pair of binoculars in hand.

"Belt on, please," she said, handing over his headset.

A minute later they were in the air, flying on a north-western heading. It didn't take long for the familiar roof of her family home to come into view and she took a westerly heading, dropping her altitude at the same time to give Garret the best view of the terrain.

"He's wearing a red shirt. On foot, obviously. I'll head for the ridge, and we can work our way back."

"Sounds good." He pulled off his sunglasses and glanced

toward the clock on the control panel.

She knew what he was thinking. They had about another hour of light before the sun went down. If they didn't find him now, they'd be searching on horseback for the rest of the night.

"We'll find him," Garret said reassuringly.

She nodded and concentrated on the ground below, correcting her heading whenever she recognized landmarks. Scrub and trees flashed by as she divided her attention between flying the Bell and searching for her brother.

They made it all the way to the western ridge, the furthest corner of Carmody land, without spotting Jed. She passed her phone to Garret. "Can you see if you can get a signal and call Casey, check that Jed hasn't turned up?" she asked.

Garret checked for reception then gave a shrug. "One bar. I'll give it a shot."

She kept scanning the fence line as he waited for the call to connect.

"Call failed. I'll try again."

Sierra turned her head to respond and caught a flash of something blue in her peripheral vision. She straightened, craning her neck, but they'd flown too far for her to see whatever it might have been. She took the Bell in a sweeping turn, doubling back.

"Where am I looking?" Garret asked, picking up on her tension.

"Near the trees. I thought I saw something . . ."

"There. Against the tree."

Sierra's heart gave a painful squeeze as she spotted Jed

leaning against a twisted tree. His chest was bare, his leg stretched in front of him. The red shirt Eva remembered had been wrapped around his calf to create a bandage over his jeans, and the options ran through Sierra's mind as she looked for a safe place to land.

Broken leg or snakebite.

Please let it be a broken leg.

Because the only truly dangerous snake in Montana was the prairie rattlesnake, and its bite could be deadly if a person didn't get medical treatment fast enough. Five years ago, one of the Johnson kids had been bitten while out hiking and hadn't been able to get to help in time. His organs had shut down one by one over the next few days before he'd died.

Panic rose up, choking her. Then she blinked and got a grip. She had to land the Bell and get to Jed.

She concentrated on putting the Bell down on the uneven ground. It wasn't her best landing, but it was more than adequate and she switched off the engine and wrenched the door open in almost the same move.

She ran the short distance to the tree, alarm racing through her when she saw that Jed hadn't changed positions since she'd spotted him from the air.

"Jed!" She fell to her knees beside him, her fingers going to his neck to find a pulse.

His skin was hot and clammy to the touch. She sagged a little when she felt his pulse beneath her fingertips, steady and strong.

He was alive. Thank god.

Garret knelt beside her, and she saw he'd stopped to grab the helicopter's first aid kit.

"He's breathing. Hot and clammy," she said.

"I'm guessing snakebite," he said.

She nodded, then touched her brother's hand. "Jed. Can you hear me? Just give my hand a little squeeze, or open your eyes if you can. Whatever you can do."

His eyelids fluttered and she felt his chest rise and fall as though he was trying to speak.

"Don't speak if it's too hard. It's okay. We're going to get you to the hospital," she said.

Garret was inspecting the makeshift shirt-bandage Jed had wrapped around his left calf.

"I don't want to disturb this. Based on what I can remember about snakebite, the less movement the better, yeah?" He started rolling elasticized bandage over the top of Jed's shirt, reinforcing what her brother had done.

"Zero movement, limb at heart level, medical care as quickly as possible," Sierra said as she lifted Jed's heel very gently to allow Garret to pass the bandage under Jed's leg.

"Think you can help me carry him?"

Sierra considered her brother's six-foot-three form. As fired up and terrified as she was, she was tempted to say she could handle her share of his weight, but he was a muscular guy.

"There's a tarp in the hold," she said.

Garret leapt to his feet and took off, understanding without her asking that she wanted to be the one to stay with her brother. Leaning closer, she pressed a hand to his forehead and winced when she felt how hot he was.

How long had he been sitting out here like this? How long had the snake venom been seeping into his body, poisoning everything it touched?

"Jed . . . I love you so much. Please be okay," she said, a horrible fear gripping her.

What would she do if he died? He'd been mother and father to her for thirteen years. He was the steely spine of their family. She couldn't imagine the world without him in it.

"Let's spread this out, get him onto it, and get back in the air ASAP," Garret said as he ran back to join her.

She nodded, glad of the instruction and the chance it gave her to pull herself together. Together they spread out the tarp, then Garret grabbed Jed beneath the armpits and swiveled him around on his butt to get him away from the tree trunk. He shifted behind Jed then and dragged him the short distance onto the tarp. Jed stirred a little as his injured leg bumped along the uneven ground. Sierra told herself it was a good sign—he was still conscious, albeit barely.

Once he was on the tarp, she and Garret each grabbed a corner and put their backs into pulling it and Jed toward the helicopter. It was by no means easy or smooth, but it was for sure better than them having to force Jed into walking or her trying and failing to carry him. Garret manhandled Jed into the passenger cabin once they arrived, stretching him out on the floor between the two bench seats before getting in and positioning himself so he could support Jed's head against his chest and brace both of them with his feet if need be.

The moment they were settled, she slammed the door shut and scrambled into the pilot's seat. The main rotor fired up with its usual mechanical roar and she did the quickest preflight check in the history of mankind before opening up the throttle and lifting the collective for takeoff.

Her palms were sweaty on the controls as she turned toward town. By car, it was a twenty-minute drive. By air, she should be able to make it in close to five if she went hard, and that was exactly what she intended to do.

She opened up the throttle and picked up the radio, finding the frequency for Marietta hospital. It was hard to keep her voice from shaking as she told them she was inbound, ETA five minutes, with a thirty-two-year-old male with suspected snakebite. Fever, clammy skin, semiconscious.

"Roger that. We will be standing by," the hospital replied.

One question kept bouncing around her head as they flew: what if they were too late?

The thought made her stomach lurch and she blinked away tears.

Don't you dare lose it, Carmody. Jed needs you to be at the top of your game.

She sucked it all back in, forcing herself to calm down, and pushed her fears away. There would be plenty of time to engage with them once she'd gotten Jed safely on the ground.

She checked the mirror and could see Garret had his head bowed as he spoke near Jed's ear. Reassuring him, she imagined.

She flashed back to the moment when she'd done the same thing for his father not so long ago, urging him to be okay, assuring him help was close. This time she was the one in the pilot's seat, though, and she hoped she could live up to

Jack's calm, efficient competence.

The first houses on the outskirts of Marietta flashed into view, then she was flying over Main Street, aiming for the hospital and the well-marked helipad on the roof. She could see hospital staff standing by with a gurney, their faces pale blurs as she approached. Then she concentrated on landing as quickly and gently as she could. The moment she felt the thud of the landing skids hitting the rooftop she switched the main rotor off and signaled for the medical crew to approach.

Clambering out of the cockpit, she pulled the passenger door open and stood back to let them do their thing.

Garret stayed in place, supporting Jed, until the team eased Jed out and onto the gurney. Sierra had to press her hand to her mouth when she registered that his breathing had become shallow and labored, his chest rising and falling rapidly. She remained frozen in place as they wheeled him toward the hospital entrance, terror rushing through her body in a cold wash.

"He only started breathing like that as we were landing," Garret said, his arms coming around her.

She allowed herself to sink into the comfort of his embrace for a full five seconds before pulling back. "I have to tell Casey."

Garret pulled her phone from his pocket and passed it over. She made the call, feeling shaky now the flight was over.

"We're on the way to the hospital," Casey said when he picked up. "We saw you fly over, heading for town. Figured you'd found him."

"He's been bitten by a snake. Case . . . He's not good. I don't know how long it's been since he was bitten, but he was having trouble breathing when we landed."

For a moment the only sound was the car engine. She guessed Casey was grappling with the same panicky thoughts she was, dread and hope and fear all mixed up in a chaotic tangle.

"We need to call Jesse," Casey finally said, his voice tight.

"I'll do it," Sierra volunteered.

He was driving, and she'd prefer he concentrated on the road.

"We'll be there soon," Casey promised and she ended the call.

"Here."

A folded cotton square was pressed into her hand, which was when she realized she was crying. She looked at Garret in despair, unable to stop the flow now she'd acknowledged it.

"I've got to call Jesse," she said.

Garret took the handkerchief from her, then wiped her cheeks and pulled her back into his arms. "Deep breaths. In, then out. That's right. Give me another couple for good measure," he said, his voice vibrating through his chest and into hers.

She sniffed, then blinked as the out-of-control feeling passed and he let her go.

"Thanks," she said, not quite meeting his eyes. Then she pulled up her brother's number on her phone.

Jesse answered just as she was starting to worry she'd be flicked across to voice mail, and she passed on the bad news as succinctly as she could.

"We're in Plentywood. We'll dump the trailer and find a stable for Major and be with you guys in six hours," Jesse said in his no-nonsense, decisive way.

"Okay. Drive safely. I love you," Sierra said.

"Love you, too, Squirrel."

For once Sierra didn't wince as her brother used her childhood pet name.

"How long can we leave the Bell here on the roof?" Garret asked.

"Not long. But I'm not going anywhere until I've had an update on Jed," Sierra said, turning toward the hospital entrance.

Chapter Twenty-One

GARRET WALKED BESIDE her as they made their way into the emergency department. The nurse at the busy emergency reception informed them that Jed was being assessed and treated and they needed to wait for further updates.

Sierra wanted to argue, but Garret's arm came around her shoulders and steered her toward a couple of empty seats. "They probably haven't got anything to tell you just yet. They'll be getting the antivenom into him, stabilizing him, making him comfortable . . ."

"I didn't realize you had a medical degree," she said, but there was no heat in her words, just bewilderment, and his arm tightened around her shoulders.

"I've got a degree in hospital waiting rooms," he said.

She sat and he took the seat beside her, keeping his arm around her shoulders. She wanted it there—needed it there—because reality was really starting to sink in now and she was so hyped up on adrenaline it felt as though her insides were vibrating.

Unable to keep still, she started bouncing her heel, the repetitive jitter oddly comforting. Garret dropped a kiss onto her temple.

"He's young, he's fit, he's healthy. He wrapped up the site of the bite and stayed still. He's going to be okay, Sierra."

"You don't know that," she said. "You can't promise that."

He fell silent, his gaze dropping to the floor. Her stomach dipped and she realized she'd been waiting for him to contradict her and guarantee her brother's survival, even though they both knew he couldn't do that.

"Sierra."

She looked up and Eva and Casey were there, bringing their own sense of urgency with them.

"Thank god you found him," Eva said, throwing her arms around Sierra.

"I should have gone out and checked on him when he didn't come back on time," Casey said, running a hand through his already tousled hair.

"How many times have any of us been back to the house exactly when we said we would be?" Sierra said. "Ranch work is done when it's done."

Casey nodded, but his mouth was still pressed into an unhappy line.

"Jesse and CJ are coming as soon as they can. They're six hours away in Plentywood, and they need to find someone to look after Major so they can dump the trailer," Sierra reported.

Casey checked his watch, then settled into the chair beside Sierra. "You okay?"

She shrugged, unwilling to give voice to all the different

ways she was afraid.

"He's the toughest bastard I know. And more stubborn than a mule," Casey said.

"I know. But you didn't see him."

A few more tears escaped then and Garret passed her the handkerchief again, his arm once again a heavy, reassuring weight around her shoulders. At some point she'd have to think about the fact that they were supposed to be over, but not now. Now she needed him to keep her steady and focused and sane.

Fifteen minutes later a dark-haired doctor came out to tell them they'd administered three vials of antivenom and Jed's vital signs had stabilized. He said it would be a while before they knew if more antivenom was needed and how much damage had been done and that they probably wouldn't know more until morning.

"But he's going to be all right?" Sierra confirmed.

The doctor hesitated. "I can't say that yet. Usually this antivenom is effective if it's administered within six hours of a bite. At this stage, we have no idea how long ago that was in Jed's case."

Sierra swallowed against a sudden rush of nausea. She could see plain as day what the doctor wasn't saying. Jed could still die.

"We're going to transfer him to intensive care. There's a private waiting room up there for family members. Someone can sit with him, but only one person at a time. Someone will come and let you know when he's been transferred."

The doctor made a point of making eye contact with them all before disappearing back into the busy emergency department.

Sierra felt Garret shift beside her. "We should probably clear the helipad," he said.

She nodded, grateful to have something to concentrate on. The Bell wasn't really fitted out for night flights—most civilian helicopters weren't—but it wasn't fully dark yet and it was only a short run back to the Tate place.

She stood. "I'll be back as soon as I can," she told her brother and Eva.

Garret was silent as they took the elevator to the helipad. She climbed into the Bell and took her place behind the cyclic, her hands wrapping around the familiar grip. Then she took a deep breath.

"Okay?" Garret asked.

"Okay enough."

She went through her preflight check, made radio contact with Marietta airport, then lifted off. It was twilight, but there was still enough light left for her to be able to identify several landmarks along the way. Car headlights marked the freeway near the Tates' home, then she saw the Tate house, the front light spilling onto the porch and surroundings. She flicked on the powerful spotlight beneath the belly of the Bell and the luminescent paint on the helipad sprang to life. Less than a minute later they were on the ground, the rotors slowing overhead.

"Tell me what to do to help you put it away," Garret said.

He helped her place the tow cart and maneuver the Bell into the hangar, then walked her straight across to the garage, beeping open his father's car. He called his mother during the drive in, explaining the situation, in case she was worried about his late arrival and sudden departure.

Sierra stared at the darkened landscape outside the car window, fear once again creeping up on her now she had nothing to occupy her. Garret's hand landed on her knee, and she realized she was bouncing her heel again. He caught her hand in his and placed his hand over it against her thigh. She glanced at him, half a dozen questions in her mind, wondering what all of this meant when he'd been so certain, so adamant last night that they were over.

Was he simply being kind, supporting her through these dark hours, or was he ready to rethink his decision?

She returned her gaze to the darkness outside the car, unwilling to ask for clarification right now. That probably made her a coward, but frankly she didn't give a damn. Her beloved oldest brother might die and she couldn't bear it. She needed Garret tonight. Tomorrow he could break her heart all over again, but not tonight.

GARRET WATCHED AS Sierra did yet another circuit of the family waiting room, stopping to twitch a stack of magazines into a neater arrangement, pausing at the other end of the room to read a public health announcement about flu vaccines. She was wired with adrenaline, still edgy with shock despite the fact they'd been sitting in this too-familiar space for two hours now, and he estimated that this was at least her tenth lap of the small space.

It was impossible to be in this gray little room and not remember the long trip home from Italy and the fear and preemptive grief he'd felt as he'd waited to find out if his father would survive his stroke. And now Sierra was enduring the same helpless cycle of dread and hope, her eyes bloodshot from too much crying, her slim body held tight, and it made his chest ache to know she was hurting and he couldn't do anything about it.

If he could, he'd take her pain away, take it on himself. But that wasn't the way grief and fear worked. All he could do was wait and watch and try to do what little he could to make life easier for her for the next few hours or as long as it took for them to come out the other side of this.

He glanced across at the other person in the room, curious about Casey's partner. Eva sat on the couch, knees tucked under her, her focus inward. With her short, punky-blond hair and colorful tattoo she wasn't exactly a typical Marietta local, but the way she looked at Casey and Sierra and the way she talked about Jed told him she was well and truly entrenched in the Carmody family.

He was about to suggest doing another coffee run, figuring it would give Sierra a chance to burn off more nervous energy, when the door to the waiting room slammed open.

"Where is he? Please tell me he's still okay," Mae said.

Gone was the smooth, corporate hard-ass he'd been dealing with the past couple of weeks, and in her place was a more familiar Mae dressed in faded jeans and T-shirt, her hair wild and curly. Freckles stood out against the pallor of her skin as her gaze bounced from him to Sierra to Eva in desperate demand.

"He's doing okay. He's had three doses of antivenom. Casey's with him now," Sierra said, coming over to give the other woman a hug. "It's a bit of a waiting game at the moment to see how much damage the venom did before he got treatment. No one has any idea how long he was lying out there after he was bitten."

Mae ducked her head, but not before Garret caught sight of the tears trembling on the tips of her lashes.

"Here. Sit down," Eva said, standing and drawing Mae over to the couch, Sierra encouraging her from the other side.

"Sorry," Mae said. "I know you're all probably really worried yourselves. I didn't mean to burst in here like a drama queen."

"No one's being a drama queen," Eva said soothingly.

Mae nodded and sniffed, then offered Eva a watery smile. "I'm Mae, by the way."

Eva's smile was wry. "Yeah, I kind of guessed that. I'm Eva, Casey's girlfriend."

"You're the one who painted the mural on the old grain elevator near town," Mae said, her eyes lighting with recognition. "My mom sent me a link to a news article. I knew your face looked familiar."

"Yep, that's me," Eva said, handing Mae the box of tissues on the table.

"Thanks," Mae said, grabbing a handful.

While she was busy blowing her nose, Eva shot Sierra a "where did she spring from" look.

"I texted Mae earlier," Sierra explained. "I thought she might want to know."

Which meant Mae must have dropped everything to jump in the car and hightail it from Helena to Marietta so quickly.

Interesting, given she was theoretically engaged to some other guy whose name was definitely not Jed Carmody. Garret couldn't help wondering how her fiancé felt about her racing to the bedside of her ailing ex.

Confused, he suspected, at the very least.

The door opened again and Casey entered, stretching his back and scratching his belly. "Tag team. You're it, Sierra." He froze midstretch when he saw the new arrival sitting between Eva and Sierra on the couch.

"Mae?" he said, his expression comically surprised.

"Hey, Casey. How are you doing?" she said.

"I've been better," he said.

"Yeah, me too," Mae said. Standing, she came across to give him a big hug, which Casey returned with equal affection.

"I'm going to head in and sit with Jed. Unless you'd like to see him?" Sierra asked.

Mae went very still. Then she shook her head. "I won't. Thank you. He doesn't want a stranger at his bedside."

"You're hardly a stranger," Sierra objected.

"It's been a long time, Sierra," Mae said, her tone more firm now. "I'll just wait with you guys for a bit, if that's okay."

"Of course it's okay," Casey said. He gave her a small smile. "You look exactly the same."

Mae lifted a hand to her hair and Garret met Sierra's eyes over the other woman's head. They both knew that when she was in Helena, Mae presented a very different face to the world.

"I'll see you soon," Sierra said, giving Mae's shoulder a squeeze before heading for the door.

Garret followed her out into the corridor, wanting to check in with her, to make sure she was doing okay. "I was going to do another coffee run. Want me to grab you one and bring it in?"

"That'd be great, thanks." Her gaze went to the closed waiting room door. "You know, all these years, I've always felt so sorry for Jed because it was so obvious he wasn't over Mae. I figured she'd probably moved on. When we heard she was engaged last year, I thought, 'well, that's it. It's definitely done.'"

"You can still love someone even though you're not with them. Even though you've found a different kind of love with someone else," he said. "The world is full of love stories that never quite made it."

Sierra frowned, her gaze darting to his face and then away again. She nodded, then turned toward Jed's ward. She'd only taken a few steps when she turned back, hands clasped together at her waist.

"Garret . . . I don't want to be one of those stories. I don't want to have to think about what we could have had for the rest of my life because you want to protect me from something that I'm more than tough enough to handle. Jed's lying in there, and if he doesn't make it . . . I don't know how I'm going to get through it without you. Because that's what people do when they love each other—they're strong for the other person when they can't be strong for them- selves, and I need you to be strong for me tonight, and I need you to let me be strong for you, too, and help you face whatever's coming down the track. I need you to let me love you. I need you so much." Her chin wobbled and her eyes overflowed with tears, and he couldn't get to her fast enough to pull her into his arms.

"Don't. I'm not going anywhere. I promise. I'm sorry about last night. I love you. I love you so much. I just freaked out, that's all. I love you too much to ever let you go. Which probably makes me a selfish asshole, but I can live with that if it means having you in my life."

"Garret Tate, you are the least selfish person I know," she said, pulling back enough to look into his face. "You're the man I want to spend the rest of my life with, no matter what that looks like. No matter what we have to wade through. Like I said last night, you are it for me. I am done."

Her hair was a tangle down her back, her eyes swimming with tears, her cheeks blotchy with emotion—and she'd never looked more beautiful to him. Holding her face in his palms, he pressed a kiss to her lips, tasting the salt of her tears, feeling the way she was shaking, the depth of her response to him.

The depth of her love for him.

He was the luckiest man on the planet. In the universe.

"I got you, Sierra. And I'm not going anywhere."

"I've got you, too, Garret. And you're stuck with me."

He laughed a little at that, and so did she. Then she pressed her cheek to his chest, right over his heart. "Please, never push me away like that again," she said in a small voice. "I understand why you did it, but I never want to feel like that again."

He closed his eyes against the knowledge he'd caused her

pain. "I'm sorry. And I promise I'll never play the noble dickhead again."

She huffed out a laugh. Then she tilted her head up for his kiss, and for a moment the world righted itself as they sealed their promises to one another.

The sound of a nurse exiting one of the nearby rooms made them pull apart, and Sierra smiled self-consciously at the other woman before stepping out of his arms.

"I don't want Jed to be alone," she said apologetically.

"I know. I'll bring your coffee in soon, okay?"

"Thank you." She turned away, then turned back again. "I love you."

"Love you too," he said.

She nodded and walked down the corridor to the door to Jed's room, easing it open quietly and slipping inside. Garret waited until she was gone before closing his eyes and taking a deep breath.

He'd nearly fucked it up. He'd nearly broken the heart of the woman he loved and deprived himself of the happiness he knew he could find with her.

But he hadn't, because Sierra hadn't let him. He figured he was going to have a lifetime of her saving him from his worst mistakes. He hoped he could do the same for her. That was his plan, anyway—the two of them saving each other for the rest of their lives.

He gave himself a shake before stepping back into the waiting room. Three heads came up expectantly and he smiled apologetically. "Just me, sorry. Gonna do a coffee run. Who's in?"

He took down their orders and made his way through

the quiet of the hospital to the nearest coffee vending machine. Five minutes later he was heading back with five coffees balanced in his arms.

"Thanks, man," Casey said, coming forward to relieve him of a couple of cups when he returned.

Garret delivered a cup to Sierra, then returned to the waiting room and sat opposite Eva and Mae. They were all silent as they sucked down coffee, absorbed in their own thoughts. His were focused on Sierra, on what might happen in the next few hours and days, on what she might need, on how determined he was that he would see her through this, no matter how it turned out.

Because her happiness was his happiness. He understood that now.

Leaning back into the couch, he settled in to wait.

SIERRA WAS DEEP in a dark, dreamless place when a gentle touch on her arm woke her.

"Sierra," Garret said, and she lifted her head from where she'd been sleeping against his chest.

Eva and Mae were also blinking back to wakefulness, unfolding themselves from the pretzel shapes they'd assumed to catch a little shut-eye through the long night at opposite ends of the couch, while CJ and Jesse stirred from where they were sitting on the floor, their backs to the wall. They'd arrived in the early hours of the night, tense and weary after the long drive and eager for good news that no one had to give.

Now they were focused, like Sierra, on the gray-haired

doctor standing in the doorway, a tired-looking Casey standing behind her. Dr. Wittin had taken over Jed's care when he'd been transferred from the ER, but this was only the second time she'd come to give them an update.

"Sorry to interrupt your rest. I'm sure you must all be beat. I wanted to let you know Jed's latest tests have all come back and it's looking good. Liver function is strong, kidneys are normal. His heart rate is still a little high, but that's not unexpected given the situation. All things considered, I'm cautiously optimistic your brother has a good chance of making a full recovery," she said, her mouth curving into a smile.

Sierra sagged against Garret's shoulder, relieved tears burning the backs of her eyes. She'd cried more in the last twenty-four hours than she had in the last ten years, but apparently she had an everlasting supply.

"He just woke up. As in, properly woke up," Casey reported. "Told me I should be home getting some sleep, because someone's going to have to do all the work today."

Sierra's laugh sounded a little strangled even to herself, but it was so typical of Jed that his first thought was for the ranch.

"Let me guess—then he wanted to know if Pedro made it back okay," Jesse said, standing and offering CJ a hand to pull her to her feet.

"Bingo," Casey said, rewarding Jesse with a big grin.

Everyone laughed, the relief palpable in the room.

"I'll leave you to it, but just so you know, if he stays stable for the next few hours, we'll transfer him to a normal ward sometime later today. And if that goes well, you can expect him home in a couple of days. Snakebites can be tricky, with some side effects not showing up for a few days, so we'll want to keep him under observation," Dr. Witten said.

"Thank you so much for taking such good care of him," Sierra said.

"I'm thrilled I was able to give you such good news," the doctor said, then she lifted a hand in farewell and slipped back out into the corridor.

"Oh my fucking god," Eva said, leaning forward and pressing her hands to her face. "He's going to be okay. Hallelujah."

Sierra's face hurt she was smiling so hard. She turned to Jesse. "You go in first to see him. We get to see him all the time."

Plus Jed and Jesse had only recently reconciled. It wouldn't surprise her one little bit to learn that Jesse had been carrying an extra burden of regret and anxiety as he drove through the night to reach his brother's side.

"If that's cool with everyone else?" Jesse asked.

It was, and he left the room, eager to go see his brother.

Mae stood, gathering her jacket and handbag and looking around to see if she'd forgotten anything.

"You're going?" Sierra guessed.

Mae nodded. "I need to get back to Helena."

Sierra had been conscious of the other woman's phone pinging a few times during their vigil. Each time Mae had tapped back a brief message, her expression unreadable, but clearly she'd decided it was time to get back to her life. And her fiancé.

"You don't want to just say hello to Jed? I think it would mean a lot to him that you came," Sierra said.

Mae's face went pink but she shook her head. "I can't. I have to go. Tell him . . . Tell him I'm really happy he's going to be okay." She blinked rapidly, then closed the distance to give Sierra a brief, fierce hug. Then she turned and hugged everyone else.

"Thanks for letting me wait with you all," Mae said with a small smile. "Stay well." Then she escaped to the hallway.

They were all silent for a moment. Then Casey said what they were all thinking. "Well, that is going to set the cat among the pigeons. Who's going to tell him?"

Sierra shook her head. She'd been thinking about it all night. "No one's going to tell him, not yet. Let's wait till he's home and strong again. You know what he's like—he hates being sick. He'd think she only came because she thought he might die. He'd see it as pity or something because he's a big doofus idiot."

Eva was nodding in agreement. "Seconding this idea. Jed needs to be back on his feet first. It'll hit him differently for sure when he's feeling less off balance and vulnerable."

CJ cleared her throat. "You know there's a chance Jesse's already told him, right?"

They all stared at each other. Then Sierra shook her head again. "Whatever. It's small potatoes. He's going to be okay. That's the important part." She turned to get Garret's take, and he smiled at her and wrapped an arm around her from behind, pulling her back against his chest. She took comfort from his warm, solid presence, something that was quickly becoming a habit.

A month ago, she'd have walked past him on the street with barely a flicker of recognition. Today, all her dreams were tangled up with him, and that was something she wouldn't change for anything in the world.

As if he sensed her thoughts, Garret tightened his arms across her chest and she felt him press a kiss to the crown of her head. She smiled to herself, then noticed CJ watching her with a small smile of her own. Sierra wiggled her eyebrows at her brother's girlfriend, unashamed for her family to see how far gone she was. After all, she'd had to put up with all of them and their public displays of affection and heated glances. Turnabout was more than fair play.

"Okay. Who's next?" Jesse said from the doorway, and Sierra flicked a look toward Casey, her eyebrows raised in question.

She desperately wanted to look into her big brother's eyes, but she wasn't about to deny Casey that comfort either.

"You go," Casey said, waving her off.

Sierra threw him a grateful look, then turned and pressed a kiss to Garret's mouth. "I won't be long."

"I'll be here," he said, his gaze steady.

Her heart felt very full as she made her way to Jed's room. It felt strange just barging in now he was awake, even though they'd been going in and out all night, so she paused to knock briefly before opening the door. His head turned toward her, his mouth curving into a tired smile when he saw it was her. "Squirrel, I hear you may have just saved my life. Knew those flying lessons would pay off some day."

For a moment Sierra couldn't speak. Her throat was so clogged with relief and gratitude and love. Then she rushed forward and threw her arms around her brother, managing to get tangled in the lines stuck to his chest along the way.

"When I saw you lying against that tree . . . I swear, Jed, I thought we'd lost you," she whispered, too afraid to say the words any louder in case she tempted fate.

"It'll take more than a snakebite to see me off," Jed said, but there was a gruff note to his voice and when she lifted her head she could see he understood how touch and go it had been.

Disentangling herself from the monitor leads, she sank into the chair by the bed. "How are you feeling?"

"Like I got tackled by a rhino."

She smiled and took his hand, holding it in both of hers. "Last night I promised myself there were some things I wanted to say to you if I got the chance. Things I've never said to you before. So brace yourself to feel uncomfortable."

"Sierra, come on, you don't need to—"

"Yes, I do, Jed Carmody, because too many people go through life assuming that the people they love will always be around and that they understand how important they are to each other. When Mom and Dad died, you held our family together through sheer willpower. You gave up your education, you gave up Mae, and you took on all of us and the ranch as well, and you made it work, Jed. You filled the hole Mom and Dad left and made us feel safe and loved. You kept a roof over our heads and helped with my homework and put up with Casey's terrible guitar playing."

"Don't forget the bit where I made it impossible for Jesse to stay," Jed interrupted, his tone flat.

"I didn't say you were perfect. And Jesse has his own

share of responsibility to carry for that." She squeezed her brother's hand and looked him in the eye. "I love you so much. I'm so proud you're my brother. Thank you for always being there for me."

Jed shifted his head on the pillow, casting his eyes to the ceiling, and she knew he was fighting a rush of emotion. After a second he met her gaze again, and she saw his eyes were shining with unshed tears. "I love you, too, Sierra. And I'm proud as a person can be to call you my sister. I'm proud of all of you. We've had some fuckups along the way, but we mostly we managed to make it work."

"Except for a few minor mishaps, like snakebites leading to near-death experiences. Little things like that," Sierra said.

"Exactly," Jed said.

She talked to him for a few more minutes, but she could see he was tiring and she told him to get some rest so he could stay on his doctor's good side and get the transfer to the regular ward that had been promised.

Then she let herself out into the corridor where she found Garret waiting for her.

"Wanna go for a walk?" he suggested.

She nodded and he ducked his head into the waiting room to let the others know they'd be back in ten minutes or so. Then he took her hand and they made their way out of the hospital. Someone had had the foresight to plant a contemplation garden off to one side of the hospital grounds and they walked among the trees, soaking up the early morning sunlight and the fresh air.

"He's okay?" Garret asked after a moment or two.

"He's good. Tired and weak, but good."

"You know, I've been wondering where all the good luck was lately. Happy for Jed to hog the lion's share," he said.

She smiled at him. "You telling me you didn't get lucky when I agreed to cover for Jack when he hurt his back?"

"That wasn't luck, baby. That was destiny," Garret said, and he used their joined hands to pull her closer.

Stepping into the circle of his arms felt like coming home, and she lifted her face eagerly for his kiss. As always, the press of his lips and the stroke of his tongue lit a fire in her blood and it wasn't long before she was regretting how public the garden was.

She felt Garret's mouth curve into a smile against her own.

"Later," he said.

"For what?"

"For the dirty thoughts you're thinking right now."

She smiled in turn. "Is that a threat or a promise?"

"It's a commitment, which is better than both those things," he said, and then he kissed her again and she lost the ability to think altogether.

Epilogue

Three Months Later

"AND THEN ONE last signature here, Gideon."

Garret watched from the doorway of the living room in his parents' home as Alec Stone handed his father yet another document to sign. It took his father longer than usual to scrawl his name using his left hand, but he was getting better and better at using his nondominant hand every day, and although he still slurred his speech when he was tired, he'd been able to communicate effectively for several weeks now.

Other progress had been much slower. He was still unable to walk, his weak right side creating too much drag to make it safe for him to move around independently. There had been some recent gains with grasp and release exercises with his right hand, however, and Garret's mother remained hopeful that soon his father could progress to a walker.

Garret had no idea if her optimism was founded or not. He'd been too immersed in saving the business to keep up with the day-to-day wins and losses of his father's rehabilitation.

It had been a rough three months, to put it mildly. Tate

Transport had lost nearly thirty percent of its customers in the fallout from the commercial bribery scandal. Garret was hopeful he had stopped the slide at this point, thanks to a lot of reassurances, sharply renegotiated contracts, and new commitments to transparency and accountability.

Perhaps not surprisingly, the clients they'd lost had been the ones who had participated in his father and Ron's kickback scheme. There had been five cases the DA was able to prove in total. More than enough to attract hefty fines and jail terms, if the DA had chosen to go in hard. Fortunately for his father, there had been little appetite to lock up a man who had recently suffered a major stroke. It probably hadn't hurt that his father had made multiple judicious political donations over the years either. Consequently, Alec Stone had been able to negotiate a settlement that kept his father and Ron out of jail. The fines would eat into the company's bottom line for years to come, and there was no telling how long the shadow of this scandal would be in terms of the business's reputation, but Garret was starting to believe that the worst was over.

Finally.

His father handed the pen to his mother as Alex took the final documents from the table.

"All signed, like a good boy," his father said, glancing over his shoulder to offer Garret's mother a roguish smile.

Some things never changed. Gideon hadn't said it outright, but Garret suspected his father considered his current legal difficulties the price any astute, aggressive businessman paid for success. Gideon had rolled the dice, and for many years he'd won until finally he'd lost. *C'est la vie.*

It was just as well he would never be in a position to act on his beliefs again—as part of the settlement with the DA, his parents had signed undertakings to ensure they would never again be officers of the company.

It was all on Garret's shoulders now. Over the past months, despite all the challenges and stressors he'd had to stare down, he'd come to realize he was happy about that. He could make a difference there, and with good people surrounding him, he was confident he could rebuild what was lost.

His phone vibrated in his pocket, and he pulled it out to see Marco had texted him a picture of the warehouse in Seattle taking receipt of the latest shipment of espresso machines from Italy. Multiple pallets were piled high with stock. **Gonna need a bigger warehouse!** the message said. Garret smiled to himself and tapped back a quick response. **This is where being the silent partner has its advantages.**

After much discussion with Sierra and his friends, he'd decided to hang on to his share of the business. It never hurt to diversify, and he still felt a sense of ownership even if he wasn't in the trenches with Jay and Marco anymore. He wanted to see how high they could fly.

He registered the time as he put his phone away and pushed away from the door frame.

"I need to go pick up Sierra," he told his parents before catching Alec's eye. "We'll be ready to take off for Helena in half an hour, give or take."

"I'll be ready," Alec said, his throat bobbing as he swallowed nervously. He'd white-knuckled it all the way during the flight from Helena this morning, and Garret suspected he'd white-knuckle it all the way back.

Some men just weren't meant to fly.

"When will we see you again?" his mother asked, her expression hopeful.

He and Sierra were based out of Helena permanently these days, the daily commute a thing of the past, and this was the first time he'd seen his parents in nearly two weeks. Not out of design, but he'd be lying if he said he felt the need for more contact.

"Not sure. Maybe next weekend. I'll let you know," Garret said.

He knew his mother felt the new distance between them. She was working hard to build a bridge and earn his trust again but while he appreciated the effort, he wasn't sure he'd ever be able to let go of his wariness where his parents were concerned. The bottom line was that they lived by a very different set of values than he did, and he wasn't about to put himself in a position where they could demonstrate that again.

After saying his goodbyes, he let himself out the front door then walked to the garage and pulled on his leather jacket. Two minutes later he was zipping down the road on the Ducati, heading for the Carmody ranch.

He'd ridden and driven this route a lot over the past three months, reprising the habits of his teen years. It had taken a while, but he'd managed to find the old, easy rhythm with the Carmody brothers during those visits, something he was grateful for, given all the potential roadblocks that had stood in the way of that happening.

That didn't mean they wouldn't come hunting for him if

he was ever stupid or careless enough to hurt Sierra. On that Garret was very clear, but that was fine with him because he knew he was the luckiest man alive, and he wasn't about to risk what he had for anything.

Sierra must have heard him coming because she was standing on the porch when he arrived. A cool breeze lifted her long dark hair off her shoulders, and she stood tall and slim as she watched him dismount. Then she took the porch steps two at a time as she came to greet him. The warmth of her body as it met his, the strength of her arms as they came around him, the press of her mouth on his . . . To the day he died, he would never get enough of her.

"Hey," she said when she'd finished kissing him hello. "How did it go?"

"All signed. All we have to do now is pay the fines. And the legal bills," he said wryly.

"The easy part," she said.

He laughed, because he knew she understood exactly how much he'd been hustling to find the money without cutting staff and going into steep debt. "Yep. So easy."

None of this had been easy. The press coverage had been every bit as brutal and thorough as Greg had predicted. The business repercussions had been scary and stressful. For a while there it had felt as though every day was worse than the last.

But every night he'd come home to Sierra, and she'd provided the rock-solid base he'd needed to dig deep and endure. She'd made him laugh when he'd thought he couldn't, and she'd distracted him in the best possible way.

She'd loved him. Stood by him. Believed in him.

Looking into her eyes now, he was hit with a sudden, dizzying thought. If his father hadn't had his stroke, if Garret hadn't been dragged away from the life he'd made for himself in Seattle, he might never have crossed paths with her again.

He shook his head, needing to shake the thought loose. He didn't want to imagine his life without her in it. Couldn't, not now. She was a part of him, just as he was a part of her.

He heard the bang of the front screen door and glanced over as Jed made his way down the front steps.

"Garret," Jed said, offering him a dip of the head by way of acknowledgment.

"Jed," Garret said, mimicking the action.

Apart from a notable leanness and some deeper lines around his mouth and eyes, Sierra's brother had recovered well from his brush with death, his stride long as he made his way to the barn.

"I'm guessing he still hasn't said anything about Mae?" Garret asked, even though he already knew the answer. Jed had been silent on the subject of his ex ever since he'd learned she'd visited him in hospital.

"Not a freaking syllable," Sierra said. "What more does the man need? She came to his bedside because she thought he was dying. Clearly there are still feelings there."

"But she's still getting married in a month's time," Garret said. "That hasn't changed."

He understood a little of where Jed was coming from. The other man had pushed Mae away thirteen years ago, and she'd gone on to forge a new life for herself—complete with a thriving forensic accounting consultancy and a high-flying fiancé. Jed had never confided in Garret, but Garret suspected Jed figured he'd had his shot at Mae and messed it up. What right did he have to rock the boat she'd built for herself?

"He drives me crazy sometimes," Sierra said, still frowning.

Garret pulled her back into his arms. She came willingly, her frown falling away.

"Allow me to distract you from the crazy," he said. Then he kissed her, and she melted against him, hot and willing.

"What time's your first charter tomorrow morning?" he asked.

Now they weren't commuting, he'd found a way to generate income for Tate Transport and give Sierra her dream at the same time. Most days she flew charter flights out of Helena, ferrying people to Big Sky and other tourist destinations, or flying scenic routes over the abundant natural beauty that surrounded Helena. Business had been slow initially, but word had started getting out lately and all the indicators were that the Bell would soon be adding a nice little bump to the bottom line at Tate Transport.

"I don't have to be at the airport till nine," Sierra said. "Why? What have you got in mind?"

He smiled and shook his head. "That would be telling. You'll have to wait till we get home."

Not that the lake house would be home for much longer. It was currently on the market, waiting for someone with fifteen million dollars and a hankering for a view to come along. Once that happened, he and Sierra would find somewhere more their speed to live.

"Tease."

"Takes one to know one," he said, because she was more than capable of a little sensual torture herself.

She laughed, her green eyes dancing, and he had to dip his head to kiss her again.

"I fucking love you so much," he said against her lips.

Her fingers wove into his hair and their kiss became fierce and fiery. When they came up for air she pressed her forehead against his, her hands still tight in his hair. "I love you too. So much. So much."

It was a perfect moment, the latest in a series of perfect moments he'd had with this woman, and he let himself savor it—the feel of her body against his, the cool fall air on his face, the blue arc of Montana sky overhead, the knowledge that she was going to be by his side for the rest of his life, up for whatever adventures or challenges came their way.

It was going to be a beautiful, wild ride—and he wouldn't have it any other way.

The End

Want more? Check out Cassidy and Jesse's story in *The Cowboy Meets His Match*!

Join Tule Publishing's newsletter for great reads and weekly deals!

If you enjoyed *More Than a Cowboy,*
you'll love the other books in....

The Carmody Brothers series

Book 1: *The Cowboy Meets His Match*

Book 2: *The Rebel and the Cowboy*

Book 3: *More Than a Cowboy*

Available now at your favorite online retailer!

More books by Sarah Mayberry

Tanner
The American Extreme Bull Riders Tour series

Almost a Bride
The Great Wedding Giveaway series

Make-Believe Wedding
The Great Wedding Giveaway series

Bound to the Bachelor
The Bachelor Auction series

His Christmas Gift

Available now at your favorite online retailer!

About the Author

Sarah Mayberry is the award winning, best selling author of more than 30 books. She lives by the bay in Melbourne with her husband and a small, furry Cavoodle called Max. When she isn't writing romance, Sarah writes scripts for television as well as working on other film and TV projects. She loves to cook, knows she should tend to her garden more, and considers curling up with a good book the height of luxury.

Thank you for reading

More Than a Cowboy

If you enjoyed this book, you can find more from all our great authors at TulePublishing.com, or from your favorite online retailer.

TULE
PUBLISHING

Printed in Great Britain
by Amazon

34047278R00209